CASSANDRA VEGA

His Red Carnation

Cover art by Turning Pages Designs

This book was professionally typeset on Reedsy.
Find out more at reedsy.com

Contents

Please Note

This book includes explicit sexual content. It's intended for readers 18 and over.

Some content and trigger warnings include:
Addiction and relapse (alcohol and drugs)
Cheating (not between main characters)
Kidnapping
Threats of violence
Domestic violence
Mention of suicidal thoughts
Mention of PTSD

Also:
My understanding of the U.S. government and military might not be completely precise, but I've done my best. Like everything else in this book, it's a work of fiction ;)

Translations

Te quiero mucho – I love you so much

 Pobrecito – poor baby

 Hermano – brother

 ¿Qué coño? – what the fuck?

 ¡A tomar por culo! – To hell with this!

 y lo juro por Dios – I swear to God

 La madre que te pario – you son of a bitch

 tramposo hijo de puta – cheating son of a bitch

 Mamá, ¿estás bien – mom, are you okay?

 déjame calmarme primero – let me calm down first

 Hablas español – you speak Spanish?

 Por eso – that's why

 ¿Qué coño has hecho? ¡Maldita zorra! – what the hell have you done? You asshole/bitch

 Esto es culpa tuya – this is your fault

 con la maldita diabla – with the fucking devil

1

Sloane

I sat on a hard, uncomfortable plastic chair, my eyes fixed on the damp grass in front of me. The warm, wet spring air made my black silk dress cling to my skin, and the plastic beneath me stuck uncomfortably to the backs of my thighs.

"Sloane, sit up straight," my mom muttered under her breath as she settled next to me.

I scoffed but straightened my back. The last thing I needed was to be scolded this early in the morning, especially on my eighteenth birthday. And especially at a funeral.

Grant, my bodyguard since I was a little girl, had suddenly dropped dead at forty-nine. Heart attack, they said. He was a healthy retired Navy SEAL, someone my dad had known since their twenties. His death had shocked the entire family—and made us all a little suspicious.

My father was in his third year as President of the United States. President Jacob Martin. Everyone adored him. At forty, he was the youngest president ever elected, and people constantly compared him to a younger Patrick Dempsey. He was a beloved retired Navy SEAL, a national "hero" with a long list of medals and awards. The praise was endless.

But my mom, Ana—she was my hero. A fierce advocate for women's and LGBTQ+ rights, environmentalism, and animal welfare. Yet, she was always in my dad's shadow. I got it, he was the President. But one day, I knew she'd be the one in his shoes. Confident, graceful yet tough, and the most beautiful woman I'd ever seen. With her dark brown hair, hazel eyes, and Spanish and Mexican heritage, she turned heads. She just turned forty a few days ago, right after Grant died.

His death had left us all on edge. The autopsy confirmed it was natural, but it was still jarring, losing someone so close so suddenly. Each of us had our own bodyguard, and now I was without one. My mom had kept me within arm's reach ever since, which only added to my restlessness. We were close, but I needed my space. And now, one of Dad's other military buddies was going to be my new "protection." I couldn't remember much about him, except that I hadn't seen him since I was little. Was it Callan? Callum? Whatever his name was, he was supposed to be at the funeral, and I wasn't thrilled about meeting the man who'd soon be shadowing my every move.

I loved Grant, but I hated—no, I *loathed*—having a body-guard. Actually, I hated being the President's daughter alto-gether. No sneaking out to parties, no smoking weed in my room while my parents were away. I wasn't allowed to live like a normal teenager. I wasn't just Sloane. I was President Jacob Martin's daughter.

The funeral service began after Dad sat down beside me, stiff and silent. I could feel the weight of his grief—he was deeply upset over his friend's death. I was shaken too. I'd never lost anyone before. My legs bounced up and down as I stared at the rings on my fingers, completely tuning out the eulogist's words.

"Pay attention, Sloane," Dad whispered, leaning in close.

I rolled my eyes and looked up, not trying to be disrespectful, but everything about this felt uncomfortable. My long brown hair clung to my skin, damp from the humid spring air, and my heels pinched painfully at my feet. My chest felt tight, the ache of sadness making it hard to breathe, but I fought to keep it all inside. The eulogist talked about Heaven and loss, and as I bit my lip, a tear slipped down my cheek. I quickly wiped it away, shifting in my seat, my gaze drifting over the rows of bodyguards standing nearby.

That's when I saw him.

My heart dropped—not from grief, but from something else entirely. Awe. Desire. A man with a short beard, slicked-back brown hair, and full, pouty lips stood among the security detail, arms folded in front of him. His face was set in a hard scowl, but his dark Ray-Bans hid his eyes, making him even more mysterious. The black, tailored suit he wore hugged his muscular frame, and I could see the faint outline of tattoos on his hands and fingers.

I had never been so instantly attracted to someone in my entire life. He had to be older than me, *much* older, but that only turned me on more.

"Sloane, pay attention," Mom repeated, snapping me out of my thoughts.

I jerked my head back toward the eulogist, but my mind kept wandering back to Hot Bodyguard. *Holy shit—is he my new bodyguard?*

The idea consumed me for the rest of the service. I couldn't tell where he was looking behind those sunglasses, but he stood perfectly still, like a statue. His presence alone was electric, captivating, and I found myself sneaking glances, my thoughts spiraling into places they shouldn't. There was no way a man like him would ever look twice at an eighteen-year-old like me. I didn't even know if I had any real sex appeal—I was just a virgin that fantasized about sex probably way too often.

But just by looking at him, I could tell he was experienced in all the right ways. And now I was fantasizing about him...

"Sloane, come on, baby," my mom said, standing up and breaking me out of my fantasy.

I jumped up quickly, hoping the sudden movement would catch his attention. I glanced over, and sure enough, his head was turned our way. My heart pounded hard in my chest as we made our way to our SUV, but soon I lost sight of him in the crowd of familiar faces. People I knew greeted me, placing their hands on my shoulder as I passed, but I didn't hear a word they said. I was too distracted, my mind still reeling from the brief moment of eye contact.

Finally, we reached the SUV, and a door was opened for me. I slid into the very back row, sinking into the cool, leather seat. The air conditioning hit my face and I closed my eyes for a moment, letting the chill calm my racing heart. Mom and Dad lingered outside, chatting with more familiar faces. That's when I noticed Hot Bodyguard slipping into the driver's seat.

My breath caught as I watched him adjust the rearview mirror. Before I could stop myself, the words tumbled out.

"Um...who are you?" My voice was quieter and more hesitant than I intended.

He paused, the mirror stopping just as his sunglasses reflected back at me. Slowly, he turned around.

"Miss Sloane," he said, his deep voice rumbling through the

air. "I'm Callan Holt. I'll be the head of security detail on your behalf."

The way his forehead wrinkled when he spoke, the slight furrow of concentration, paired with those full lips, was almost too much. I stared, my lips parting in response, but before I could say anything, my mom climbed into the SUV, followed by Dad.

"Oh! Callan! You're already here," Mom said warmly, resting her hand on the passenger seat in front of her.

"It's nice to see you, Mrs. Martin," Callan replied, polite and professional.

Mom scoffed lightly. "Cal, you know you can call me Ana."

Dad climbed in next to Mom, settling directly behind Callan. As the door closed, he reached out to clasp Callan's shoulder.

"Callan," Dad said, his tone grateful. "Thank you so much for being here."

Callan let out a soft exhale that sent a swirl of butterflies through my stomach. "Of course," he said, his voice steady. "I wish it were under different circumstances, but I'm glad to be here, Jake."

Another bodyguard slipped into the passenger seat up front, and soon the SUV began to move, the interaction between me and Callan still hanging in the air.

I shakily buckled my seatbelt, my eyes fixed on the back of Callan's head. Mom and Dad talked quietly between themselves, but all I could think about was how in the fuck I was going to handle having the hottest guy I'd ever seen around me almost 24/7.

"Uh...Dad, are we going home now?" I asked softly, leaning toward the middle row of the SUV.

"Yes, sweetie," Dad replied, glancing back at me before

turning to smile at Mom.

I watched them for a moment, my heart warming at the way they looked at each other. Mom was crazy about Dad, and Dad was obsessed with her right back. Their constant PDA grossed me out sometimes, but deep down, they were everything I wanted in a relationship. The way they looked at each other with so much love—it made me long for that kind of connection myself.

The ride back to the house—the White House—was short, but it felt like forever. All I could think about was getting to my room and fantasizing about my new bodyguard. I wanted to touch myself just by looking at him. Fuck, this was like the start to all the smutty books I read.

"Honey, Callan is going to take you inside. Daddy and I need to get some work done in the office," Mom explained as the SUV came to a stop.

"I'm sorry, Callan...did I introduce you to Sloane?" Dad asked as we stepped out of the vehicle.

I hopped out, feeling a little unsteady, but Callan was there instantly, his big hand firm on my elbow. I glanced up, and there he was—sunglasses off, standing tall with a slight smile on his lips. The sight of him up close made my breath catch.

"Um..." I managed to breathe out.

"He'll be the head of security for you, baby. Please don't give him a hard time. He's one of the good guys," Dad teased with a smile.

Without waiting for my response, they both walked off, leaving me alone with Callan. My heart hammered in my chest as I met his gaze, his hazel-green eyes watching me with a hint of amusement, like I was doing something entertaining. It was only then I realized he was still holding my elbow.

"You okay there?" he asked lightly, finally letting me go.

"Um…yeah." I smiled nervously, pushing some hair out of my face.

He studied me for a moment. "I got a quick little tour earlier. Should I take you to the living quarters upstairs?"

Yes. Take me to my bedroom and strip me bare.

"Uh, yeah, sure. Do you need a more extensive tour? I know my way around pretty well," I said, trying for a playful tone that bordered on flirtatious.

Callan raised his eyebrows, clearly caught off guard by my comment, but there was a glimmer of amusement in his eyes.

"Whatever you'd like," he replied.

He was at least a few inches taller than me, even with my heels on. At 5'5", that had to put him around six feet. His cool, unbothered demeanor was almost infuriating, like nothing fazed him, and I did my best to act like it did nothing to me.

"Cool. Follow me," I said, keeping my voice steady as I started walking, my heart racing.

2

Callan

Jake had told me earlier it was Sloane's birthday. Eighteen. Old enough to make her own decisions, but still young enough that I had no business noticing the sway of her hips as she walked ahead of me.

But I fucking noticed. Her silk dress clung to every curve, and her high heels clicked against the floor, making her ass jiggle with each step. Girls didn't look like this when I was her age—granted, that was twenty years ago.

She tossed a glance over her shoulder, catching me mid-stare. *Fuck.* She probably thought I was some creepy old dude. But instead of calling me out, she smiled.

"There are lots of little secret shortcuts around here. I'll have to show you them sometime." She raised an eyebrow at me before turning around and continuing down the hallway.

It was wrong to even have these thoughts.

I don't remember her as a kid. I just remember Jake had a daughter. That was it. Back then, when he was still governor of New York, he pulled me out of a spiral I barely survived. I was strung out, half-dead, all the way down at rock bottom.

Jake saved me.

And now I was staring at his daughter, who was fucking walking in front of me in that dress and giving me a hard on.

It was wrong in so many ways.

"It's my birthday, you know. What a celebration, right?" She scoffed, rolling her eyes as she finally walked beside me, giving me a full view of her gorgeous face.

"Happy birthday," I said, probably with a little too much enthusiasm.

She gave a small laugh and rolled her eyes. "Thanks. Today wasn't exactly how I imagined spending my eighteenth birthday, you know?"

"Well, how would you have wanted to spend it?" I asked, scanning the hallway of the living quarters, doing my best not to stare at her for too long.

She stopped in front of the kitchen and sighed as I turned back to face her.

"I don't know, honestly. I'm not allowed to do much," she said, her tone laced with the rebellion of a typical teenager. I couldn't help but laugh a little, shrugging.

"If you weren't Jake's daughter, how would you want to celebrate?" I asked.

Her eyebrows twitched slightly as she looked at me. "It's weird hearing someone call Mr. President by his real name," she said with a laugh.

I shifted my weight, feeling a little more at ease. "Yeah, well, he'll always be Jake to me. I'm not fucking calling him Mr. President," I said, laughing along with her.

She smiled, biting her lip as she stared at me. It made my dick twitch. I had to look away.

As she leaned against the wall, she crossed her arms. "I'd

want to get a tattoo."

I glanced at her as her eyes traveled over me, finally landing on my hands in my pockets.

"Yeah? What would you get?" I tried to sound casual, but all I could picture was a tiny cherry on her perfect ass.

She shrugged, her gaze dropping to the floor. "I've always wanted Ferdinand the Bull. It's my mom's favorite book, and I love the message behind it."

I smiled. Beautiful and thoughtful—yeah, I was in deep fucking trouble.

"How many do you have?" she asked, her eyes wide with curiosity.

My fucking dick twitched again.

"A lot." I shrugged, trying to downplay it. No way could she know how much her excitement was turning me on.

She narrowed her eyes, biting her lip to hide a smile. It was driving me insane. "Can I see them?"

Is she flirting with me? I looked away, licking my lips before I could stop myself.

"Yeah, maybe later. Do you need anything? I'm heading into the kitchen." I desperately needed to get away from this girl. No, she wasn't just a girl—she was a woman, and she was already doing things to me.

She sighed, a hint of disappointment in her expression.

"No, I think I need to lie down. I'll see you later." She turned toward her bedroom door, then glanced back at me. "I need your number. You know, in case of an emergency." She bit her lip, smiling again. *Fuck.*

"Right. I'll text it to you. I already have yours."

She gave a slow nod, lingering at her door. "I'll need a ride later too. Around seven or eight."

I blinked. "For what?"

She shrugged. "You'll see." Then she quickly shut the door behind her.

I stood there, stunned. Was she even allowed to plan impromptu trips like that? And was I really going to question her?

Fuck that. She could do whatever she wanted. And I'd be right there to protect her.

3

Sloane

I was probably pushing my luck. Callan didn't seem remotely interested in me—he barely even looked my way. He probably thought I was just some little puppy, trying and failing miserably to flirt. Did he even notice? I'd only tried flirting a handful of times in my life, and nothing ever came of it. Was that because I was the President's daughter or because I was just bad at it? Maybe both.

The moment I told him I needed a ride, I decided I'd go get a tattoo. Something about Callan and finally being eighteen made me want to do something out of character. Normally, I was the straight-laced, quiet, follow-the-rules type—a straight-A student who wouldn't dare curse in front of adults. I had always wanted to be the rebellious girl with tattoos, blue hair, and a 'fuck it' attitude toward authority. But I never was—probably because I didn't want to give my dad any more stress or negative press. He had enough to worry about, leading the free world and all.

So what exactly would be the problem if his eighteen-year-old daughter got a tiny, hidden tattoo? With her hot new bodyguard tagging along, preferably behind her, fucking her with his tattooed hands gripping her hips?

Back in my room, I felt around my wet pussy as I laid in bed under the covers, the image of Callan's strong hands on my body enough to get me worked up. I put one hand to my breast under my T-shirt, playing with my erect nipple. *His full lips on my neck, one hand reaching over to rub my clit as he pounded me from behind*...my orgasm quickly and fiercely approached, a quiet moan escaping my throat as I came to my fantasy.

I gasped when there was a knock at the door. I removed my hands from my wet spot and breast and feigned sleepy eyes as I covered my whole body with blankets.

"Come in," I called.

Mom stepped inside, still in her black funeral dress and heels. She gave me a small, sympathetic smile as she closed the door behind her and made her way over to the foot of my bed, sitting down gently.

"I'm sorry your dad and I rushed back to work so soon. How are you feeling? Did you and Callan get to know each other?"

I nodded quickly. "It's fine. I'm okay. And yeah, we did. He seems nice." I shrugged, trying to sound casual.

Mom nodded, a slow smile creeping onto her face. "Isn't he hot? In that bad boy kind of way? I always thought so," she said, laughing softly.

"Mom!" I laughed, feeling my cheeks flush. "He's Dad's friend!"

She shrugged with a playful smirk. "I'm still a hot-blooded woman. Don't you think he is? You're probably too young to notice. He's very sweet, though. He'll do a good job watching you."

My face burned. If only she knew how much I wanted him

watching me just a few minutes ago.

"No, yeah. He's hot," I admitted, trying to play it off. "But like, way too old." No way could Mom know about the crush I was developing.

She shook her head teasingly.

"I asked him for a ride later. I'm going to get myself a birthday present," I added, feeling a little thrill at sharing it with her. I'd never tell Dad, but I told Mom everything. *Mostly* everything.

Her eyebrows lifted in surprise. "And what kind of present would that be?"

I bit the inside of my cheek, a nervous habit. "I'm gonna get a tattoo. A small one. Like, on my back or something," I said quietly.

Mom immediately smiled. "Please don't get a tramp stamp. Anywhere but your lower back. Please." She laughed.

I scoffed, laughing with her. "I'm not getting a tramp stamp. I want to get a little red carnation."

Her face lit up. "Spain's national flower. Oh, baby. *Te quiero mucho.*" She squeezed my hand warmly.

"I love you too." My tone turned serious. "But please, don't tell Dad."

She scoffed, rolling her eyes. "You think I'm going to tell your father? You want him to kill *me*?" she teased. "No, save that for when you're thirty-five."

* * *

My heart raced when I got a text from Callan.

It's Callan. Here's my number.

I smiled, trying to come up with something witty to say.

Callan, it's Sloane, the 18-year-old you have to babysit.

I hit send and instantly regretted it. I didn't want him to see me as a little girl. But his response came quickly.

Ha. You're funny. Pretty sure you can take care of yourself, but it's my job. Sorry you think of me as your babysitter.

I bit the side of my lip, debating my next move.

I don't think of you that way at all. I hit send, my heart racing. What would he make of that?

Good. Now where do you need a ride to at 7 or 8?

I smiled to myself.

It's a surprise. Meet me in the hallway at 7:30.

What I really wanted to do was pull him into my bedroom and get on my knees in front of him. I instantly got wet at the thought.

Okay. I'll see you then.

I glanced at my phone—it was 6:30 p.m. Time to get ready and wear something that would show him I wasn't a little girl anymore.

It was still warm, so I could easily wear another dress. I slipped into a cute summer skater dress, flared and super short. The best part was the low-cut neckline that highlighted my breasts. I slid on a thong, already imagining where I'd get a tattoo on my back, secretly hoping Callan might catch a glimpse of my ass. I was proud of my curves—they came from my mom, and people never stopped admiring her body, even though she was so much more than just her looks.

I glanced at myself in the mirror, adjusting the white floral dress before slipping on a pair of white low-top Converse. Grabbing a cardigan from my closet in case it got chilly, I started on my makeup—thin winged eyeliner, a touch of pink blush, and dark pink lipstick. If my dad saw me like this, he'd probably have a heart attack. Luckily, he was still buried in work downstairs.

I stood up and gave myself one last look in the mirror, smiling as I turned around, satisfied with how I looked. I took a quick glance at my phone—7:25 p.m. *Perfect.* I grabbed my purse and stepped out of my room, only to find Callan leaning against the hallway wall. He was still in his suit from earlier, but without the jacket and tie. His white shirt was unbuttoned at the top, and his sleeves were rolled up, exposing more of the tattoos that covered his forearms. My heart pounded like it was about to leap out of my chest.

His eyes widened slightly as he looked at me.

"Hey," I greeted quietly, shutting the door behind me.

His jaw tightened. "Hey. You ready?" His face was serious, and he didn't take his eyes off me, making me feel suddenly self-conscious.

"Uh huh." I nodded.

He glanced down the hallway, then back at me. "Are you going to tell me where we're going now?" His raised eyebrows hinted at mild annoyance.

I fought back a smile, feeling a little mischievous. "I'll tell you in the car. Let's go." I turned and headed down the hallway, fully aware of him following behind me. I swayed my hips on purpose, just like earlier.

We headed down the stairs and through the side corridor that led to the Presidential cars. Callan opened the back door for me, but I shook my head.

"I want to sit up front."

I walked around the car, opening the passenger door myself and slipping in quickly. Callan got in the driver's seat, side-eyeing me.

"Okay. Now what?" he asked, his elbow resting on the armrest between us. His muscled arms looked like they were about to burst out of his shirt. My heart pounded as I stole a quick glance before looking straight ahead.

I typed the tattoo shop's address into my phone and placed it in the center cup holder. As Siri announced the directions, I could feel Callan's eyes on me.

"I'm not fucking taking you to get a tattoo," he muttered, clearly exasperated.

I turned to him, narrowing my eyes. "Yes, you are," I shot back.

He shook his head quickly. "No way. Your dad would kill me."

I rolled my eyes. "My mom gave me her blessing. Now please, let's go."

Callan stared at me, as if weighing his options. I noticed his eyes flicker down to my cleavage before he quickly looked away.

"Fuck," he muttered under his breath, starting the car and heading toward the tattoo shop just minutes away.

4

Callan

Watching Sloane walk out of her bedroom in that fucking dress with her pretty pink lips had me fucking dying. The things I wanted to do to her, like bend her over and grab that perfect ass and shove my dick so hard in her that her sweet little voice screamed my name. And then sitting beside her in the car, noticing her tits shaking as she bossed me around and rolled her eyes at me. I wanted to fuck her mouth with the way she talked back to me. But goddamn it, I needed to clear my head and stop thinking about my friend's daughter. My friend's barely eighteen-year-old daughter. And now I was taking her to a fucking tattoo shop. Of course Ana would approve—she's always been a firecracker. I remember back in our twenties, at a party, when some drunk asshole grabbed her ass. Without missing a beat, she turned around and slapped him so hard, the whole room went silent. She didn't even flinch, just stared him down until he slunk off like the piece of shit he was. That was Ana—fierce as hell, and Jake fucking loved her for it. I saw the same fire in Sloane. She played the good girl, but I could tell there was a wild side under there. The way she flirted with me, a guy twenty years older, screamed rebellion. Did she even realize she was doing it? Because it was driving me fucking crazy and if she kept doing it, I wouldn't be able to help myself. I'd fucking rip that pretty little dress off of her if she asked me to.

We pulled up to the tattoo shop a few minutes later. She jumped out of the car and stomped her way to the entrance, and I hurried to catch up. She always stomped around like she was on a mission to fuck shit up. I wondered if she even realized how much confidence she radiated—it was surprising coming from an eighteen-year-old.

Before I could even try, she yanked the door open and walked right in.

The place was packed for a Thursday night. Sloane headed straight to the front desk and started chatting with the receptionist, a tattooed guy who didn't look much older than her. The way he stared at her, openly ogling her, pissed me off. I couldn't make out their conversation over the loud music, so I moved closer, resting my hand on her back—almost possessively. Just touching her soft body made my dick twitch. She glanced over at me, her eyes widening for a split second, her body relaxing from my touch, before turning back to the tattooed kid.

"This your dad or something?" he joked.

"No, you know exactly who she is. I'm her fucking muscle. So cut the jokes, asshole. You got a private room or something? She needs privacy."

He gaped at me, clearly realizing who I meant. His eyes flicked to Sloane, narrowing.

"Holy shit, it *is* you. You're Sloane Martin." He continued to blatantly check her out, and I had to hold back the urge to clock him.

"So? Do you have someone who can tattoo me?" she asked quietly, almost as if she were embarrassed.

"Yeah, for sure. Uh, here...follow me." He got up and gestured for us to head down a hallway.

Sloane shot me a pissed-off look. "Could you maybe *not* mention who I am to everyone we talk to?" she muttered.

Fuck. "He was being a fucking jackass," I argued.

She glared at me. "You could've told him off without mentioning who I was," she snapped.

I stayed silent as she walked ahead, following the jackass into a private room. I needed to start considering her feelings more. I wasn't used to dealing with famous, beautiful teenage girls—especially ones that I wanted to fuck. And not just fuck—I already cared about her. I wanted to protect her. I didn't want anyone even looking at her, let alone talking to her. I'd never felt this kind of possessiveness toward a woman before.

"Just fill this out. I'll have someone come in for you soon," the loser muttered, handing Sloane the paperwork before walking out and closing the door behind him.

She sat down and started filling it out.

"I'm sorry," I said quietly, taking a seat across the room. There was a chair next to her, but I didn't think she'd want me being that close to her at the moment.

She shrugged. "It's fine. It's just...it's rare that I get to go somewhere and be anonymous." Her eyes stayed fixed on the paperwork.

I nodded. "I get that."

Finally, she looked up at me and smirked. "So, you're my *muscle?*"

I laughed, feeling a little embarrassed. "I just wanted to give him some shit. Honestly, I think you've got enough muscle for the both of us," I teased.

She licked her lips, her eyes drifting to my arms. If I didn't know any better, I'd say she was checking me out.

"I don't know," she said as a slow grin appeared on her lips. "I was kind of looking forward to seeing that muscle."

Jesus Christ. I instantly had a semi, but thank fuck someone walked in before I said something I regretted.

"Shit, it *is* you." Another hipster kid walked in, gawking at her like an idiot.

Sloane's smile faded as she gave a small shrug.

"This is great. What can I do for you? You're eighteen or...?" He glanced at me, almost questioning.

"I'm eighteen. I want a red carnation. A small one," she answered confidently.

What happened to Ferdinand?

"Okay, cool. Where do you want it?" he asked, sitting down on a swivel chair near the reclining chair.

Sloane hesitated, glancing at me for a moment before turning back to him. "Beside my ribcage."

"Got any example photos? I'll draw something up for you—just show me what you had in mind."

I watched as she pulled out her phone and handed it to him. Then it hit me—how the fuck was she going to get a tattoo in that spot without lifting her dress, exposing herself to this shithead?

"Cool. This won't take long. I'll draw something up and come back," he said, quickly walking out. I felt a twinge of nervousness being alone with her again.

"I thought you wanted Ferdinand the Bull?" I asked, hoping to steer the conversation away from where it had been heading.

Sloane shrugged off her cardigan, leaning over slightly, her perky tits stealing my attention for a second.

"That's my next one. I just wanted something small tonight."

She stood up and started checking out the tattoo designs framed on the walls.

"Are you going to show me any of yours?" she asked, still not looking at me.

I glanced down at my left forearm. "There's an anchor here. Pretty self-explanatory."

She glanced over, her gaze lingering on my arm with a spark of desire.

"How many do you have?" she asked, curiosity all over her face.

I thought for a second. "I don't know. Over thirty, at least."

Her eyes widened. "Holy shit. Over thirty? Where are they all?"

Fuck, there goes her eagerness again.

I shrugged. "Everywhere. Mostly my upper half."

Her eyes scanned my body. My dick involuntarily twitched again.

"You sure you want it on your ribcage? That's right on the bone. Might hurt a little."

Her eyes flicked to my lips before meeting mine. "I can handle a little pain."

Did she fucking know what she was doing to me? Did she know I'd imagine her bent over, slapping her ass and pulling her hair?

"I'm sure you can," I muttered, keeping a straight face.

No, you fucking idiot. Don't flirt back with her.

She smiled shyly at me. *So, she can dish it out, but she can't take it? Oh fuck that, I'd make her take it.*

I was saved by the hipster idiot again.

"How's this?" he asked, handing her a tablet with what I assumed was his drawing.

She smiled at him, and it made me jealous as fuck. "Perfect."

He pulled out a flat, cushioned table and started laying a paper sheet over it. I noticed Sloane standing there, looking uneasy.

"I'll have to lay down?" she asked.

He glanced at me, then back at her. "Yeah, if you want it on your ribcage."

She looked at me and then back at him.

"Okay. I just...I don't have anything to cover my bottom half."

I stood up immediately. "We should go then." There was no way I could handle seeing her ass on display and not doing a damn thing about it. Worse, I didn't want that hipster fucker seeing her like that either.

The guy raised his hand. "No, it's all good. I'll grab you a paper blanket. We use them all the time."

Sloane glanced at me, then nodded. "Yeah, that's fine." She smiled warmly at me, almost like she was trying to calm me down.

I reluctantly sat back down.

"Here." The douchebag pulled a paper blanket from a drawer. "Just uh, get situated and comfortable, and I'll be right back."

He nodded at me and left the room.

"I'll give you some space," I said, heading for the door, but Sloane stopped me.

"Wait."

I turned back to her expectantly.

"It's okay. Just...don't look." Her wide brown eyes stared at me, hopeful.

I sighed, nodding as I turned around and crossed my arms.

I heard the crinkling of the paper as she got onto the table. My mind wandered, imagining what her juicy ass looked like laid out on that table. Was she wearing a thong? Boy shorts? Nothing?

"Okay. You can turn around."

I hesitated but turned, and immediately my eyes caught her bare ass under the paper blanket. It wasn't pulled down nearly enough. Her ass was even better than I'd imagined, and my mouth practically watered. I quickly looked away, reminding myself that she wasn't trying to show it off to me. Or...was she?

"You're not covering much. Might want to pull it down more," I muttered, my eyes fixed firmly on the floor beside me.

She giggled quietly, sending a shock straight to my dick. "Whoops." There was crinkling of the paper again.

"Yeah, whoops. Better fucking fix it before that asshole sees your ass."

"Which asshole, you or him?" she teased.

I glanced up, and her ass was still peeking out.

"Sloane, it's fucking clear as day. Pull the blanket down." I was pissed, knowing someone could walk in and see her completely exposed. I averted my eyes back to the floor, desperately trying not to march up to her and grab her, claiming her body the way I'd been dying to do all day.

"I'll cover it up before he comes back in. This is just for you." Her voice was breathy and quiet, with a seriousness that hit me hard.

My eyes shot up to meet hers. The paper blanket barely

covered anything now. She was wearing a pink thong—if you could even call it that—practically swallowed by her perfect, plump ass. I couldn't take my eyes off of her—my dick grew hard and was desperately trying to break free from my pants.

"Sloane, don't do this," I warned her.

She bit her lip, smiling. "Don't do what?"

"Don't be fucking coy. I'm your dad's friend. I'm fucking twenty years older than you." My angry voice didn't match the way I felt inside, fucking eager and ready to spread open her legs and fuck her on that table.

"So? I'm eighteen. I can do what I want. And who I want," she argued back. "What, you don't think I'm good enough to fuck?"

Her voice was strained and full of hurt.

I quickly shook my head. "You don't think I want to fuck you? No. You're *too good* for me to fuck. You're too fucking pure. Too fucking beautiful and sweet."

She smiled quickly, but the knock at the door made both of us jump. Sloane hurriedly pulled the paper blanket down, finally covering her ass.

"Better?" She raised an eyebrow at me, almost mockingly.

I didn't answer. "Come in," I called out.

5

Sloane

My heart pounded so hard I could feel it in my ears. It wasn't because of the tattoo I was about to get—it was because Callan had just admitted that he wanted to fuck me. But he wouldn't. Too pure? Too sweet? Too beautiful? None of those were good enough excuses. What did I have to do, beg him?

The needle piercing my skin barely registered. All I could think about was Callan—the way his eyes darkened when I purposely showed him my ass. Around him, I became the girl I always wanted to be: fearless, rebellious, flirtatious. And I knew he couldn't resist me. He'd been checking me out since the car ride, his gaze tracing every curve of my body like a silent confession. He didn't even bother hiding it.

But now he sat in the corner, avoiding looking at me, his eyes glued to his phone. Not a single glance in my direction. The heat from his earlier attention still lingered on my skin, and I couldn't believe I'd actually had the nerve to flaunt myself like that—was I really that horny? Something about him fueled this heated desire in me, a fire that burned hotter the more he resisted. I wanted to be the girl he couldn't stop thinking about, the one who made him lose control.

But instead, it seemed to piss him off. He wanted me—I could feel it—but he fought it every step of the way. And that only made me want him more. I wanted to push him to the edge, make him want me so badly that he couldn't help himself. I wanted him to snap, to give in to the tension between us.

"All done. Wanna take a look?" The tattoo artist handed me a mirror, snapping me out of my thoughts.

I angled the mirror toward my ribcage, revealing a dainty little red carnation with a green stem. It was perfect.

"I love it. Thank you." I handed the mirror back to him before he covered the tattoo, then pulled my dress down before removing the paper blanket.

I glanced over at Callan; his eyes were locked on the floor as he stood and pulled something out of his pocket.

"Thanks. Use this tip to forget you saw Sloane here." He handed a wad of cash to the tattoo artist.

I rolled my eyes, grabbing my cardigan and purse off the chair.

"Yeah, for sure. Thanks, man." The tattoo artist walked out, leaving the door open behind him.

I sighed, placing my hand on my hip. "I could have paid for that," I mumbled.

"You're welcome," Callan replied with a mocking smile.

He started to walk out but then stopped, raising his eyebrows when he noticed I hadn't moved. "What?" he asked, his irritation still clear.

"There's another place I want to go," I said, though I wasn't even sure where. I just knew I didn't want to go home yet.

His expression shifted, suddenly nervous. "And where's that?"

I hesitated, trying to come up with something. I couldn't exactly say what I really wanted—which was to be in the backseat of the SUV with him fucking me senseless.

"I'm hungry," I blurted out.

He blinked, seeming caught off guard. "The kitchen can make you something at home."

"They can't make me crepes from Crepeaway," I countered.

His forehead creased as confusion crossed his face. "What the fuck is Crepeaway?"

I giggled. "Come on, I'll show you."

Callan hesitated but followed me out. I let him open the SUV door for me this time, wanting the sight of me bending over to remind him of what he'd seen earlier. He slammed the door shut as I settled into my seat.

I could feel his irritation as I glanced at him when he got in. "No need to be an asshole just because you saw my ass," I said, keeping my voice casual, though my heart raced, daring him to react.

He buckled his seatbelt and gave me a sidelong glance as he started the engine. "You don't need to keep reminding me that I saw your ass."

Backing up, he placed his hand on the back of my seat as he checked the rearview.

"What, you want to forget?" I snapped, irritation bubbling up.

I was starting to regret being so forward with Callan. He wasn't giving in. What was I going to have to do to push him over the edge?

He stayed quiet for a moment. We stopped at a red light and he glanced over at me.

"Sloane, you have no idea how gorgeous you are. Why would

you want to bother with an old guy like me?"

His words hit me hard, sinking my heart to the floor. I stared at his full lips, unable to stop imagining how they'd feel against mine.

"You obviously have no idea how hot you are, Callan," I shot back, my pulse quickening. He seemed taken aback by my response.

A honk from behind jolted us—the light had turned green. Callan focused back on the road, and we drove in silence to the dessert place a few minutes away. After parking in a garage a few blocks from our destination, he cut the engine.

Unbuckling my seatbelt, I looked at him with a nervous smile. "So...should we make out now?"

He glanced at me, his expression tight, the lines on his forehead betraying his inner conflict.

"Are you a virgin, Sloane?" His eyes were hard, though his dilated pupils told a different story.

My breath quickened. "Why does that matter?" I asked softly.

He licked his lips, never breaking eye contact.

"It matters because if you are, it'd make me even more of a creep for wanting to fuck you."

I narrowed my gaze. "Virginity is a social construct, Callan. An outdated, misogynistic one at that. It shouldn't be the deciding factor on whether or not it's 'creepy' for you to want to fuck me."

His lips curved into a surprised smile. "You're so fucking feisty, Sloane."

I bit my lip, sensing his guard lowering. In one quick movement, I swung my leg over into the driver's seat, straddling him effortlessly, my hands landing on his shoulders.

"Fuck," he breathed, his hands instantly grabbing my ass, squeezing tightly.

My hips instinctively started moving, grinding against him. I couldn't control it, my body responding on its own. His eyes locked on mine, darting between my lips and eyes as the heat between us grew. I felt his erection pressing against my drenched panties.

"I can't do this, Sloane," he whispered, his grip on me never loosening.

I ignored him, crashing my lips against his, moaning as his soft mouth urgently claimed mine. His hands slid under my dress, guiding my hips to move along his hard cock. I moaned again, the sensation overwhelming, feeling like I could come just from dry humping him.

Suddenly, he pulled his lips from mine. "Wait, wait—" He stilled me, and I let out a whine of frustration.

"Backseat," he murmured.

Oh my God, is this really happening? I scrambled off him and climbed into the spacious backseat, kneeling as I waited for him to join me. He practically jumped in beside me, quickly unbuttoning his shirt. I straddled him again, helping him shrug off the fabric, revealing even more glorious tattoos before he swiftly lifted my dress and tossed it aside.

"Fuck," he muttered, his eyes roaming over my body.

"Show me that muscle of yours now," I breathed, my fingers already finding his zipper.

Without hesitation, he lifted his hips, shoving his pants down to his knees. My breath caught when he pulled down his boxer briefs, revealing his thick, massive cock. I dropped to the floor of the SUV, wrapping my hands around him without a second thought.

"Take it, Sloane. Take it all in your mouth," he commanded, gathering my hair into a makeshift ponytail with his hand.

I licked my lips and opened my mouth wide, barely able to take in the head of his cock.

"Look at me, baby," he commanded.

I quickly lifted my gaze to meet his, his full lips slightly parted as he watched me. I'd never given a blowjob or even a handjob before, and here I was, taking in the biggest cock from the hottest man I'd ever seen. I bobbed my head up and down, keeping my eyes on him, watching the rapid rise and fall of his tattooed chest.

"Come here." He released my hair and pulled me up, his fingers hooking under the waistband of my thong, sliding it down until it hit the floor.

"It's gonna hurt, baby. I'll go slow," he whispered as I positioned my knees beside him, hovering over him.

I smiled, leaning closer. "Like I said...I can handle a little pain."

He licked his lips before pulling me in for a passionate, hard kiss. As our mouths moved together, I lowered my hips, positioning myself over him. The head of his cock began to push inside me, stretching me in a way that made me gasp.

"Oh my God," I moaned, breaking away from his lips.

"Nice and slow, baby," he murmured. "Let me fill you up, inch by inch."

He was right—it hurt. But my slickness helped me ease down on him. The feeling of him filling me was even more incredible than I'd imagined.

"Oh fuck, Callan," I whined, freezing as I fully took him in.

"You feel so fucking good, Sloane," he muttered, his hands gripping my ass tightly.

I slowly began moving my hips, my clit brushing against his cock with every movement, my body trembling in response.

"The things you do to me, baby," he whispered into my ear before pressing his lips softly to my neck.

Pleasure rippled through me as I ground against him faster, the pressure building, my nipples hard and pressing against his firm chest.

"I'm gonna come, Callan," I moaned, grabbing his hair for support as I moved faster, chasing the release.

"Come on my cock, baby. Go on," he urged, his voice rough against my neck as he gently tugged my hair.

His words sent me over the edge, and I came hard, the pleasure crashing through me as I let out sounds I didn't know I was capable of, overwhelmed by a release like nothing I'd ever felt before.

"Fuck," he groaned as I slowed my hips. "I need to bend you over and watch your ass bounce against me."

Still catching my breath, I lifted myself off him and quickly got on my knees, bracing against the cushioned back seat. He grabbed my hips, guiding me until I was bent over, facing the rear window. His cock slowly pushed into me again, every inch of it reigniting the pleasure coursing through me. I moaned as he filled me once more.

"You okay?" he asked, a hint of concern in his voice.

"Yes," I breathed. "Fuck me."

He gathered my hair in his fist and, without warning, plunged into me fully—hard and fast.

"Your fucking pussy, baby...it's perfect," he growled.

"Spank me," I blurted out.

He didn't hesitate, his hand landing on my ass with a firm smack. I gasped, the sting sending a rush of heat through me, mixing with the pleasure of his cock filling me completely. The fullness made me crave more, my body begging for it.

"You like it rough, huh? You want me to pound your pussy?" he asked, smacking my ass again.

"Yes...fuck me hard, Callan," I moaned, another orgasm building fast.

"I knew you were a naughty fucking girl the moment I laid eyes on you this morning." He picked up the pace, reaching around to rub my clit. "And now you're *my* naughty fucking girl, aren't you? You're mine, baby. All. Mine."

"Yes! I'm your naughty girl!" His words, combined with the pressure on my clit, pushed me over the edge again. I came hard, and his grunts grew louder as his hips quickened, pounding furiously until he let out a deep, guttural moan.

His movements slowed, and we both caught our breath as I collapsed against the seat, my body melting from the intensity.

"Fuck!" Callan suddenly grunted, frustration evident as he pulled out of me.

I turned, confused, watching him hurriedly pull up his pants and boxer briefs.

"What?" I asked, still breathless and unsure, sitting back on my ass.

"We shouldn't have done that, Sloane," he hissed, quickly sliding into the driver's seat.

I scoffed, still feeling his cum dripping from me, and he was already spiraling into guilt?

"I wanted to do it, Callan. We're two consenting adults," I argued, grabbing my dress and slipping it back on. "And from what I'm feeling between my legs, I'm pretty sure you wanted it too."

Callan let out a small laugh. "Don't get me wrong—that was

fucking amazing. But it was still wrong." His tone grew more serious with each word.

I climbed into the passenger seat, frowning. "I still don't get why it's so wrong. Because you're older than me? That's it?"

He scoffed, starting the engine. "That's one of many reasons. The biggest being that I'm your fucking dad's friend."

"I'm not asking you to marry me. We just had sex. It's not that big of a deal."

Frustration bubbled up inside me. I couldn't even enjoy the fact that I'd just had sex for the first time—with probably the hottest guy I'd ever sleep with.

"Yeah, well, you're dodging a bullet, Sloane. You don't want a scumbag like me." He pulled out into downtown traffic, eyes fixed ahead.

I rolled my eyes, crossing my legs. "Do you always beat yourself up like this? And where are we going?"

"Yes," he snapped, his voice tight. "And I'm taking you home."

6

Callan

What an idiot. What a huge fucking idiot. My dick had completely taken over the moment Sloane climbed on top of me, her perfect body making my mind go blank. I couldn't even last one day without fucking a beautiful girl who threw herself at me? I've had better self-control with strippers throwing themselves at me in alleyways. And that would've been a hell of a lot better than fucking the eighteen-year-old daughter of the President of the United States—the girl I was supposed to protect.

So fucking stupid. But she was too perfect, too irresistible. Maybe if I kept being an asshole, she'd lose interest. But I didn't want to be an asshole. She was smart, funny, and so damn easy to talk to. And now I'd fucked up her first time by immediately telling her I regretted it. The truth was, I didn't regret a thing. I wanted to live inside that girl's pussy, worship her, lose myself in her. I wanted to disappear to fucking Fiji and spend the rest of my life following her, watching her stomp ahead of me, rolling her eyes at every step.

I'd never felt like this about anyone before. I didn't want to just fuck her—I wanted *her*. I *needed* her. I needed her to be mine. And it was never going to fucking happen.

She didn't say a word as she got out of the SUV, slamming the door behind her. I'd probably already fucked it all up. But I couldn't just run after her—what would that look like to everyone else?

I needed to clear my head. But first, I had to make sure she got inside safely.

"Don't follow me," she snapped when she noticed I was behind her.

"That's literally my job, Sloane," I shot back.

She spun around, flipping her hair over her shoulder, clearly pissed; it only made me want her more.

"I'm going inside now. See? Bye." She stormed through the side entrance of the house, disappearing from view.

I sighed heavily and made my way back to my car—my own car, a 1969 Mustang. I started the engine and drove the short five minutes to my downtown apartment, just a few blocks from where Sloane and I had fucked. I parked in the garage and headed up the elevator. My small apartment was still cluttered with boxes; I hadn't had time to unpack since arriving in D.C. just two days ago.

Jake had called me, panicked, asking me to drop everything I was doing in Virginia to come out here. He said he didn't trust anyone else to protect his family. And look at the great job I'd done in just twelve fucking hours.

As I took off my shirt, undressing for the shower, I was surprised to hear my phone vibrating on the bathroom counter. As much as I wanted Sloane's scent to linger on me forever, I needed to wash away my sins in the heat of a shower. Grabbing my phone, I saw a text from her. It was an image, but my phone was locked, so I couldn't see it right away. I unlocked it, and there it was—Sloane's perfect, bare ass filling the entire screen. My dick instantly hardened.

A follow-up text popped up as I gaped at the photo. **Next time in my ass?**

"Jesus fucking Christ," I muttered.

She was persistent, and I wanted her so fucking badly. My cock throbbed, and I knew I'd have to jerk off immediately.

There won't be a next time, Sloane.

I grew more frustrated with each passing second, furious that I couldn't have her the way I wanted.

Okay, sure. Look how long it took you to give in today.

I shook my head—she wasn't wrong. Without replying, I pulled out my dick and started stroking myself, thinking about that perfect ass.

What are you doing? Jerking off?

I ignored her text, focusing on the image in my mind—her ass bouncing on my cock. Only a minute later, my phone buzzed again—FaceTime. *Fuck it.* I accepted, and her screen lit up with the sight of her perfect pink pussy, her fingers swirling around her clit. She was smiling in the background.

"You *are* jerking off, you pervert," she teased.

My breathing hitched, my strokes speeding up as I watched her play with herself.

"Play with your tits," I muttered, my voice rough.

"Bossy, huh? I thought this wasn't going to happen again," she teased, but still grabbed her full tit, pushing my restraint even further.

"Doesn't count. I'm not touching you," I responded quickly, trying to hold off my orgasm.

She laughed softly. "Still counts to me. Let me see your big cock in your hand."

Sitting down on the closed toilet, I angled my phone to show her, but my eyes stayed glued to the screen, watching her.

"I want my mouth around it again. I want you to shove it down my throat," she breathed, her hand slipping back between her legs.

"Fuck, Sloane," I groaned, feeling the pre-cum drip into my fingers.

"What would you do to me if I were there right now?" Her voice turned quiet, serious, as her gaze locked with mine through the camera.

"I'd turn you around and give you another slap on your ass for trying so hard to fuck me," I blurted out.

She giggled. "And then?"

I wasn't going to last long. Her sweet little voice talking dirty pushed me closer to the edge. "And then I'd spread your legs, get on my knees, and taste your sweet pussy."

She moaned, eyes fluttering shut. I watched as she brought her fingers from her pussy to her mouth, slowly licking them clean.

"I can still taste your cum," she whispered.

"Fuck," I groaned. "Make yourself come, baby. I'm gonna explode."

My load shot up, landing on my hand as I drained every last drop. Her moans echoed through the phone, the screen shaking, but I couldn't see her.

Panting, I stared at my phone, waiting for her face to reappear. Finally, she came into view, smiling at me—suddenly looking a little shy.

"I want you," she whispered, settling into her bed.

Fuck, I want her too.

"I know. I want you too," I admitted.

She smiled wider. "I like hearing you say that. For a minute, I thought I was delusional or something," she teased.

My jaw clenched involuntarily. "I want you. It's just...it can't be a thing." *As much as I fucking want it to be.*

Her smile faltered, and the silence stretched between us. I wiped the cum off my hand into my boxer briefs and tossed them aside.

"I can keep a secret if you can," she finally murmured.

I shook my head. "It's too risky, Sloane."

I swear I saw her eyes glisten.

"My dad's too busy to notice anything," she countered softly.

I sighed, shaking my head again. "Maybe. But everyone else won't be as busy."

She bit her lip, glancing away. "Are you married or something?"

I let out a laugh, the idea absurd. *Yeah fucking right.*

"No, baby, I'm not married," I finally answered.

Her expression hardened. "Fine. I'll make you change your mind. You'll see," she said with determination. "Meet me here tomorrow morning. I need another ride."

* * *

I sat in the yellow oval room with Jake and Ana the next morning. I was tense—having to look Jake in the eye after fucking his daughter the night before had my conscience weighing heavily.

"I hope Sloane hasn't been too much of a handful." Jake laughed. "She's a good girl. But she is very determined to get her way. I heard she made you take her to Crepeaway last night."

My heart sank, and I cleared my throat, forcing a laugh. "It hasn't been a problem. She's...she's a sweet kid." My face heated up as I glanced at Ana, only to catch her giving me a knowing look.

"Good. I just worry, you know? Now that she's eighteen, I don't want people to think...fuck, I don't know. I don't want her to be taken advantage of," Jake continued.

I nodded, taking a quick sip of my coffee. "I get that."

I could hardly look him in the eye; this was the man who'd saved my life when we were SEALs, and I'd repaid him by fucking his daughter.

"She's going to tour Georgetown University today. We'd love to go with her, but we have to leave for Hiroshima for the summit meeting," Ana chimed in, resting her hand on Jake's thigh.

Jake glanced between Ana and me. "She's interested in women's and gender studies," he added proudly. "Just like Ana."

Ana smiled and shrugged. "I know she wants to get far away from D.C. Berkeley is her top choice. You'll probably have to take her there this spring too," she added.

I was too afraid to ask, but I did anyway. "Has she graduated high school?" Eighteen or not, if she was still in high school, I was going to flip the fuck out.

"She finished school early in the fall. She won't officially graduate until next month," Ana explained.

I blinked, nodding, not sure how to process that.

Jake looked over my shoulder. "Someone's ears must have been burning."

I turned, and my stomach dropped. Sloane walked into the room, wearing a white crochet crop top and ripped jean shorts that clung to every curve. The same white Converse she wore while we fucked last night stood planted firmly next to me.

"Good morning, baby." Ana reached out to squeeze Sloane's hand.

"Good morning," she said to her parents, then turned to me with a smile. "Hey."

"Good morning." I smiled back, keeping my expression polite as I willed myself to stay calm.

"I was just telling Callan that he'll be keeping an eye on you while Daddy and I are in Japan for a few days," Ana explained.

Sloane flashed a quick smile at her mom. "I can take care of myself. But thanks," she said coolly, leaning against the couch beside Ana, now facing me.

"He won't get in your way, honey. He just has a job to do," Jake added.

Sloane shot me a grin, and as fucked up as it was, I was excited to get some extended alone time with her.

She bit her lip, crossing her arms. "Fine. But you'll have to take me to Crepeaway again."

7

Sloane

It was so easy to keep breaking Callan's walls down. I knew exactly how he'd react when I sent that picture, so I was ready for the call. I knew he wouldn't be able to resist watching me play with myself. And when he told me he wanted me, my stomach swirled with butterflies.

I couldn't quite pinpoint what it was about him that made me want him so badly. Sure, he was hot—*so* fucking hot—but it was more than that. He had the foulest mouth and the toughest exterior, constantly trying to close himself off. Was it just the toxic masculinity he'd been taught to hide behind? Every time I chipped away at those walls, I felt a little victory. But really, I didn't know him all that well, did I? Maybe he just needed time to open up. Maybe trying to jump his bones at every chance I got wasn't the best way to get to know him...

The thought of my parents being gone for two days filled me with excitement—I wouldn't have to leave Callan's side. The real question was, would he want to stay by mine?

We spent half the twenty-minute drive to Georgetown in silence. As we stopped at a red light, I glanced over at him and instinctively placed my hand on his thigh. It felt natural, my palm resting on the fabric of his pants, feeling the muscle underneath. He quickly gave me a sidelong glance, offering a small smile.

"Hi," I said, suddenly feeling shy.

He smiled back. "Hi."

"We don't have to stay long. I don't really want to go to Georgetown. I'm just going on this tour to appease my parents."

The light turned green, and he accelerated smoothly.

"Where do you want to go then?" he asked, his curiosity piqued.

Anywhere you are.

"Berkeley. Or Stanford."

He nodded. "So, you've got your heart set on California?"

I shrugged. "I don't really know. I want to take my time deciding," I explained.

He smiled briefly, glancing over at me before returning his focus to the road. "Didn't take your time deciding on me," he joked.

I laughed. "You're about the only thing I've ever jumped into. Or onto," I teased.

He swallowed hard, giving a small nod. "And why's that?"

I turned to stare out the window. "I'm still trying to figure that out."

The car fell into silence for a moment. "You're wasting your time on me, Sloane. You could have any man you want."

I rolled my eyes without meaning to. "I don't want just any man, Callan. I want you."

He sighed, the weight of his breath heavy. "I'm the only man you've ever had. How do you know you don't want something else?"

My cheeks grew hot. "So...what? You want me to go fuck other guys before I can decide on you?"

His jaw tightened, and he shook his head. "I don't even want you *looking* at another man, Sloane. But it's not about what I want," he growled, his voice rough.

My pussy clenched, and I could feel the wetness soaking through my underwear. "So it's about what I want? Haven't I made it *abundantly* clear what that is?" My heart raced with frustration, my voice trembling slightly.

He stayed quiet for a moment before finally speaking. "We're here."

* * *

Georgetown was beautiful, but it still didn't change my mind about not wanting to go there. Callan stayed a few feet behind me and the tour guide, a handsome, eager counselor in his thirties who showed us around with a bit too much enthusiasm.

"We'd love to have you here, Miss Martin," the counselor said as we wrapped up at the main offices.

"Thanks. It was nice meeting you." I shook his hand and headed back toward Callan's SUV.

Ever since Callan made it clear he didn't want anyone else to have me, all I could think about was him taking me back to his place and properly fucking me. The moment he slid into the driver's seat, I placed my hand on his thigh again.

"Will you show me your place?" I asked sweetly. "Please?"

He stared at me, as if weighing his options.

"Sloane, you know I can't do that," he breathed, his deep, low voice sending a jolt straight between my legs.

I couldn't help but pout, disappointment clear on my face. His eyes softened.

"You know what will happen if we go to my apartment," he murmured quietly.

I sighed, pulling my hand from his thigh as I looked out the window.

"I just want to spend time with you. Can you come back and just...hang out with me?" I asked, almost begging.

"Of course, baby," he replied softly.

My stomach flipped at the way he called me *baby*. Hearing him say my name was always a thrill, but this? This was better than anything, especially because he said it outside of sex.

I quickly smiled and turned to him, the sight of his full lips making me crave them all over again. I hadn't planned on making a move on him at the White House, but now I wasn't so sure.

On the way back, I connected my phone to the car's Bluetooth, sharing all of my favorite songs with him. I was a huge fan of female bands from the '90s, especially those from the riot grrrl movement, like Bikini Kill and Bratmobile.

I noticed Callan grinning from ear to ear as we listened to "Demirep" by Bikini Kill.

"What?" I laughed, turning the volume down.

"I like it. You're a good little punk rock riot girl," he teased with a laugh.

"A good one, huh?" I asked, surprised that he knew about the movement.

He nodded. "Doesn't surprise me, though. They're badass, just like you."

I couldn't stop beaming. "What music do *you* like?"

He glanced over at me as we pulled up to the house. "Everything. Rap, hip hop, metal, classical. The Beatles. I'm a man of many tastes."

He cut the engine, and we lingered in the car for a moment. Now I was grinning just as wide.

"I like getting to know you. What else? Where did you live before you came here?" I asked eagerly.

He looked down at his hands. "Virginia. I was undercover there for a while. Glad to leave it behind, though."

That piqued my curiosity. "What kind of undercover stuff?"

He side-eyed me, shaking his head. "Stuff I'm not allowed to talk about. Come on, let's go inside."

* * *

I led Callan into the hall where bookshelves lined the walls and a grand piano sat off to the side. I sat down at the piano, playing casually while he browsed the books. As I began to play "Let It Be," I drifted into my own world, softly singing, my eyes closed to fend off any stage fright. After the chorus, I stopped and opened my eyes, realizing Callan was now sitting next to me, his soft, kind eyes locked on me.

"Sloane, you're amazing," he whispered, sitting close, though he wasn't touching me.

My cheeks flushed as I looked down at the keys.

I shrugged. "I play occasionally. When I feel like it."

He chuckled softly. "The Beatles are my absolute favorite. But the way you just sang it—that's my favorite version now."

Tears pricked at my eyes. It was the best compliment I'd ever received. I wanted to kiss him so badly, and it broke my heart that I couldn't—not here, not now.

"Come on. My room." I stood quickly and headed down the

hallway.

"Sloane," he called, still rooted to the seat as I glanced over my shoulder.

I stopped and sighed, walking back toward him. "Please. I just want your company. I won't try to make a move on you. I promise," I whispered, hoping he'd believe me.

He looked conflicted, glancing down the hallway before letting out a heavy sigh. Finally, he nodded and stood up slowly. "Okay."

He followed me into my room, and I made sure to lock the door behind us. The space was fairly neat, with touches of my personality scattered throughout—framed photos of old movie stars on the walls, a desk overflowing with journals and books, and several plants hanging by the window. Callan kept his hands in his pockets, glancing around until he stopped at my bookshelf.

"*Birthday Girl?*" he asked, scanning my smut collection. Of course, he'd pick the age gap and forbidden romance shelf.

"Yeah, I...uh, like romance. Spicy romance." I laughed, kicking off my Converse and sitting on the bed.

He turned to me, eyebrows raised. "Why doesn't that surprise me?"

I smiled and rolled my eyes, glancing out the window at the light rain drizzling down.

Changing the subject quickly, he moved to sit in the chair at the far end of the room—putting as much distance between us as possible. "So, how long have you been playing piano?" he asked, crossing his legs and revealing a pair of argyle socks under his black suit. Seeing him like that only made me want him more.

"I don't know. Ten years?" I guessed. "I taught myself when

I was younger."

Callan looked genuinely surprised. "That's impressive. You continue to surprise me." He smiled, his gaze lingering on me.

My cheeks heated up again, his compliments making me feel dizzy with pride.

"What about you? Do you play any instruments?" I leaned back on the bed, letting my legs dangle as I watched him.

"Some guitar. Not very well, though—mostly just for fun." He shrugged. "I spend most of my time working on my '69 Mustang and my motorcycle."

Why did the fact that he had a motorcycle and a classic car turn me on?

"Well, you're obviously good with your hands."

I hoped he'd catch the double meaning, and by the way he narrowed his eyes and flashed a sly smile, I knew he did.

"It's raining out. You want to watch a rainy-day movie?" I asked casually, though my real hope was to get closer to him, craving the warmth of being near him again.

He was quiet for a moment, staring down at the floor.

"What movie do you have in mind?"

I grabbed my laptop off the nightstand and opened it. "Come help me pick one," I said with a smile, eager to draw him closer.

Callan didn't move. I glanced over at him and patted the bed beside me. "I won't touch you. I swear."

He let out a heavy sigh—the kind I was starting to expect whenever he felt the need to argue. Slowly, he got up, slipping off his suit jacket and draping it over the chair. He took his time walking to the bed, pausing to look out the window before his gaze finally landed on me.

"Okay. But no romance flicks."

8

Callan

I didn't know why I kept saying yes to situations I knew I wouldn't be able to resist. And now, here I was, sitting on Sloane's bed, just inches away from her as she streamed *Jurassic Park* on her laptop. She wasn't even born when that movie came out. I shook my head at myself, fucking pissed that I'd let this happen—I was falling for the President's eighteen-year-old daughter, the very girl I was supposed to protect. And not just any girl—she was the daughter of my Navy SEAL shipmate, someone I'd known for twenty years. *Fuck.*

We watched the movie in silence, side by side, and the tension between us was undeniable. She kept her promise—not once did she try to touch me. And somehow, I hadn't touched her either. But when thunder suddenly roared outside, making Sloane jump, she laughed at herself and glanced at me. She was so damn beautiful, it felt criminal. And it wasn't just her looks—her soul felt older than eighteen. I had no doubt she was smarter than me. What the hell did I know, anyway? So what if I had a master's degree and was a fucking Navy SEAL? The woman sitting next to me could start and end wars if she wanted. She could do anything without breaking a sweat. And I was crazy about her.

So it didn't surprise me when my hand slipped onto her thigh after she jumped from the thunder. I kept my eyes on the screen, but I could see her glance at me from the corner of my eye. I was too afraid to look at her because I knew that if I did, I wouldn't be able to resist kissing those perfect, full lips.

As we watched Jeff Goldblum almost die, Sloane gently rested her head on my shoulder, her hand slipping on top of mine that was still on her thigh. I'd already broken my own rule, so why was she still holding back? I couldn't focus on the movie anymore—all I could think about was the smell of her vanilla-scented hair and the warmth of her hand on mine.

"Callan," she whispered.

I shut my eyes tightly, savoring the way my name sounded on her lips.

"Hm?" I responded quietly.

She didn't say anything. Instead, she nuzzled her nose against my shoulder, carefully scooting closer.

"Sloane. We can't." My voice was strained, and I could hear the lack of conviction in my own words.

"I know. We're not," she whispered back.

My heart raced, and I could feel my dick hardening. *Fuck it.* I turned toward her, cupping her face as I pulled her in for a heated kiss. She responded immediately, her hands tangling in my hair as she swung a leg over me, straddling my lap. Her grinding against my growing erection sent a shock through me, and I quickly slipped my hands under her top, pulling it over her head, forcing our lips apart. I couldn't stop myself from staring at her perky, full tits before leaning down to take one in my mouth, pulling her closer.

Her warm, soft body turned me into a fucking animal as she kept grinding on me, tugging my hair, soft moans escaping her lips.

"Come on, baby. On your back. I want to taste your pretty pussy," I growled, laying her down and tugging her shorts off in one swift motion.

She eagerly helped, yanking them off before pulling at my tie and unbuttoning my shirt. I shrugged it off quickly and spread her legs open, my mouth watering at the sight of her wet, trimmed pussy. Her eyes locked onto mine, filled with desire, as I knelt between her legs, placing them over my shoulders.

I pressed my lips to her slit, spreading her open with my tongue and tasting her sweetness. Her moans grew louder, and I couldn't help but growl into her as I licked deeper, hungrily devouring her.

"Oh my god...Callan...I'm gonna...come," she whimpered.

I chuckled with delight as I stuck two fingers inside of her and circled her clit with my tongue. Her thighs pressed against the sides of my head as she grabbed a pillow and screamed into it, her body trembling as she lifted her hips up and down against my face. I didn't slow—I continued to play with her clit, wanting her to come on my face over and over again. Without fail, she screamed into the pillow again, her fingers tangling in my hair as she pulled me closer, grinding against my face.

"Fuck, baby. You have the sweetest pussy I've ever tasted," I said before I began to gently kiss the inside of her thighs.

"Callan. Fuck me," she begged, throwing her pillow to the floor. "Please. I need you inside of me."

I didn't hesitate to stand up and remove my pants and boxer briefs, letting my aching cock spring free as I watched her gorgeous body waiting for me.

I quickly hovered over her and kissed her passionately, gently scanning my hand across her body and tits while my other pressed down against the bed for support. She squirmed as I put my fingers to her wet pussy, gently pushing one inside of her; I loved feeling her arousal for me. I removed my finger and pulled my lips from hers, sticking my wet finger into her mouth. She sucked on it as she looked up at me with lust, a smile clear on her lips. *Fuck, I need to be inside of her.* I grabbed my cock and started to tease her pussy by rubbing myself up and down her slit.

"Please!" she continued to beg, pulling my hips toward hers.

I chuckled, then quickly thrust myself into her, forcing her to whimper as she dug her nails into my back. I watched her big, full tits bounce up and down as I slowly thrust in and out of her, taking my time feeling her pussy stretch for me.

"Harder. Faster," she ordered eagerly.

"Wait, baby. You just feel so fucking good," I said into her ear before putting my lips to her neck.

She turned her head, seeking my lips, and our passionate kiss only drove my hips to move faster, thrusting deep inside her. A loud moan escaped her, and I broke away from the kiss, sitting up on my knees as I pulled her legs to my chest and began thrusting again. I watched her tits bounce with every movement, gripping her legs tight while pounding into her, her hands clutching the comforter. The sight of her body, the sound of her breathy moans—it was almost too much. I knew I wouldn't last in that position, so I pulled out, flipping her onto her knees.

"Fuck me hard," she demanded, pressing her ass against my thighs.

I let out a soft laugh, but her eagerness made my knees weak.

"Oh, baby. I'm gonna fuck you until you can't see straight." I thrust back into her quickly, gripping her hips as I pounded her, mesmerized by the way her ass bounced with every movement. The sight had me fucking hooked. I knew exactly how to make her come again; sliding an arm around her, I teased her clit while keeping my hips driving hard into her.

"Oh, fuck," she whimpered as she fisted her comforter, her pussy clenching around my cock.

The feeling of her tight pussy coming for me pushed me over the edge—I came instantly, a deep growl rumbling from my throat beneath the sound of Sloane's whimpers. My hips slowed as we both caught our breath, but the familiar guilt started creeping back into my gut. I couldn't keep pulling away after we fucked; I knew it hurt her. But she couldn't expect this to keep happening...even if it did.

I pulled out and collapsed onto my side, tugging her close. She immediately wrapped a leg over me, pressing herself against me, our sweaty bodies tangled together. Her hand found my beard, her fingers gently stroking my face.

"You started it," she teased, almost reading my thoughts.

I chuckled. "I can't fucking help myself. You're like my Kryptonite."

She giggled. "Hmm. Does that make you Superman?'"

I smiled down at her, her deep brown eyes gazing up at me with a zeal that sent flutters through my chest, turning me to mush. I fucking loved her. I never wanted to leave her side. Two days—that's all it took for me to fall for this girl. It was terrifying.

"Nah. I could beat Superman's ass," I joked with a grin.

Her eyebrows lifted in amusement. "I bet you could. Look at you," she mused, running her fingers along my arms. "You're a beast. How'd you get so buff?"

She was flattering me, but I didn't mind soaking it in.

"I work out a lot. If I'm not on the job, I'm either at the gym or working on my car."

She sighed dramatically. "Work, work, work. You need a vacation. You should take me to Fiji. Or Hawaii," she teased.

God, I'd fucking love that. Sitting on the beach with my beautiful girl beside me, warm sand on our feet, the sun giving her olive skin a cute little suntan.

"Hmm." I laughed, but it came out half-hearted. "I wish." The reality of it all started to sink in. This was too forbidden, too fucking complicated. It could never last, no matter how much I wanted it to.

Sloane's frown deepened as she searched my face. "I wish you'd tell me what's on your mind. Your thoughts are safe with me."

There it was again—that fucking old soul wisdom. She'd be a great fucking therapist.

"I can't because it doesn't matter. Everything I'm thinking about you would turn to dust the second I said it out loud."

She was quiet for a moment. "Not if we didn't let them," she said softly.

I sighed, shaking my head. "We can't, Sloane. You know it, I know it," I said, my voice dry and emotionless, even though I wanted to cry into a pillow.

She let go of me and sat up in bed. I followed her.

"Why keep doing this, then? I've already caught feelings. I really like you, and it hurts so badly when you say these things."

I was pushing her away. Maybe it was for the best. Maybe she could live a normal, happy life with someone her age—not worrying about taking care of an old man like me years down the road.

"I thought my thoughts were safe with you? And now you're mad because I'm telling you the truth?" I shot back.

She scoffed, standing up to grab her clothes. "I didn't say I was mad. But you can't just say those things and expect me not to feel hurt. I wish, just once, you'd tell me you cared about me after we fucked instead of saying shit like that," she yelled, pulling on her underwear.

I sluggishly grabbed my clothes and began to dress, the heaviness in my chest making every movement feel like a chore. I hated that I was hurting her. All I wanted was to fucking kidnap her, take her to Tahiti, change our identities, and spend every second of the day fucking while I told her how much I loved her.

"I'm sorry, Sloane. I don't like hurting you," I admitted quietly, sitting still on the bed with my shirt hanging open and my pants half-buttoned.

She shrugged, crossing her arms, her voice soft but firm. "Maybe we should only see each other when it's absolutely necessary. This...this hurts too much," she said, motioning between us.

I nodded because she was right. "Okay." My voice was flat, defeated. Hers wasn't much better.

She watched me stand to finish getting dressed, slipping on my shoes. Every part of me wanted to drop to my knees and tell her how much I needed her, how much I loved her. But instead, I just walked out the door, saying nothing, and sat at the piano in the hallway, hating myself more than I ever had.

9

Sloane

I was going to be petty, and I didn't care. It wasn't like me, but Callan had me doing and saying things that were so out of character. I needed to show him I was worth the fight. And if that meant going out with another guy to make him jealous, then so be it.

I texted my mom that night as I lay in bed, crying off and on, feeling sorry for myself. I wanted so badly to text Callan, but I couldn't give in. If he wanted to talk, he could text me first.

Hey Mom. Who was that guy you said I'd like? The son of that one guy?

I had half paid attention when she'd mentioned some twenty-year-old she thought was adorable. Apparently, they met at a dinner, and she was impressed enough to get his number for me. She was always trying to play matchmaker, much to Dad's dismay.

James Miller? Mayor Miller's son?

I rolled my eyes, sighing. I didn't want this James guy—I wanted Callan.

I guess? What was his number again? I wondered how

56

suspicious I sounded, trying to get a guy's number while my parents were out of town. Mom was pretty open-minded, though.

She texted back the number, then added: **Please be careful. Let Callan know where you'll be.**

I laughed to myself. How ironic. **Thanks, Mom.**

I copied and pasted his number, sending a quick text. **Hey. This is Sloane. Embarrassingly, I got your number from my mom.**

Setting my phone down, I grabbed my laptop off the end table, wondering what Callan was doing. My phone vibrated only a minute later.

Hey Sloane. I'm glad to hear from you. I didn't think I would, haha. What's going on?

I sighed, texting back. **Not much. Where do you live again?**

I needed to be persistent if I was going to make Callan jealous. **I'm off-campus at Georgetown. Wanna hang out or something?**

I smiled, feeling like my plan was working. Glancing at my phone, I noticed it was 8:07 p.m.—not too late for dinner. **Yeah. Meet for dinner?**

He replied almost instantly. **Yeah, that would be cool. I know a good place downtown. I'll text you the address. Meet around 9?**

I was already dreading it. **Sounds good. See you then.**

* * *

I slipped into my most flattering dress—a yellow silk mini that hugged my curves and showed off my best assets. Chunky heels and bold red lipstick completed the look. As I walked into the hall, I glanced around, hoping to spot Callan. The rain had stopped a couple of hours ago, but the sticky heat lingered in the air, even indoors.

"Sloane." Callan's voice came from behind me.

I turned, and there he was, leaning against the hall, his eyes roaming over me. He took me all in, and the ache of wanting him flared up inside me. But apparently, he didn't want me enough.

"Where are you going?" His gaze dipped briefly to my cleavage before he shoved his hands into his pockets.

"I forgot I had a thing tonight. A dinner thing." It wasn't a lie, but I wasn't exactly telling him the whole truth either.

"What dinner thing? With who?" he pressed, stepping closer, his expression shifting to something serious, almost concerned.

"You don't want to know," I muttered, turning on my heel to walk away.

"Sloane." He grabbed my arm and spun me around.

My heart raced, desire surging hot and fast. My chest rose and fell rapidly as I stared at him, every nerve in my body screaming for him to throw me into my bedroom and fuck me senseless.

"I promise you don't want to know," I whispered, Callan's face only inches from mine as he hovered above me.

His expression flickered between anger and concern. "Tell me."

"Let go of me," I argued, trying to keep my voice steady.

He ignored my plea. "Tell me, Sloane."

I sighed, pulling myself free from his grip. "My mom set me up with this guy. Long before we ever...met." I crossed my arms, staring anywhere but at him. "We're having dinner downtown.”

Callan licked his lips, his eyes darkening with anger when I finally dared to glance up at him.

He let out a short, disbelieving laugh. “You’re not fucking doing that.”

My mouth dropped open, and I laughed in disbelief right back. “What?”

“You’re gonna go on a fucking date when we just fucked a few hours ago?”

Was he seriously judging me?

“You’re the one who said we can’t do this,” I hissed, feeling my own anger bubbling up. “You don’t get to dictate what I do or who I see.”

Callan fell silent, but the anger simmering beneath the surface didn’t fade. He looked like he was wrestling with what to say next.

“I’m driving you there. And you’re not fucking going anywhere else with him,” he growled before storming toward the stairs. I quickly caught up with him.

“You’re really going to drive me to a date?” I scoffed, trailing him down the stairs.

“Mmhmm.”

Maybe he really doesn’t care about me. I followed him to his SUV, and he held the passenger door open for me, but I brushed past him, opening the door behind the driver’s seat and slamming it shut.

“So, where are you meeting this fuck face?” he asked as soon as he started the engine.

“Downtown. Here.” I leaned forward, typing the address into the built-in GPS, catching the familiar scent of his woodsy cologne as I moved back to my seat.

As the car began to move, I stared out the window, willing Callan to say something—*anything*. The only thing that kept running through my head was, *pull over and fuck me right now.*

After a few minutes, he finally broke the silence. "So, who is this idiot?"

I sighed, holding back a smile, enjoying the jealousy in his voice.

"I don't know. His name's James. He's some mayor's son."

Callan scoffed, saying nothing more until we reached the restaurant in the heart of downtown.

"Don't let this fucking kid touch you," he warned as I opened the door. "I'll be right here, Sloane—"

I slammed the door shut behind me, cutting him off. Flipping my hair, I glanced back through the window, catching Callan's scowl. *This is such a bad idea.*

As I walked into the restaurant, regret hit me instantly—I had no clue what James looked like, and now I felt completely out of place as curious eyes followed me. Pulling out my phone, I shot him a quick text.

I'm here, but I have no idea what you look like.

I scanned the room nervously until I spotted an attractive guy approaching. Brown wavy hair, a big, bright smile with dimples, medium build, taller than me, wearing casual jeans and a bomber jacket.

"Sloane, hey. I'm James," he said, extending his hand for a shake.

He was cute, but he was no Callan.

I smiled. "Hey."

He gestured toward the restaurant. "I've got a table for us outside. A little more privacy that way," he explained, sounding a bit nervous.

He's sweet. "Okay, after you."

I followed him through the crowded restaurant and out a side door that led to a cozy outdoor space, small tables adorned with lone candles flickering in the middle. Only two other couples were nearby, neither paying any attention to us. I felt a little more at ease.

James pulled out my chair for me, then sat across from me.

"So, um." He smiled nervously. "What made you decide to text me tonight?"

I glanced down at the table, guilt creeping in. I was using him to make Callan jealous, and that didn't sit right with me.

"I, uh...I don't really know." I laughed softly, feeling a bit embarrassed. "I guess I just wanted some company." I shrugged, meeting his eyes again.

He nodded, offering a small smile. "I'm happy to keep you company."

Under different circumstances, I'd be thrilled to be on a date with him. He was sweet, attractive, and kind. But I was already tangled up in whatever this thing was with Callan.

I quickly changed the subject. "So, you go to Georgetown?"

He nodded. "Almost a senior. I'm a psych major. What about you?"

The waiter arrived, placing water and menus in front of us before leaving. As soon as he walked away, I answered.

"I'm actually graduating next month. Haven't decided on college yet, but it's looking like Berkeley."

James smiled, nodding. "I love it out there. I almost went to Berkeley too."

"Oh, really?" My voice sounded too excited—I didn't want to be excited for anyone but Callan.

We continued with small talk, and I started to feel more at

ease. James was sweet, but I knew by the end of the meal that I didn't want to see him again, at least not romantically. How was I ever going to move on from Callan? James was great and all, but Callan...Callan was a real man—fierce, ungodly attractive, and impossible to forget.

As I laughed at a joke James made, a familiar figure caught my eye. Turning my head, I saw Callan walk through the side door, his stride purposeful, his face twisted with unmistakable anger.

"Sloane. I've been trying to reach you," Callan said in his deep, low voice, not even sparing a glance at James.

"Uh...my phone's in my purse," I explained, fumbling for the small bag hanging off my chair.

"We need to get you home. I can't explain right now, but we need to leave. *Now.*"

I looked up at him, eyes wide, my heart racing with anxiety. *What the hell is going on?*

"I hope everything's okay," James chimed in, his voice uncertain.

I glanced at James, then back at Callan.

"Now, Sloane. It's urgent." His tone was sharp, impatient, his eyes still refusing to acknowledge James.

"Uh...okay." I stood up, frowning at James. "I'm sorry, James. It was nice meeting you."

"Yeah—" he started, but Callan grabbed my arm and pulled me away before he could finish.

I hurried to keep up, nerves eating at me as a hundred worst-case scenarios flashed through my mind. *What if someone hurt my dad? Or worse...*

"What's going on?" I asked as we rushed out of the restaurant into the warm, sticky night air.

Callan didn't answer, gripping my hand and leading me several blocks away from the downtown chaos.

"Please, Callan. Tell me what's going on. Is my dad okay?" I asked, my voice trembling as tears welled in my eyes.

He stopped, glancing back at me. "Yes. Your dad's fine. Everything is fine." He picked up the pace again, pulling me into a narrow alley.

Frustration boiled over. "Stop, Callan," I snapped, yanking my hand free from his.

He spun around, and even in the darkness, I could see his chest rising and falling rapidly, his eyes dark with intensity. Without warning, he pressed me against the wall, his body close, heat radiating between us.

"You think I'm gonna let some fucking boy touch you? You're *mine*, Sloane. You're fucking *mine*," he growled, then crashed his lips against mine, the kiss rough and desperate.

My mind went blank as I wrapped my leg around Callan, his hard body pinning me firmly against the wall. He hoisted my other leg up, lifting me effortlessly, my dress riding up as he grabbed my thighs. His erection pressed against my already dripping pussy, grinding into me with a desperate urgency. I heard his zipper slide down as he freed one hand from my leg.

"You win, baby. You fucking win," he breathed, quickly swiping my panties to the side and thrusting into me with an urgent need.

"Fuck, Callan," I whined into his ear, wrapping my arms around his shoulders as I bounced on his cock, my slickness making every movement fluid, his thick length sliding in and out with ease.

The friction against my clit sent me spiraling, my body giving in to a sharp orgasm. A low moan escaped my lips, half aware that we were out in public but too far gone to care.

"My cock is the only one you will ever come on. You understand me, Sloane?" His voice was rough, and he tugged my hair back, forcing me to look into his dark, intense eyes as he kept grinding into me.

"Yes, yes—" I moaned, my body trembling as another orgasm rushed through me, my eyes fluttering shut just as Callan let out a deep, throaty groan.

His hips slowed, and he trailed kisses along my neck and shoulder before his lips found mine. He kissed me hard, fierce, and possessive, and in that moment, I knew—Callan was mine.

10

Callan

I knew Sloane went out with that kid just to make me fucking jealous. And it worked. Watching her walk out of her room in that short dress, her tits bouncing, red lipstick making her look fucking stunning—it instantly had me hard. I was in way over my head with this shit, and offering to drive her to that kid was the stupidest thing I could've done.

I parked a few blocks away, standing against the wall across the street, watching them sit and talk. She was fucking laughing. Too comfortable, with her hand resting on the chair, her tits bouncing every time she laughed. And that asshole was checking her out whenever she looked away. It was infuriating.

I had to get her out of there.

Before I knew it, my feet were already moving toward them, my mind spinning. I didn't even have a plan, but there was no way I was letting her finish that date.

I hadn't planned on fucking her in the alley, but she had me so worked up. Her feistiness drove me wild, and being inside her—it released all the anger I'd been holding. Her pussy was like my fucking anger management.

When I told her she'd won, it surprised me. I hadn't even thought about it, but the words slipped out. And she knew exactly what I meant. I couldn't live without her. If we had to keep this a secret for the rest of our lives, I didn't care. I just wanted her, however I could have her.

I held her hand as I drove the few blocks to my apartment. I needed her close, in my arms until she was sick of me. My place would give me that freedom.

When we walked in, Sloane looked around like she'd just stepped into the Louvre. It wasn't even 700 square feet—just a place that reminded me of a hotel suite. But it worked for me.

"Your place is so cute. I love it," she mused, setting her purse down on the kitchen counter.

"Cute?" I repeated, slipping off my suit jacket.

She glanced back at me with a playful smile. "Cute in size. Super manly," she teased, her eyebrows raising in amusement.

Having her in my apartment, in my space, put me in such a good mood that I felt like a little fucking schoolboy.

I rolled my eyes, slipping off my tie and shirt. The moment she noticed I was shirtless, her eyes widened as she checked me out. She bit her lip, shrugging her heels off, which made her look even shorter and sweeter. Slowly, she walked toward me, placing her hands against my chest with a look of awe.

"You're so fucking sexy," she whispered, her eyes locking with mine.

I let out a soft laugh. "Look in the fucking mirror, baby."

She smiled and rolled her eyes. "Take the compliment. Does no one ever tell you that? Because I find that hard to believe."

Her hands stayed on my chest as I grabbed her wrists, bringing them up to my lips and gently kissing the top of each hand.

"I don't let anyone close enough to give me compliments," I admitted quietly.

Her eyebrows lifted. "That doesn't surprise me. When was your last relationship?"

I laughed again, but it felt hollow. "Relationship? Fuck. Years ago. I don't have time for a relationship."

The moment the words left my mouth, I knew she'd take it the wrong way. Her hands slid off my chest, and she stepped back, her eyes wandering around the apartment again. *Fuck.*

"Sloane, I think we should talk about this," I said, grabbing a stool from under the kitchen island, feeling the tension rise between us.

She froze for a moment, then nodded before sitting on the stool next to me. I spread my legs slightly, pulling hers between mine as I held her hands.

"I can't stop thinking about you. This is the first time I've ever felt like this, and it scares the shit out of me. I don't know how we're going to make this work, but I want to. I want you so fucking bad."

The hard line of her lips softened into a smile, and she squeezed my hands, looking down at them as she played shy.

"I want to do this too. I'm crazy about you, Callan," she said softly, peeking up at me through her lashes.

That feeling deep in my chest tightened. I already knew it—I fucking loved this girl. But I couldn't say it yet. I didn't want to rush things and fuck it all up.

"You wanna stay here tonight, baby? Maybe help me fix this place up?" I asked, glancing at the boxes scattered around the apartment.

Her smile brightened, revealing a small dimple in her cheek that made my chest ache. *Fuck, she's beautiful.*

"I'd love to."

* * *

Sloane had slipped on one of my T-shirts while helping me unpack, and seeing her in it made something stir inside me—an even deeper possessiveness than before. I knew I had to keep unwiring the ingrained misogyny that had shaped me over the years. Growing up in a military household, then joining the military, and later becoming a government agent—none of those environments exactly fostered equal rights or feminism.

That fact became glaringly obvious when Sloane's phone vibrated on the kitchen counter just before midnight, right as I was about to suggest we head to bed. I grabbed it quickly, realizing it was from that stupid fucking kid she went on a date with. The screen was locked, so I couldn't read the message.

"Who is it?" she asked, noticing the scowl I knew was plastered on my face.

"That fucking kid you went on a date with. What does it say?" I handed the phone to her as she stood in front of me.

Her brows pulled together, but she glanced down and read it. "He's just asking if everything is okay," she said, holding the phone up for me to see.

I grabbed the phone and started scrolling through their conversation. My blood boiled when I saw she'd only planned the date an hour before she left.

"I thought your mom set you up with him. You *initiated* it?" My voice came out harsher than I intended.

Her eyes widened in anger. "I was mad at you for acting like you wanted nothing to do with me. I wanted you to realize what you were missing out on," she snapped back.

For some reason, seeing her pissed off turned me into fucking mush. Maybe something was wrong with me for finding an angry woman so damn endearing—or maybe it was just *her* and that goddamn beautiful face.

"Alright, well, you're not talking to him anymore," I finally said, setting her phone down on the counter.

She planted her hand on her hip, her eyes narrowing. "Just because we're making this a 'thing' doesn't mean you get to dictate what I do."

There was my fiery fucking feminist. I couldn't argue—because she was right. But that didn't make me any less jealous.

"So, what then? You want to keep talking to that fuck face?" I asked, bitterness seeping into my tone.

Sloane paused for a moment, then burst out laughing. I couldn't help but crack a smile too.

"No, I don't. But that's not the point," she said, her tone lighter now. "It's hot when you're possessive and tell me I'm yours, but actually *telling* me what to do in real life? Not so hot."

Now I was the one laughing. I loved how she called me out on my shit, and her honesty just made me fall harder.

"Okay, baby. I'm sorry," I finally whispered, cupping her face and pressing my lips gently against hers.

A soft moan escaped her throat, pushing me over the edge. Without breaking the kiss, I scooped her up and set her on the counter. She opened her legs, wrapping them around my waist, pulling me closer.

"Fuck. I can't get enough of you, Sloane," I murmured, trailing kisses down her neck.

She let out another soft moan. "Give me your big cock, Cal," she purred, her voice thick with need.

I quickly slipped her panties off, tossing them to the floor. "Let me see you on your knees first, baby."

Her smile widened as she slowly removed my T-shirt from her body, then slid off the counter and knelt before me. Her eyes, wide and eager, locked on mine as I pulled off my pants, my hard cock straining beneath my boxer briefs.

"What do you want to do with my cock?" I teased, watching her gaze fixate on me, filled with desire.

She bit her lip and smiled. "I want it in my mouth. I want you to fuck my face."

Holy fucking shit. Hearing her talk dirty was quickly becoming my new favorite thing.

"I might have to shove it in there. You think you can take me?" I teased, my voice low.

She nodded eagerly, her eyes full of anticipation.

"Use your words, baby," I coaxed, wanting to hear more.

"I can take you. I'll be your good girl and open wide." Her voice was sweet but laced with something dark, and it almost pushed me over the edge.

"Where'd you get such a dirty mouth, huh?" I asked, grinning.

She giggled, teasing. "From my spicy books. Aren't you glad I read them now?"

I let out a soft laugh. *Of course.* "Maybe. Let's hear more of that filthy mouth," I said, placing my hand on the back of her head and pulling her toward my cock, rubbing it against her face through my briefs.

"Mmmm," she moaned. "I want your big fucking cock to choke me, Daddy."

I stopped and pulled away. "Daddy?" I repeated.

She looked up at me with wide eyes. "What? You've never had anyone call you Daddy during sex before?"

I felt conflicted. Here I was, old enough to be her dad—*her dad's friend*—and she was calling *me* Daddy. It twisted something inside me, a mix of guilt and desire, making my pulse race and my head spin.

"You wanna call me Daddy?" I asked, rubbing my cock on her face again.

"Yes, Daddy." She smiled eagerly.

"You want to be my good fucking girl and choke on my cock?" *Fuck, I'm gonna burst.*

"Only if you'll come deep down my throat, Daddy."

Jesus fucking Christ. "Baby, you're gonna make me come just by flapping your gorgeous fucking mouth like that."

She giggled, and it was the perfect moment to yank her hair back, pull my cock out, and shove it into her mouth. Sloane moaned, her wide eyes watering as I pushed deeper into her pretty mouth. I couldn't hold back any longer. Pulling her up, I bent her over the counter, desperate for a taste of her.

Spreading her legs, I dove right in, burying my mouth against her pussy, my tongue working its way inside as I smothered myself with her. She moaned, and I added a finger, feeling her push back against me, urging me on.

Without a second thought, I moved my mouth from her pussy to her ass, licking her hole like a fucking ice cream cone.

"Fuck! Oh my God!" she screamed.

I furiously fingered her while I ate her ass, then inched my finger to her clit, forcing a loud moan from her as she rode my hand.

"I'm coming. I'm coming—"

Her hand reached back, grabbing my hair with a surprising

force that made my dick throb even harder. She slowed her hips, letting her upper body collapse onto the counter, panting and laughing.

"Oh my God, that was fucking incredible," she breathed out.

"Your ass is fucking incredible, baby. Now come sit on my cock." I stroked myself as I stood up, palming her ass and giving it a light tap, waiting for her to take what we both needed.

She turned and pushed me towards the couch, then shoved me down on my ass once we reached it. *God, she's fucking amazing.* She widened her legs to hover on top of me and then quickly sat on my cock, gasping as she inched herself in deeper. Her full tits bounced in my face as she rode me, moving faster and faster, and I knew I was close to exploding as she tilted her head back, her hands gripping my thighs for support.

"You still want my cum in your throat, baby?" I said between hitched breaths.

"Yes, Daddy," she moaned, her hips continuing to grind on me.

I kissed her before I lifted her up and sat her on her knees. I stood up and stroked myself in front of her full lips.

"Please. I need your cum." She smiled and opened her mouth wide.

That's all it took—I grabbed the back of her head and shoved my cock in her mouth, my load shooting directly into her throat. I refused to let my eyes close with pleasure as I watched her take my load, her gaze never leaving mine.

She moaned and smiled before my cock ever left her mouth.

"Fuck, baby. I need to make you my wife," I joked as I pulled out of her mouth.

She stood up, her lips still slick with my cum, and kissed me deeply.

"Let's do it. I'm yours."

11

Sloane

I knew Callan was joking about making me his wife, but I wanted to make him sweat for a minute. He'd put me through the wringer so many times, I figured it was my turn.

"Let's go tomorrow," I said, widening my eyes dramatically. "We can fly to Vegas and elope. No one has to know."

His brows furrowed, and I could see the flicker of fear on his face. I couldn't hold it in—I burst out laughing, collapsing onto the couch.

"You fucking terrify me, baby." He laughed, grabbing my legs and kneeling in front of the couch.

He pulled me close, kissing me with that familiar passion, then effortlessly lifted me up and carried me to his bed.

Naturally, sleep was impossible. I was too excited just being around Callan, spending the night in his apartment like a real adult...like his real girlfriend.

As he lay next to me, sleeping peacefully, I quietly got up and wandered into the living room. I turned on the small light above the oven and began moving around, opening cabinets and peeking into the boxes we hadn't unpacked yet. One box caught my attention—it had a few pictures inside. I pulled out one of my dad and Callan, younger, standing side by side in their Navy uniforms. A tug pulled at my heart as I finally started to understand what Callan must be feeling.

He and my dad had been through so much together. Dad said he didn't trust anyone else to look after me. And now here I was, throwing myself at Callan while he wrestled with his conflicting emotions—betraying my dad or being with me. Guilt washed over me, but my feelings for Callan ran deeper than anything else. Wouldn't Dad understand that I...*holy shit, that I love him*?

The realization hit me like a tidal wave. I'd never loved anyone the way I loved Callan. Sure, I was young, but how had I found someone as intriguing, intelligent, and undeniably hot as him? The physical attraction was overwhelming, but it was the deeper pull toward him that I couldn't fully comprehend.

I gently placed the photo back in the box and slipped quietly back into bed, wrapping my arm around him snugly. My fingers traced soft circles on his chest and stomach, and I fell asleep with a smile on my face.

* * *

I woke to the sound of the shower running in the nearby bathroom. Blinking my eyes open, I realized the sun was already high in the sky. I reached for my phone on the nightstand—10:45 a.m. I quickly hopped out of bed, grinning at the thought of catching a glimpse of a naked, wet Callan.

Quietly, I pulled back the shower curtain and found him with his back to me, his gorgeous ass on full display as he stroked himself with a steady rhythm.

"Excuse me, I think that's my job," I announced loudly, making Callan jump and spin around, startled.

"Fuck, baby. You scared me." He laughed, letting go of his cock.

"Didn't get enough last night?" I teased, stepping into the shower and eyeing his hard cock.

He grinned, his eyes dark with desire. "I woke up and saw your beautiful body, but I didn't want to wake you, so I came in here instead."

I tried to hold back my smile, but it crept up anyway. "Next time, wake me up. I don't want to miss any of *this*." I gestured to his body, my eyes lingering.

He slid his hand to the back of my head, pulling me in for a tender kiss. My pussy was instantly dripping, and it wasn't just from the water streaming down our bodies. My hands found his cock, and I began to stroke it slowly with both hands. He moaned into my mouth, slipping one hand between my legs and quickly sliding a finger inside me.

"It's dangerous for us to be alone like this. We're never gonna fucking get anything done," he breathed against my lips.

I giggled, leaning into him. "What's wrong with that?"

"Fuck, I just want to feel your wet pussy for the rest of my life. Stay here with me and never leave," he murmured, his voice thick with desire.

"I think they'd come looking for us," I teased, my eyes fluttering open as I stroked him faster.

He stared down at me, slipping another finger inside and pressing his thumb to my clit. The sensation made my breath hitch.

"I want to feel you come on my fingers," he growled, his

voice low and possessive. "I want this tight pussy to clench around them, and then I'm gonna come all over your pretty face."

Holy shit. "Yes, Daddy. I want you to come all over my face and then help me lick it clean."

He moaned and pushed me against the shower wall, his fingers moving faster, thumbing my pussy with determined precision.

"I'm gonna come," I gasped, my hips bucking toward his hand as I lost my rhythm on his cock, my eyes squeezing shut.

"That's right, baby. Come for me," he growled in my ear.

The sensation of his hard cock in my hand and his fingers inside me sent a powerful orgasm ripping through me, a scream escaping my lips as Callan groaned loudly. When I opened my eyes, he pushed me down onto the shower floor, stroking himself furiously.

"Open your mouth, my pretty little slut," he commanded, his voice thick with pleasure. I did as he said, and he released his load onto my mouth, chest, and face.

His warm cum covered me, and I brought a finger to my breast, swirling it in the liquid before bringing it to my lips. I looked up at him, moaning exaggeratedly as I tasted him.

I smiled. "So tasty, Daddy."

His eyes widened with arousal as he lifted me up, kissing me hard. Then he pulled back and began licking his cum off my chest. The sight of him tasting himself off my body turned me on more than I ever imagined.

"You're fucking amazing, baby," he murmured, pausing to press a kiss to my cheek.

"I'm so happy, Callan. I don't want this to end," I admitted, a flicker of fear rising in my chest as I remembered the realization I had last night.

His eyebrows twitched slightly as he looked down at me, confused. "It's not going to end. We're gonna make this work, baby. You're mine, remember? I'm all yours."

I felt tears well up, surprised by the surge of emotion. It was hitting me—his guilt over us being together, the weight of it all. I was terrified that eventually, it would take over, and he'd leave me.

"Hey...baby. It's okay. I love you," he said, wrapping his arms around me tightly. "*Fuck.*"

My heart dropped to my knees. I pulled back, looking up at him, my heart racing. He looked terrified.

"You love me?" I asked quietly, my voice trembling.

He nodded slowly, and the moment he did, I felt an overwhelming surge of joy. *Yes. FUCK yes.*

"I love you too. So now you're stuck with me," I said, grinning.

He laughed, nodding. "And that makes me the fucking luckiest man on earth."

* * *

I knew I had to return home at some point, but with my parents away until the next day, I took full advantage of every moment with Callan. I watched him get dressed in his suit while I slipped back into my dress from the night before, my mind spinning with the fact that he loved me. He'd told me first, which I wasn't expecting, but even with his confession, fear still lingered.

What if my parents found out?

So what? I was a grown woman, and he was a grown man.

But the questions haunted me—would they disown me? Would they disown him? Guilt twisted in my chest as I thought about Callan potentially losing his friendship with my dad, yet he was still here, still choosing me, despite our fears. It meant that our relationship mattered to him more than anything else. The thought kept bringing tears to my eyes.

I walked up behind Callan as he adjusted his tie, slipping my arms around him. I breathed in his scent, feeling the strength of his body under my hands, and in that moment, it felt like we had been together forever. He placed his hands over mine, turning his head to look at me.

"I love you, baby. Let me make you come and scream my name one more time before I take you home."

12

Callan

I let the L word slip out while comforting her, and she didn't even bat an eye. In my entire thirty-eight years, I'd only told one other woman I loved her—besides my mother. It wasn't something I threw around lightly. But fuck, I'd never felt this way about anyone before. Not even close. Sloane, my old-soul baby girl, was wife material. But that needed to wait...at least a few more months. *Right?* When she joked about eloping in Vegas, I almost told her I'd book the next flight.

As I held her hand on the drive back to her house—the fucking *White House*—I still couldn't wrap my head around it. My girlfriend lived in the White House, and she wasn't just the president's daughter, she was *Ana's* daughter. The most powerful man in the world? Yeah, that was intimidating, but it was fucking Jake. But Ana? I was almost more afraid of her reaction. I wouldn't put it past her to put a fucking hit out on me.

Once we got to her room, Sloane changed into ripped shorts and a tight crop top that showed off her perfect tits. Meanwhile, I was still stuck in a damn suit trying to be professional, even though I knew I'd probably spend the whole day in her room. I made myself comfortable, taking off my jacket and tie, rolling up my sleeves. It was way too fucking hot for all those layers.

I sat in the chair by the wall, watching her stare out the window, wringing her hands.

"I wish we weren't confined to my room and your apartment," Sloane said as she walked over and settled on my lap. "Don't get me wrong, I'll take you however I can have you. But wouldn't it be nice to like, go on a real date or something?"

I'd thought about that a lot—how much I hated that I couldn't just take her out, hold her hand, kiss her in public whenever I damn well pleased. But then an idea hit me. *Fuck yes. She's going to love this.*

"Maybe we can make that Fiji trip happen," I joked, pulling her closer and pressing my lips to her neck.

She turned to look at me, hope lighting up her face. "Don't tease me with that," she said softly, her voice filled with longing.

I sighed, brushing a strand of hair from her face. "I know, baby. Soon."

* * *

When I asked Sloane to stay the night at my place again, her eyes lit up. I knew we wouldn't get many more chances like this once Jake and Ana were back in town, so I wanted to make the most of it.

I also had something else planned.

My heart pounded like a jackhammer as I put the plan into motion. I swapped out my suit for jeans and a T-shirt, hoping she wouldn't suspect anything. I never did this kind of thing, but Sloane brought something out in me I'd never felt before. I needed to show her how much she meant to me. I kept glancing at my phone, waiting for the signal, and I could tell Sloane was starting to pick up on something.

"Is everything okay?" she asked, glancing over at me from the kitchen as she rummaged through the fridge.

"Yeah, everything's fine. You want to order a pizza or something?" I tried to shift the conversation, keeping things casual.

She paused, eyeing me suspiciously. "Sure..." I could tell she wasn't fully convinced. *Note to self—never lie to her.* Not that I ever would.

"Okay. What toppings? There's a good spot downtown I'll order from."

Before I even heard her answer, my phone buzzed—the text came in. Everything was ready.

"Ah, fuck, did you hear about the shooting stars tonight?" I blurted out, improvising. "Wanna go check them out?"

I wasn't sure if she'd be into it, but her face lit up immediately.

"Yeah, where?" she asked, excitement in her voice.

I stood up and took her hand. "We can see them from the roof."

We took the elevator to the top floor, then climbed the stairs to the roof. As soon as I opened the door, the twinkling lights overhead came into view. Sloane gasped, her eyes wide as she took in the scene before us. A projector and screen were set up, blankets and pillows arranged front and center. Rose petals were scattered across the ground, and a bucket of sparkling cider sat chilling on ice. The pizza had been ordered long before I even asked her.

"What is this?" she asked, turning to me, her mouth slightly open in surprise.

"We're not in my apartment or your room. It's a date, baby."

A smile tugged at her lips as she shook her head in disbelief.

"You did all of this?" Her voice trembled, and her eyes shimmered with unshed tears.

"Yeah. Do you like it?"

A soft laugh escaped her. "Do I like it? I *love* it. It's perfect. Thank you, Callan."

She rose up on her toes and kissed me, her lips warm and soft against mine, making my dick twitch. I clenched my jaw, knowing that if I pulled her any closer, we'd end up fucking, and I wanted this to be a proper date.

"There's pizza on the way. Come on." I gestured to the blanket and took her hand, leading her over.

"How did you plan all this? You were with me all day." She sat down and crossed her legs, eyes still roaming the rooftop in awe.

I sat next to her, tugging off my boots.

"I pulled a few strings. There's a great party planner in DC. Told her I needed something special for two." I smiled, glancing around, pleased with how everything had turned out.

Sloane took my hand. "I love you, Callan. This is all...it's so perfect." Tears shimmered in her eyes again. My baby was emotional and it was taking some getting used to. I wanted to kiss her tears and tell her everything was okay, but I realized everything *was* okay. More than okay.

"I love you, baby. You're perfect," I said, lifting our intertwined fingers to my lips and pressing a kiss to the back of her hand.

She smiled, biting her lip before glancing around at the cozy setup.

"What are we watching?" she asked as her gaze shifted to the screen.

"It's an old one—*Harvey*. Jimmy Stewart. One of my favorites," I explained, picking up the remote from the wooden tray beside the chilled sparkling cider.

Her face lit up. "Oh, I love his movies! I've always wanted to see this one. The one about the imaginary friend rabbit, right?"

A warm flutter stirred in my stomach, like butterflies had taken over. If I hadn't fallen in love with her before, this moment would've been it.

"Yeah, that's the one. Fuck, are you sure you're eighteen? You know more about shit than I do," I teased, chuckling.

She smirked, a playful glint in her eyes. "Age has nothing to do with it."

I raised an eyebrow mockingly. "Are you saying I'm an idiot?"

Her laughter filled the air. "I'm surprised you picked up on that."

I widened my eyes in a fake gasp, then darted my hands to her sides, tickling her without mercy. Her laughter was like a drug, making me feel like I was becoming the man I'd always wanted to be. *Fuck, I love her.* By the time I stopped, she was crying from laughter, and I found myself hovering over her, pinning her arms beside her head. I grinned down at her as she bit her lip, her eyes silently pleading for a kiss. Leaning in, I pressed my lips firmly to hers, my body already reacting. I was never going to get enough of this girl.

I pushed my hips into hers, and she wrapped her legs around me, pulling me in tighter.

She abruptly pushed me back, glancing toward the rooftop door.

"Don't worry, baby. I thought of that. I hired someone to watch the door," I said, my voice low and reassuring.

Her smile returned, and she pulled me back in, our kisses growing deeper and more intense. It was almost as good as being inside her. *Almost.*

Sitting up, I tugged her shorts and underwear down in one swift motion before unzipping my jeans and freeing my cock. I stared at her, licking my lips, hungry for her in every way.

"I want you to fuck my face," I said as I began to stroke myself.

She sat up quickly. "What?"

My inexperienced, sweet girl. "I want you to sit on my face and ride it, baby."

Her lips parted with a smile. "Okay," she responded shyly.

I laid on my back and pulled her on top of me, eager to get her sweet pussy in my mouth. Her gaze darted around before settling back on me, her uncertainty slowly melting away. She positioned her knees on either side of my head, inching closer. I grabbed her full ass with both hands, gripping tightly as I pulled her down, eager for the taste of her. When she finally pressed her warm, perfect pussy against my mouth and began to grind, it was like she already knew exactly what to do, moving with confidence that sent a thrill through me. I held onto her thighs, not wanting to touch myself for fear of coming too quickly; if I had to, I'd come just by looking at her. I went between sticking my tongue far into her wet pussy to teasing her clit with quick motions. I watched her on top of me with her tits jiggling and her mouth parted, her eyes closed with pleasure. Her thighs began to tremble under my hands and her soft moans made it clear she was about to come. I moaned, the sound rumbling through me and into her. Her response was immediate—a loud, breathy whimper escaping her lips as her hips slowed. She let her hands fall to the ground above my head, her body trembling as she rode the high of her release.

"Oh my God," she cried out, quickening her hips again, chasing another orgasm.

She came again, her loud cries filling the air, and in that moment, I knew—her riding my face was my new favorite thing. Watching her lose herself in the pleasure I was giving her, the way her body responded to my mouth, made my cock throb painfully. It was thrilling, knowing I could bring her to that edge over and over.

"Fuck me now, Daddy," she whispered, sliding down my body, her wetness leaving a trail on my shirt.

I looked up at her with a grin. "Why don't you hop on my cock, baby?"

She smiled back, then took hold of my cock and guided herself onto me, wasting no time as she began grinding fast. Her pussy wrapped around me, taking every inch like she'd fucking mastered it. Her moans told me she was close again, and I wanted to take her pleasure even further. I wet my finger with my mouth, then reached around her, teasing her ass gently. I eased just the tip in, barely applying pressure, and her eyes shot open, wide with surprise as her hips stilled.

"This okay, baby?" I asked, unsure if I was pushing too far.

"Yes, fuck! Keep going," she demanded, grinding down on me even harder.

I pushed my finger further into her, feeling the tight heat of her body as she moved faster on my cock. I was so fucking close but I needed my baby to come first.

"Oh, God. Yes. Yes! I'm coming," she moaned, her voice breathless and shaking, and that was all it took. I finally let go, groaning as I came inside her, my grunts mixing with her sweet cries of release.

Her body collapsed onto mine, and I gently pulled my finger from her ass, trying to catch my breath.

"Please, please fuck my ass next time," she whispered into my ear, her voice a mixture of exhaustion and desire.

I chuckled, hugging her tight against my chest. "As you wish, baby."

We spent the rest of the night watching *Harvey*, eating pizza, and snuggling close. Sloane draped her leg over mine as I pulled the blanket over us, holding her tight, knowing I never wanted to let her go.

13

Sloane

My parents got back the next day, long after I'd already returned home and showered. Callan kept his distance, probably paranoid we'd be caught if we so much as crossed paths within fifty feet of each other. The rooftop date he planned had been perfect—everything from the sex to the movie to the cool spring night air. I wasn't sure how he could possibly top that.

Mom was in the living room with me, working on her laptop. I sat with a new Sara Cate book in my hands, but I couldn't focus on the words. My thoughts kept drifting back to Callan—his full, pouty lips, his hard, tattooed body, and his perfect, hard...

I snapped the book shut and grabbed my phone. Callan had to be nearby—his job was to literally protect me around the clock.

Hi. I miss you.

His response came instantly. **I miss you too, baby. What are you doing?**

I glanced up at my mom, still engrossed in her work, completely unaware of my distraction.

Reading, but I'd rather be making out with you. I bit my lip, smiling as I hit send.

"How was your night out with James?" My mom's voice pulled me out of my Callan daydream.

"It was fine. He was nice, but…" I shrugged. *But he's no Callan.*

Mom smiled softly and tilted her head. "Then who are you texting?" she asked, her tone casual.

I blinked, caught off guard. I hadn't expected that question.

"Taylor," I lied smoothly. Taylor had been my best friend back in New York.

Mom didn't seem to suspect anything, just nodded and glanced back down at her laptop. "Yeah? How's she doing?"

I sighed, trying to stay casual. "She's good," I replied, eyes drifting back to my phone.

There was another message from Callan waiting for me.

Maybe we can sneak it somewhere. How about a Crepeaway trip? I'm fucking aching for you, baby.

My heart skipped a beat. The idea of sneaking around turned me on more than I wanted to admit.

Meet me in my room in five minutes, I typed and hit send without hesitation.

He responded almost immediately. **Sloane, we can't fuck in your room. Not now.**

I bit the inside of my cheek, not willing to give up. **What if we just make out? Or I could give you a blowjob? Please?**

It was kind of funny, how I was begging to give him a blowjob—that seemed about right.

Fuck. You win. See you in five.

I grinned to myself. *I win again.* I stood up quickly, setting my book aside. "I'm gonna go lay down," I announced, already moving toward the hall.

"Okay, baby," Mom called back, still absorbed in her work.

I practically sprinted down the hall, bursting into my room. Glancing in the mirror, I quickly fixed my hair, smoothing out my dress, excitement racing through me as I impatiently waited for that knock on the door.

Five agonizing minutes later, Callan slipped into my room, shutting the door behind him with a quiet thud. I gave him a questioning look as he hurried in.

"I didn't want anyone to see me come in," he said, answering the question in my eyes.

I bit my lip, pushing myself against him, pinning him to the door. Our hands were everywhere, touching, grabbing, as we kissed with frantic urgency. He guided me toward the bed, our lips never parting, and sat down, pulling me onto his lap, straddling him. I couldn't get enough—he consumed me, mind and body. My hips moved instinctively, grinding against his hard cock, the friction sending heat through me. I tugged at his hair, desperate for more, frustrated by the layers of clothes between us.

A moan escaped my lips as I pressed harder, the rhythm pushing me closer to the edge.

"Baby, your book—"

I jumped away from Callan as soon as I heard my mom's voice. Turning around, I saw her standing in the doorway, eyes wide with shock. Callan stood next to me, frozen in place, mirroring my own fear. My heart raced so fast it felt like it was about to burst from my chest.

"What the fuck is going on?" she asked quietly, closing the door behind her and stepping further into the room. "What the fuck is going on? Callan? Sloane?"

I glanced up at Callan, and he looked down at me, then back to my mom. He opened his mouth to speak, but I interrupted him.

"I'm in love with him, Mom," I blurted out, my hands trembling at my sides.

Her expression shifted to one of disbelief, a laugh escaping her lips. "What? What the fuck are you talking about, Sloane? You've known him for less than a week," she argued, still reeling from the revelation.

I looked back at Callan, searching for support, feeling at a loss for words.

"Callan, you're fucking twenty years older than her. She's *eighteen*. I'm...I'm so confused right now." She sank into the chair against the wall, her gaze shifting between us.

I was taken aback that she wasn't screaming at him.

"Are you going to say something, Callan?" Her voice rose, sharp and demanding.

"I know this is crazy, Ana, but it's true. I love her. I don't know how it happened, but I love Sloane. She is...she is wise beyond her years," he said, his tone low and earnest, a mixture of vulnerability and conviction.

Mom laughed again. "You're in love with her? How did this even happen? I need you both to explain how the fuck this all happened." She stood up again, putting her hands on her hips.

"I seduced him. He fought it. He fought it hard, Mom. He didn't want to do any of this. But then it happened and now..." I trailed off, sitting down on my bed, and Callan followed, sitting close to me.

She looked between us, her eyes still wide with confusion.

"Callan, I need to talk to my daughter alone," she said quietly.

"Of course," he replied, standing up quickly and nearly bolting for the door.

Mom watched him leave, closing the door softly behind him. She turned back to me, shaking her head in disbelief.

"Is this for real, Sloane? You actually love him?" Her voice was surprisingly calm, but I could hear the underlying concern.

I nodded immediately. "Yes. I know he's older—*much* older—but something just clicked between us," I explained, my heart racing.

Mom sighed, raising her hands to her face as she shook her head. "Sloane," she groaned. "Your dad is going to have a fucking fit."

"Dad isn't going to find out," I assured her.

She smiled and tilted her head at me. "Baby, I just walked in on you and Callan making out. And we've only been home for two hours."

She had a point. "We'll be more careful," I urged her.

Mom was silent as she stared at me. I couldn't stand that she was so quiet.

"Mom, what are you thinking? I know this is crazy, but it's real. I assure you...it's *very* real between us. It's not just sex. I am...I'm *so* in love with him."

Mom blinked. "I must be crazy because as shocked as I am, I'm not mad. I'm just...I'm very shocked right now, Sloane."

I nodded. I could understand that. *But wait...*

"You're not mad?" I asked with confusion.

She sighed and got up from the chair, then slowly walked towards me and sat next to me on the bed. She took my hand and gave it a squeeze.

"I get it, baby. He's hot," she said, a laugh escaping her. "You're not one to jump into things or act impulsively, so this must be something special. And Callan wouldn't do anything this reckless unless he was on drugs again, but I'm pretty sure he's not," she joked, a playful glint in her eyes.

Oh. I didn't even know that about him. I realized we still had a lot to learn about each other.

"He's not," I assured her. "I should know. We've been inseparable for the past five days," I admitted.

She shook her head at me again. "*Dios mío, baby.*" She laughed. "Just please make sure of this one thing."

I waited for her to continue, my heart racing again.

"Please be careful in public. If anyone finds out, this could really hurt Daddy's re-election. People don't understand these kinds of things."

I nodded quickly. "I know." I stared down at the floor, feeling guilty for even risking this.

"Maybe Callan can take you to Berkeley this week. You two can have some alone time to get things out of your system, like making out without the door locked," she teased me.

I sighed with relief. I couldn't believe how supportive she was being.

"Why are you so amazing, Mom?" I asked, giving her hand a squeeze.

She smiled widely. "Because all I care about is my daughter's happiness. If you're happy, then I'm happy."

I almost started crying. "I am very happy, Mom. More than I ever thought was possible."

* * *

Mom wanted to have a private chat with Callan, and I didn't want to be stuck in my room. I stepped out into the hallway and began to play with the keys of the piano, mindlessly singing "Work Song" by Hozier, the lyrics flowing softly from my lips.

I noticed Callan slowly walking up the stairs, a big smile on his face as he watched me from the top step. I stopped when he approached, but he shook his head. "Please don't stop." He settled onto a couch in front of the bookshelf, crossing his legs and watching me intently.

I continued with the chorus, feeling my cheeks burn; I could have sex with this man, yet singing in front of him made me incredibly nervous. When I stilled my hands, he spoke.

"You have the most beautiful voice I've ever heard," he said quietly.

I raised my eyebrows, wondering how the chat went. "What did she say?" I got up and sat on the couch parallel to him.

He blinked, then shrugged. "She told me she'd kill me if I hurt you. She said to be careful. And she's scheduling a tour for Berkeley right now. She wants me to take you."

I couldn't help but smile. "She's being surprisingly support-ive."

He nodded. "I was about to get a fake passport and disappear to Costa Rica."

"She wouldn't be hunting you down—*I* would. You better never leave me," I replied, crossing my arms defiantly.

He gave me a small smile, leaning closer with his elbows on his thighs. "Baby, I'd never dream of leaving you."

14

Callan

Ana scared the shit out of me when she pulled me into a private room I didn't even know existed and pointed a finger at me.

"Callan, if you hurt her, I will make sure you are tortured and beheaded."

My stomach dropped, and I felt like I was going to throw up. But then Ana burst into laughter.

"*Ay pobrecito*, I'm just messing with you." She smiled, amusement dancing in her eyes. "But seriously, don't hurt her. She's not a delicate flower, but she's very sensitive. I know you are too. Somehow, it all works in this weird, fucked-up way."

I smiled in surprise. "Ana, you know I'd never hurt her. I'm actually afraid she'll hurt me," I admitted.

She shook her head quickly. "She'd never do that. Just please be careful, Callan. If this got out, it would be the end for Jake."

I nodded, the weight of guilt pressing down on me like a ton of bricks. "I know, Ana. We'll be careful."

* * *

I was thrilled to be alone with Sloane as we settled into our First Class seats for the flight to Oakland International Airport. Even though we couldn't touch in public, just being in her presence was enough for me. She wore a crop top that left little to the imagination, her hard nipples teasing me without her even realizing. Her comfortable gray sweats looked effortlessly stylish on her, and I was grateful I didn't have to wear my suit; I felt at ease in my jeans and T-shirt.

"I love seeing you in a suit, but God, you look amazing with your tattoos and muscles showing," Sloane whispered as we sat down, her eyes sparkling with admiration.

My dick started to harden. "Baby, I'm gonna fuck you so hard when we get to the hotel."

She giggled, turning to look out the window, her genuine happiness making my heart feel like it would fucking burst.

Sloane and I had six hours to talk, nap, tease each other, and share our favorite songs. She tried to read, but I kept bugging her, and she didn't seem to mind. No one noticed the subtle squeezes I gave her thigh under the blanket we shared. So much for being careful in public; I couldn't fucking help myself.

As we exited the terminal toward baggage claim, a sea of photographers suddenly appeared, snapping pictures of my girl.

"Whoa, whoa!" I exclaimed, instinctively stepping in front of her and spreading my arms wide. "Give us some space!"

"Sloane! Sloane, over here!" they called out, completely ignoring me.

"Back up!" I nearly reached for Sloane's hand but caught myself just in time. "Come on, baby. Let's get to the car," I whispered in her ear.

A sleek black car was waiting right outside. I guided her

into it before turning back to grab our luggage, the swarm of photographers still snapping pictures.

"Fuckers," I muttered under my breath.

I tossed our bags into the trunk and slid next to Sloane in the car.

"Those fucking guys." I pointed out the window. "Does that happen a lot?"

She sighed, taking my hand discreetly, careful not to catch the driver's attention. "Sometimes. In public places like this, especially when they know to expect me. I hate it," she admitted, her voice low.

My teeth clenched together. "I'd fucking kill every one of them for you, baby. Just say the word."

I was joking, but part of me meant it.

She smiled, letting go of my hand for a moment to quickly glance at the driver, ensuring he wasn't watching.

"Please don't. I'd rather you be with me than in jail." She gave me a sly smile, and I prayed the car would pull up to our hotel any minute so I could fuck her in every inch of our room.

After an agonizingly slow twenty minutes, we finally arrived at the hotel. Ana had booked us a place within walking distance of UC Berkeley. I grabbed our bags from the trunk and followed Sloane inside, noticing the young receptionist recognize her immediately.

"Oh! Hello, Miss Martin. Welcome to Berkeley," she beamed.

"Hi," Sloane replied warmly. "There should be a reservation under my name."

The receptionist typed away at her computer. "Yes, we have a suite for three nights. Would you like two keycards?" She glanced between me and Sloane.

Sloane looked over at me, and I tried to keep a few feet of distance between us. "Um...yes, please."

Once we hurried into our suite, I wasted no time—I grabbed Sloane by the hips and lifted her against the wall. She instinctively wrapped her legs around me, her hands finding my cheeks, pulling me in for a kiss. I needed to be inside her immediately or I'd explode.

"I need you, baby. Being so close to you for so long and not being able to touch you has driven me fucking insane," I breathed against her skin, trailing kisses from her neck to her cheek.

She moaned, lifting her hips against me, the heat between us igniting further.

"I brought lube. I want you to fuck my ass tonight, Daddy," she whispered, her voice sultry and full of promise.

She looked at me eagerly as I pulled away, and I couldn't help but wonder how the fuck I had landed this perfect sexual goddess.

"Oh, you came prepared, huh?" I teased.

She smiled brightly. "Are you proud of me?"

"So fucking proud. Are you sure you're ready?"

She nodded enthusiastically.

"You didn't happen to bring a butt plug, did you?" I asked, wanting to make this as pleasurable as possible for her and prep her slowly.

Sloane blinked, her expression shifting to one of nervousness. "No. Do we need it?"

"I mean, we don't need it. But it would help prepare your pretty little ass better," I explained gently.

Her brows furrowed. "Fuck," she groaned. "Can we go get one?"

I glanced at the clock on the nightstand: 8:30 p.m. I hesitated, but I knew that going to a sex shop at night was better than doing it in broad daylight.

"Why don't I just go?" I offered, remembering Ana's warning to be careful.

Sloane frowned. "I want to go. I've never been to one. We'll be quick."

Fuck. Why did she always manage to convince me to go along with her bad ideas?

"Baby, my cock is aching, though. We can do anal later. I need to fucking come inside you right now." I pressed my hard cock against her.

She smiled, her eyes sparkling. "I know. But won't that make it even better?"

I paused, considering her words. Fuck; she was right. I let go of her and ordered an Uber to the closest adult store.

Fifteen minutes later, we stepped into a seedy-looking store in a questionable neighborhood. The clerk behind the counter didn't even glance up at us. I headed straight for the butt plugs, and Sloane trailed behind, her eyes darting around at everything in the store.

"How's this, baby?" I held up a box containing a series of three butt plugs: small, medium, and large. "We can maybe use the first two."

Her eyes widened. "Yes. Perfect." I could tell she was nervous, but if it hadn't been her idea to try anal, I would have never pushed it.

"Are you sure you want to do this?" I glanced back at the clerk, who was now looking over at us.

Sloane nodded, a smile playing on her lips. "Of course, Daddy," she whispered.

Fuck, she was making my cock ache even more.

"Okay. I just don't want you to think I need to do freaky shit to be happy. I just need to fucking be inside you, and I'm happy," I whispered back.

She giggled, and my cock twitched in response. "I know." She looked over my shoulder. "What do you think of that?"

I turned to see a strap-on with a dildo on display. "What do *you* think of that?"

I wasn't about to admit that I'd always wanted to be pegged; it didn't feel like a "manly" thing to want, and I was still trying to get past that bullshit.

She raised her eyebrows, intrigued. "Might be fun. Should we get it, just in case?"

I smiled. "If you want, baby."

She leaned past me and grabbed it. "Let's go check out."

Thank fuck the cashier didn't seem to recognize Sloane. We took an Uber back to the hotel with our discreet black shopping bag. Once inside, Sloane ripped open the butt plug box, eyeing the contents like they were precious diamonds.

She glanced over at me as I pulled down my jeans, eager and ready. "How do we do this?" she asked, her excitement bubbling over.

"Get naked. I'll wash it and get you prepped."

Her chest rose and fell rapidly, a smile spreading across her face. "Yes, Daddy."

15

Sloane

Watching Callan walk out of the bathroom in just his boxer briefs had my pussy dripping; his muscled body, his tattoos, the sexy look on his face as he eyed my naked body on the bed had my skin tingling.

"Fuck. We're never leaving this room and you're never getting dressed again," he teased.

I was propped up on my elbows as I laid on my back, but I had to let my arms collapse as I looked over at him and put my hand to my slick pussy. I watched him as I stuck a finger inside, his mouth parted with lust as he stood in front of the bed. He set aside the butt plug and crawled onto the bed, hovering over me.

"Is your pussy wet for me, baby?" he asked in his low, deep voice.

"Yes," I breathed back, staring at his full lips above me.

I gasped when he quickly removed my hand and stuck his own finger inside of me. "Fuck, you're so fucking wet." He smiled then brought his finger to his mouth.

My pussy ached for him. "Fuck my pussy first, Daddy," I

begged.

Callan suddenly stood up, removed his boxer briefs, then hovered over me again. I pulled his hips towards mine and he swiftly thrust inside of me, his hips moving quickly, his grunts loud. He lifted my legs up onto his chest, staring at my bouncing boobs and then grabbing them and squeezing tight.

"Fuck, baby. I'm so close to coming," he moaned, now staring intently in my eyes. "Let's get that butt plug in and then I'll eat your pussy." He pulled out quickly, catching his breath.

I stayed on my back as he grabbed the butt plug, slathered lube onto it, and eyed me with a sly smile.

"Get on your stomach, baby. Relax," he said gently.

My heart started racing. I was excited for anal, but I was nervous too. I wanted to experience everything with Callan, at least once. This had been one of my fantasies since I secretly started reading my smutty books a couple of years ago.

I got onto my stomach and turned my head to see what Callan was doing. His hand palmed my ass, then he squeezed one side and opened it up for a better view. I was getting turned on just by the process. I felt the pressure from the cold, stainless steel butt plug and bit my lip as he slowly made his way in.

"You okay, baby?" he asked, looking up at me and stopping.

"Yes, keep going."

He inched his way in a little more, slowly and carefully. The feeling of it inside my ass made my whole body tingle with goosebumps. I let my head fall down below me and squeezed the pillow as Callan went further.

"Still good?" he asked hesitantly.

"Yes. Do it all," I moaned.

A small scream escaped my mouth as the biggest part went

in, and there was suddenly no more feeling of pressure or pain, just pleasure.

"It's in, baby." Callan exhaled a surprised chuckle. "How does it feel?"

"Good. Fuck me now, please," I said shakily, getting onto my knees, wholly aware of the feeling of something foreign inside of me.

Callan took my hips and slapped his cock against my pussy, making me gasp as he teased me and chuckled to himself.

"Not yet, baby. I need to taste you." He suddenly pulled my thighs towards him as I bent over onto the bed, eager for release.

His mouth kissed the lips of my wet spot, then his tongue slowly crept inside of me, wiggling at the same speed.

"Oh my God," I moaned, the butt plug somehow making everything feel more intense, more pleasurable.

Callan dug his tongue further inside of me, moaning into me and sticking a finger in beside his mouth. He suddenly took my hips and flipped me onto my back, gazing up at me with desire as he pulled me to the edge of the bed and got onto his knees on the floor. He pulled my thighs over his shoulders and stuck two fingers inside of me, then put his mouth to me and began to tease my clit with his tongue. I lifted my hips, close to coming, unable to take my eyes off of him.

"I'm gonna come," I announced, lifting my hips up and down as I chased my orgasm.

My eyes closed as I felt the explosion of pleasure that Callan forced upon me, my pussy throbbing as his tongue never stopped its pace. I was surprised as another intense orgasm hit me, and my body began to tremble with pleasure. All of a sudden, his lips parted from me, and I felt his cock slowly push into my pussy. The feeling of his size with the butt plug was overwhelming. I gasped as he inched in, his eyes wide and eager, and my thighs trembled around his body.

"You okay, baby?" he asked gently, pausing.

"Yes," I breathed quietly.

His eyes darkened as he began to thrust quickly, staring down at me with concentration. My pussy throbbed, and I couldn't help but bring my finger to my clit, rubbing gently. Callan let out a low grunt as he watched me, and I couldn't keep my eyes off of him as another warm wave of pleasure washed over me.

"Please," I exhaled between quick breaths, looking down at Callan's proud smile. "Please fuck my ass now, Daddy."

He pulled my thighs towards him again, letting my legs dangle, and he hovered over me to kiss me passionately, the taste of myself on his lips. His hand slid down to my ass and he slowly pulled the butt plug out as I held my breath. He released his lips from mine and glanced over at the lube on the end table as he stood up.

"You ready, baby?" He smiled down at me as he grabbed the lube and began to generously coat his cock with it.

I nodded, biting my lip with anticipation.

"Tell me," he ordered, stroking himself.

"I'm ready. I want your cock in my ass," I moaned eagerly.

He squeezed more lube onto his cock and then threw the bottle over his shoulder. He placed my feet onto the bed and then guided his cock to my ass. He looked up at me and began to slowly press his cock against my hole. My heart raced, desire and nervousness coursing through my body. Callan inched his way in further as he studied my face, his lips parted slightly as he continued.

"More," I begged softly as I felt a mixture of pleasure and pain.

He smiled and pushed himself in further; my legs began to shake as he went in even deeper, and I could already tell that I was going to come if he so much as looked at my clit. I gasped as he continued, and it felt like it was past the point of pain—Callan's cock was in my ass and I was ready for him to fuck it.

"I'm in, baby," he breathed, stilling himself. "How does it feel?"

"So fucking good," I moaned. "Fuck me now."

Callan's mouth widened even more as his hips began to move slowly, watching me carefully.

"Oh my God, it feels so good," I cried out.

"Yeah? You like me fucking your ass, pretty girl?" His thrusting quickened.

"Yes!" I whimpered.

"Are you going to come while my cock is in your ass?" Now he was fucking me fast and hard and my moans were loud as I clutched onto the sheets beside me, my eyes closed with pleasure.

"Yes. Please!" I begged.

Callan thumbed and circled my clit and I immediately came—I was struck with the most intense pleasure I had ever felt as I whimpered under his touch.

"Fuck!" Callan grunted, and I knew that sound: he was coming too.

My pussy continued to throb as Callan's hips slowed and he removed his thumb from my clit. I opened my eyes and saw his hot, muscled body as he gripped his hands onto my thighs.

"Callan, that was the best fucking thing I've ever felt," I

breathed.

He chuckled and leaned down to kiss me softly.

"Baby, I can confirm that your pussy and ass are the best fucking things I've ever felt too."

* * *

We didn't have to tour UC Berkeley until the next afternoon, so after we showered, I planned to cuddle with Callan for as long as possible, pressing our naked bodies together. We lay in bed, mindlessly watching reruns of *The Office*, when a commercial for a whiskey brand I'd never heard of came on. My mind drifted to my mom's comment about his past drug use.

"So, my mom mentioned you used to do drugs," I blurted out.

Callan laughed instantly.

"Yeah, babe, I did. Drugs, alcohol—anything that could fuck me up." He spoke so casually about it.

I looked up at him, one hand resting behind his head while he gazed down at me with amusement.

"When did you get sober?"

He narrowed his eyes, staring up at the ceiling as if deep in thought. "The first time or the last time?"

"Both," I replied quietly.

He shifted slightly as I continued to stare up at him, waiting for him to share more.

"I started drinking really young—like fifteen," he began. "I'd get blackout drunk. I'd steal my parents' car and take money from my mom's purse. I ended up in juvie. Eventually, I started doing cocaine, and that really fucked me up. I went into rehab when I was nineteen, and when I got out, I joined the Navy."

He looked down at me hesitantly before continuing.

"I met your dad in the Navy, as you know. We became SEALs together. We went through a lot. Jake stayed in, but I was out before I turned thirty. That's when everything went downhill. I found myself on the streets in Philly, drunk and starting fights, living out of a tent. That lasted for a couple of years, and I wanted to fucking die. I called Jake for help because he was the only person I could think of; he was the only one I hadn't ever fucked over."

A lump formed in my throat as he looked back up at the ceiling. It was becoming clear why Callan felt so indebted to my dad, why he carried so much guilt about us.

"I got back on my feet. Found a decent job. And now here I am. It's been eight years," he finished quietly.

I shook my head, unsure of what to say.

"I'm sorry you had to go through all of that. I'm proud of you, Callan," I whispered.

He smiled down at me, his hand gently caressing my cheek.

"I'd do it all again if it led me to you, baby."

My heart constricted, and tears began to flow down my cheeks. "I love you, Callan."

Just thinking about him on the streets made my lip tremble, and the weight of his struggles hit me hard.

"I love you, Sloane." He leaned down and kissed me passionately, and we slowly made love until the sun began to rise.

16

Callan

I had no idea why Ana told Sloane about my substance abuse history. The weight of it hung over me while Sloane slept peacefully in my arms. Was it meant to scare her? Had it come up casually in conversation? Whatever the reason, I just hoped Sloane wouldn't ask any more questions about that part of my life.

We woke to the sound of my alarm going off at noon. We had to get Sloane to UC Berkeley by two, and I needed enough time to fuck her in a warm shower beforehand.

I opted for a casual look—there was no way I wanted to stick out like a sore thumb in a suit on a college campus. I didn't want to draw any more attention to Sloane.

Walking beside her without holding her hand was a struggle. We'd spent the last twenty-four hours in our own little bubble, and I wanted it to last forever.

It took only a few minutes to reach the campus. An eager faculty member led us around while I kept a few feet behind, watching Sloane like a hawk. I didn't want her to get bombarded like she had at the airport, but I figured the students here had more decency than those fuckers with cameras.

As the tour guide pointed out the essentials, I noticed girls stopping to point their phones in our direction. At first, I thought I was just being paranoid, but Sloane glanced back at me, her expression uneasy.

"Can you excuse me for a second?" she asked the tour guide before walking up to me and subtly nodding her head in the other direction.

"You're causing a scene looking so hot around here," she joked, glancing down at the ground.

I looked around, and it became glaringly obvious that people were watching us. Why wouldn't they? She was the daughter of the President, and she was a fucking babe.

"You wanna go, baby?" I asked quietly, making sure we were out of earshot.

She nodded quickly, and all I wanted to do was pick her up and carry her to the hotel, Kevin Costner and Whitney Houston style.

"Alright," I said, nodding decisively. I glanced back at the tour guide and gestured for him to come over.

He approached us swiftly.

"We gotta cut the tour short. Sloane is getting too much unwanted attention. Thanks for the tour," I explained, then turned around to lead her away.

"Thank you!" Sloane called over my shoulder before turning to walk toward the hotel.

"O-okay. Thank you, Miss Sloane!" the tour guide replied, his voice trailing off.

My baby's legs were much shorter than mine, but you'd think she was a fucking giraffe the way she was striding. We finally made it off campus and past all the college chaos when she suddenly slowed and broke down in tears. Instinctively, I wrapped my arms around her—I wasn't about to just stand there and let her cry. She held on tightly, and in that moment, I didn't give a fuck if anyone saw us.

"It's going to be like this everywhere. Why bother going to an in-person college? I can do what I need to do online, right? I'll just stay in your apartment 24/7, and you'll never have to leave me, and we'll never be bothered." Her words tumbled out in a rush, her breath hitching between sobs, never lifting her head from my chest.

"We can do whatever you want, baby. You can bounce on my cock while you do your homework either way," I joked, trying to lighten the mood.

She laughed through her tears and lifted her head to look up at me; her teary eyes made my heart ache. "This place sucks. Let's go back to the hotel."

* * *

Sloane and I fucked in the shower, using my cock to help her forget all about her shitty tour experience. After we dried off, she immediately crawled into bed naked, and I quickly followed, wrapping my arms around her. As I held her close, I glanced out the window, watching the sun set and transform the California sky into a swirl of orange and pink. I gently rubbed my hand up and down her soft arm, feeling content and sleepy.

The sudden loud vibration of her phone broke the silence, making both of us jump. She grabbed her phone with a look of irritation, likely annoyed that it interrupted our peaceful moment.

I glanced over as she unlocked her phone, and my heart dropped—it was a zoomed-in photo of me from earlier at the college. I was crossing my arms, looking over my shoulder, seemingly at the camera.

"What the fuck?" I asked, almost in sync with Sloane.

She scrolled down, and I caught a glimpse of the text over her shoulder: **UM, EXCUSE ME. Sloane Gabriela Martin. Who is this fucking babe following you around UCB? Your new bodyguard?**

Sloane let out a snort, clearly amused.

"It's my friend, Taylor," she explained.

"Well, how the fuck did she get that picture?" I was too confused to feel amused or flattered.

Sloane began texting back: **Yes, that's Callan, my new bodyguard. How did you get this?!**

We both waited quietly for a response as the text bubbles appeared. She sent back a link and then added: **He's more popular than your dad right now. BABE, he's a babe.**

Sloane tapped on the link, leading us to a series of threads on a social media site. She scrolled so fast I could barely keep up.

HOT NEW BODYGUARD ALERT. Sloane Martin seen touring UC Berkeley today with hot, tattooed DILF.

More fucking stalker photos of us from afar filled the screen. There were shots of me and Sloane standing a few feet apart, her beautiful smile directed at me; one of her with her hand on her hip, glancing at me while I spoke; and another where our elbows brushed as we both looked at something the tour guide was showing us.

If the focus had solely been on Sloane, I'd have been pissed. But in a strange way, I kinda liked seeing us together. I didn't like that the attention made her uncomfortable, but I'd never had the chance to see us from the outside. From that distance, I didn't look like an old man next to her—I *liked* how we looked together.

"Hey, I have an idea," I blurted out before I could change my mind.

Sloane glanced up at me, her phone still in hand.

"Let's take a selfie." I felt like a fucking idiot using the word *selfie*, but we didn't have any pictures of us together, and I wanted to see more.

A huge smile spread across her gorgeous lips, revealing that adorable dimple. She looked back down at her phone, opened the camera app, and aimed it at us.

My heart stung at how beautiful she looked on the screen. Then there was me, appearing like an old, washed-up asshole with a permanent scowl. The lines on my forehead seemed to have appeared overnight. But when Sloane pressed her lips against my cheek, all my self-doubt faded away, and by the time she hit the shutter, I had a genuine smile on my face. She glanced at the phone and scooted closer, my arm instinctively wrapping around her. She laid her head on my chest and snapped another picture.

It was starting to sink in deeper that this girl was too good for me. She made me feel good, and why the fuck did she owe me that? She would soon find out what a piece of shit I really was. The sad truth was, I never tried to be an asshole—it just happened. Everything good in my life always seemed to run away screaming in the end. Yet, even knowing that, I couldn't help myself with Sloane. I was addicted to her. I couldn't give her up. I tried, but she didn't let me. And I was so fucking thankful for that.

Sloane lowered the phone and looked up at me with her wide, brown eyes. "What's wrong?"

Is my face that obvious?

I sighed and shook my head. "Baby, you're too good for me," I admitted quietly.

She rolled her eyes and sat up. "I don't know why you keep saying that, Callan. Why am I too good for you?"

"Because you're this fucking pure eighteen-year-old babe who hasn't done anything bad in your life. I'm a hardened thirty-eight-year-old asshole who shouldn't even be alive because of all the stupid decisions I've made." I sat up, wringing my hands together.

Sloane was quiet for a moment, staring down at her hands. Then she looked back up at me, fire igniting in her eyes. "Please stop calling me so fucking 'pure.' Would you call an eighteen-year-old guy with the same history as me pure? It's misogynistic to glorify a woman just because of her age or sexual history. Would I still be pure or 'too good' for you if I were twenty-five or thirty? If I'd slept with ten other guys? Callan, you need to cut this bullshit. Stop trying to make yourself feel bad about this situation, because you have nothing to be ashamed of. *I* initiated this, remember? I'm choosing to be in this relationship with you. I want you for *you*. I don't care about your age or whatever bad decisions you think you've made in the past."

Her passion was palpable, and tears welled in her eyes. Fuck, she was incredibly smart. I decided to keep my mouth shut and let her win this one.

"Alright, fine. Why don't you show me how fucking unpure you are by getting on your knees and sucking my cock?"

A smile flickered across her face. "It's *impure*, babe." She was fucking correcting me and I loved it. "And let's double up and film it."

My cock instantly hardened. I knew she wasn't a sweet little angel—my dirty girl was meant for me. I had to stop letting myself forget that.

"Yeah?" I shifted on the bed and took my cock out as I began to stroke myself.

Sloane licked her lips as she slunk her naked body to the floor on her knees. I hadn't even realized her phone was still in her hand until her lips wrapped around the head of my cock and the makeshift mirror appeared beside us. There was something even fucking hotter about knowing I'd be able to watch this later.

"That's right, baby." I took my hands and grabbed her hair behind her head so I could see all of her pretty fucking face. "Take in Daddy's cock like a good girl."

Fuck, did I just call myself Daddy? Who fucking cares, she's into it. Sloane moaned as she bobbed her head up and down, her eyes alternating between mine and the camera.

"Look at you, baby. So fucking pretty with my cock in your mouth. You want me to fuck your face, my sweet girl?"

She smiled with my cock still in her mouth. "Mmmhmm," she moaned out.

God damn. My hips began to move up and down quickly as Sloane drooled on my cock, gagging but never looking away from me.

"Fuck, Sloane. Where do you want me to come?" I couldn't hold off any longer—the whole concept of my cock in her mouth on camera pushed me over the edge.

"Mmm-mmmm—" She tried to speak as I slowed my hips; I chuckled to keep myself from coming.

"Your mouth, baby?"

She eagerly nodded, tears streaming down her face. I instantly continued to fuck her face, holding her head in place, making sure not to block the view for the camera. Her moans made my cock burst and pleasure took over my body, my throat grunting like a wild fucking animal.

I looked down at Sloane after I finished and she removed her mouth from my cock, swallowing my load with a smile.

"Mmm, so fucking tasty," she said sweetly.

Fuck. I was ready to go again.

She threw her phone on the bed, pushed me down on my back, and straddled me with her wet pussy teasing my cock. She leaned down and trailed gentle kisses on my chest before looking up at me with a smile. "My turn."

17

Sloane

Callan and I had one more full day before we needed to head back to DC. I was seriously considering just living in our hotel and never returning; I loved focusing solely on each other, exploring each other's bodies, and lounging around while we chatted. I kept thinking about the possibility of attending UC Berkeley, but I was certain I didn't want to go on campus. I wasn't even sure if they had an online program for Women's and Gender Studies. I'd need to do some research and figure out my options—just not yet.

The only downside to spending so much time with Callan was the guilt I could see weighing on him about our relationship. He kept trying to find reasons to gently push me away, and I continually argued against it. I wasn't sure when, or if, he would ever be completely okay with us being together. Would it be easier once Dad was out of office? Would time change things? The only thing holding me back from announcing our relationship was Dad. Otherwise, I would have proudly shouted it from the rooftops.

There were so many reasons for me to love Callan. He

was deep, whether he wanted to acknowledge it or not; his mind was always active and engaged. He was open-minded, seemingly unafraid of being challenged by a smart woman—in fact, he seemed to enjoy it. He was sweet, caring, kind, and protective. And it didn't hurt that he was easily the hottest guy I'd ever laid eyes on. I was pretty sure I'd always had a thing for older men. Was it the books I read? Was it because I was mature for my age? Even my mom didn't seem upset by our relationship. I knew it made sense, whether Callan wanted to admit it or not.

I woke up to the sun high in the sky. Callan was already up making coffee, and I admired his shirtless body as he moved around, unaware I was watching him.

"Good morning, sunshine," I said quietly as I sat up.

He turned to me with a surprised smile, setting his coffee down before crawling onto the bed, pushing me onto my back and hovering over me.

"Good morning, baby." He smiled sweetly.

I placed my hands on his strong, muscled arms. "Let's do something today. We haven't seen much around here. How about the Golden Gate Bridge?" I was trying to persuade him before we ended up staying in bed and fucking all day, which wouldn't have been a bad idea, either.

"Yeah? I'd love to. I was actually going to suggest a hike. We could find a desolate trail and fuck in nature."

He was in a good mood—horny but cheerful. I liked it.

"That sounds amazing."

I loved seeing Callan in his casual clothes almost as much as I loved seeing him naked. He threw on a sweater and gray sweatpants, and I nearly had a heart attack when I caught sight of his massive bulge, practically begging for my touch. I put on leggings and a fitted zip-up sweater, hoping to tease him just as much as he was unknowingly teasing me.

As I slipped on my tennis shoes, Callan answered his phone. I watched as a smile spread across his face while he listened. "Thanks. Be down in a minute." He hung up and raised his eyebrows at me. "I've got a surprise for you."

As soon as we exited the lobby, I noticed a huge Harley Davidson parked off to the side, with a guy sporting an eager smile next to it.

"Mr. Holt," he greeted Callan, handing him the keys.

"Thanks, man. She'll be ready for pickup tomorrow morning." Callan took the keys, and the guy nodded at me before heading back into the lobby.

"This is for *us*?" I asked, excitement bubbling up.

"Yes, baby. Here." He opened a compartment in the back of the bike, revealing two helmets. "Put this on."

He handed me a sleek black helmet and quickly put on his own. My heart raced as I watched him get on the bike. How did he somehow get even hotter? I fumbled with my helmet and slid it on, grateful I had put my hair in double French braids. I swung my leg over the seat behind Callan, wrapping my arms tightly around his strong body.

"Hold on and lean into me. Grip my body with your thighs. You should be used to that by now, baby," Callan teased, and then the engine roared to life.

My heart raced with excitement. I had never been on a motorcycle before, and the excuse to hold onto Callan in public elated me. I wondered if he did that on purpose. Plus, we had the luxury of anonymity with our helmets on. It was perfect.

I clung to Callan as he accelerated, heading off into the open road. My cheeks began to hurt from how much I was smiling.

"You okay back there, baby?" he shouted over the roar of the engine as we stopped at a red light.

"I'm fucking fantastic!" I laughed, running my hands over his chest.

"Careful, baby. We might need to make a pit stop if you keep touching me like that."

I laughed as he accelerated with the green light. I was elated, surprised by how I reacted on a motorcycle with a hot guy—how typical was that? But there was a good reason for it; it was exhilarating, fun, and undeniably hot.

We weaved through traffic on the Golden Gate Bridge, approaching the northern tip of San Francisco known as the Presidio. I was in awe, gazing out at the Pacific Ocean, almost feeling emotional. I could already tell how stunning the views from the hike would be. We pulled into a parking lot with a few other vehicles and a sign that read Bay Area Ridge Trail. Callan cut the engine and lifted his helmet, turning his head to look back at me.

"How was the ride?" he asked, resting his hand on my thigh.

I pulled off my helmet, revealing the huge grin on my face. "We need to do that more often."

Callan grabbed his backpack and stored our helmets before guiding me onto the trail, as if he knew exactly where he was going.

"I did some research. This trail is moderately strenuous, but it's secluded." He shot me a mischievous grin. "You ready for a workout?"

My heart skipped a beat; his deep voice and the way he side-eyed me made me want to strip naked and pull him into the woods. "Let's do it."

I kept my head down as we passed a couple of groups of

people who seemed unfazed by us. Callan glanced around as we slowly walked uphill, then took my hand, giving me a sly smile.

"This is truly my happy place, Sloane. Being in nature, with you, all alone. Fuck, I never thought I'd say shit like this, but you bring it out of me, baby." He chuckled, looking almost embarrassed as he laughed to himself.

I smiled down at the dirt trail and squeezed his hand. "I like when you tell me how you're feeling. Sometimes I feel like I'm into you more than you're into me," I admitted quietly.

Truthfully, it hurt when he continually tried to push me away. Callan stopped and turned toward me.

"I'm sorry, baby. You have no fucking clue how much I love you. It's terrifying. I'm just trying to get used to all of this." He lifted my chin with his free hand, forcing me to look up into his eyes.

I smiled as I met his nervous hazel-green gaze. "We need to stick together—we need to be strong together. We have to be 100% sure of this, because if it ever gets out, it's going to be tough. I'm scared too. I love you so much it hurts."

Callan's eyebrows twitched as he seemed lost in thought. "You don't seem scared, Sloane. You're so fucking tough. You could easily bust my balls if you wanted to." He laughed.

I giggled, but then my expression shifted. "I *am* scared, though. You're so unsure about all of this. I don't want you to flee," I confessed, feeling my face fall into a frown.

He looked genuinely hurt, his brows furrowing as he looked down at me. "Fuck. It's not that I'm not sure about this, Sloane. I'm just as scared that you're going to flee too. Everything good that's happened in my life has gone to shit, and it's always been my fault. I don't want to fuck this up." His voice strained, and his eyes were wide with uncertainty.

I looked down at the ground, searching for my next words. "You keep saying you've made bad decisions in your life. Your substance abuse—is that what you're talking about? Because we're all human, Cal." I looked back up at him. "Addiction is just like any other disease."

He licked his lips and lowered his eyes. "Yeah, but it's the shit I did when I was drinking and on drugs. I don't remember half of it. I was told I did horrible things, but I can't tell if it's true or not because I was too fucked up."

Now my curiosity was piqued. "Like what?"

Callan shook his head. "Can we talk about this later? I wanna enjoy this hike. I want to fuck you over there in those bushes and erase that shit like it never happened." He nodded toward the woods behind me.

I smiled, deciding to let it go for now. "Let's keep going. You can fuck me while we look over the ocean. Promise."

He moaned impatiently. "Fuck it. You're worth the wait. Come on, baby."

He turned and guided me up the trail, the tall trees casting dappled shadows as they blocked the sun. We continued along the dirt path with few breaks and even fewer people passing us. Eventually, we found a fallen tree off the path, and I climbed up onto it.

"Get your phone out. I want you to take a picture," I told Callan who stood a few feet away.

I looked around as he pointed his phone at me. I zipped down my sweater to reveal my boobs and smiled wide at a surprised Callan.

"Fuck, baby. You're perfect," he groaned, keeping his phone on me and tapping the shutter.

I quickly zipped my sweater back up and giggled as I hopped down. I had too much fun teasing Callan.

He stopped me as I tried to walk past him onto the trail by putting his hand to my arm.

"Wait just a moment, baby. Why don't you feel how hard you made Daddy's cock?" he teased, his voice low and deep again.

Butterflies swarmed my belly. He grabbed my hand and put it to his cock, making me rub the length of him over his gray sweats. My pussy was already drenched.

"I don't see the ocean just yet, Daddy," I teased back as I put my hand down the front of his sweats, grabbing onto his cock and stroking.

His eyes fluttered shut as he moaned.

"Fuck, I want to come inside your sweet pussy, baby," he breathed out before he opened his eyes again.

Watching him moan for me almost made me give in, but I wanted to keep teasing him. I quickly pulled my hand out and stepped past him.

"Come on. It looks like we're almost there," I called out over my shoulder.

"I'm gonna fucking burst," he groaned, but I could hear his footsteps behind me.

I smiled to myself. Having all this power over him was thrilling, especially after begging for him for so long.

He took my hand and hurriedly guided me up the trail. Callan remained quiet as we walked a few more minutes up a steep incline. As we grew closer to the peak, I could hear voices—there were people up there. Callan was going to be pissed that he couldn't just drop my leggings and fuck me right then and there.

"Fuck," he muttered under his breath.

Once we reached the top, the breathtaking views of the city, mountains, and sea made me forget everything else. The fog hugged the low mountains, while the setting sun painted the clouds in shades of orange and pink.

Callan gently grabbed my hand, and I turned to look at him. The sunlight cast a perfect glow on his face, highlighting his full lips, which pouted slightly. My heart swelled with love.

"This is beautiful," I said softly, unable to take my eyes off him.

He stared back at me, sincerity in his gaze. "I love you so fucking much, Sloane. I'm sorry if I've made you feel like I don't."

I wanted to cry. I wanted to stay with him in California forever, somewhere secluded, just the two of us.

I smiled at him. "I love you too. Don't forget it, babe."

We turned back to the breathtaking view, and I finally noticed the other people taking it in as well.

"Excuse me? Could you take a picture of us, please?" A woman with an accent approached us, holding up her camera.

"Yes, of course!" I said, taking her camera and pointing it at her and a few others in her group.

"*Merci*, thank you!" she smiled warmly.

"Would you mind returning the favor?" Callan asked, handing her his phone.

"*Oui*, yes!"

Callan wrapped his arm around my waist, holding me close and completely unafraid to show PDA in front of them. I smiled, clutching the back of his shirt.

"Gorgeous couple. *Merci*, thank you," the woman said before handing Callan his phone back.

I felt a flutter of joy at hearing that we were a cute couple, something I knew Callan wanted to hear. I waved as they walked away, and then Callan swooped me into his arms, giving me a passionate, urgent kiss. As he pressed his body against mine, I felt his hard cock against my stomach. He let go of me, turned me around, and quickly pulled my leggings down. I leaned against a tree and looked around for any other signs of life.

"Let's hurry, baby. I'm gonna fill your pussy up so you can have my cum dripping down your legs all the way back."

I gasped as he quickly thrust himself into me, and he fucked me as we looked over the beautiful Pacific Ocean, just as I promised him.

18

Callan

Feeling Sloane's arms wrapped around me while she sat behind me on the Harley felt like home. I wanted to keep driving until we reached the backwoods of Canada, where we could start a new life together—one where no one knew her as the President's daughter or me as the "hot bodyguard."

Hiking with Sloane and being able to hold her hand in public filled me with so much joy. I'd never felt anything even close to what I felt for her, not even with the liar who almost ruined my life. I shook my head at the thought; she didn't deserve a place in my mind. I knew I had to tell Sloane about her someday, but I didn't want her to think that what I was accused of was true. I didn't want her to have any doubt about me. Everything was just *too* perfect between us.

I knew it was stupid of me to fuck Sloane in public during our hike, but it was too fucking thrilling and my cock literally ached for her. She kept teasing me and she loved it—fuck, *I* loved it. I think she was starting to realize what power she had over me. A fucking eighteen-year-old would literally have me on my knees begging just to get a taste of her. I wouldn't do this shit for anyone else. I realized she was it for me; if this didn't work out, I didn't want any other woman. I wanted to spend forever worshiping her. I wanted to die an old fucking man with Sloane on top of me.

We returned to the hotel late after cruising around the city, and I dreaded heading back to DC the next morning. We'd have to pretend we weren't together, and I knew it was gonna fucking kill me. How was I supposed to wake up without her beside me every morning? After getting a taste of it for a few days, I never wanted to wake up alone again.

Maybe Sloane would want to stay with me. How fucking needy would that sound if I asked her to move in, even if it was just part-time? Ana knew about us, so there wouldn't be much suspicion if she didn't mention anything to Jake. I figured he was too busy being President to notice what was going on. But that thought brought an ache of guilt deep in my chest. What the fuck would happen when he inevitably found out? Maybe not this week or this year, but he would find out eventually, especially if Sloane and I became a real thing. Scratch that—we already *were* a real thing.

I didn't want to think about it anymore. Jake was the only piece of this puzzle I wasn't sure I could face. Scrutiny from strangers? Sure, I'd get over it. But from Jake? That would be a different story. It would be bad. It would be really fucking bad.

"Let's postpone our flight back," Sloane whispered as my eyes began to shut in the dark.

We were cuddled together in bed, and after the hike and multiple rounds of fucking that day, I felt completely spent. But her words perked me right up.

"Yeah? For how long?" I asked, curiosity igniting.

She sighed. "I don't know. Let's go out to the desert and do more fun stuff before we have to face the real world.”

I smiled. “Like south of here? The Mojave Desert?” It didn’t matter—I was already in.

“I don’t care. Anywhere. Wait, *fuck*,” Sloane groaned. “There’s the state dinner on Friday. I told my dad I’d be there.”

I sighed. “Okay, we’ll go back, then we can plan another trip somewhere,” I said with a smile.

I heard her softly laugh. “UCLA next?”

I could easily picture us cruising down the Pacific Coast Highway on a Harley.

“Perfect.”

* * *

I was ready to go into full bodyguard mode at the airport, but luckily, I didn’t have to. Sloane and I were left unbothered the entire time, which allowed us the freedom to get handsy under the blanket in First Class again. She rested her head on my shoulder for half the flight, either reading or napping, and for the other half, we laughed together watching a goofy Adam Sandler movie. But as we got closer to DC, an uneasy feeling settled in. We’d be back in secret mode, and I fucking hated it.

Ana was quick to greet us when we returned.

“Well, hello you two.” She eyed us as we sat in the hallway near the piano, far apart from each other. It was killing me.

“Hey, Mom.” Sloane got up to give Ana a hug, and I could hear the sadness in her voice; she didn’t want to be there either.

“What’s with you two? Did you enjoy the Bay Area?” Ana asked, glancing between us.

Sloane nodded as she sat down on the couch opposite me. “Probably too much. We didn’t want to leave,” she replied, a small smile barely breaking through.

Ana sighed and nodded as she sat down next to her. "Daddy is taking the day off to have a family day before the state dinner tomorrow." I felt a pang of jealousy towards Jake for some reason. It couldn't possibly be because he was "Daddy" to Sloane too. I never heard her call him that. And how fucking weird would it be for me to get jealous over *that*?

Sloane looked up at me, then back at Ana. "Callan doesn't have to leave today, does he?" Her voice sounded desperate, and I felt the same way.

Ana looked over at me with sad eyes. "Of course not. He's welcome. I mean, he's family too, right? Maybe not in the way Daddy thinks," she joked, turning to Sloane.

Neither of us laughed.

"*Ay, dios mio.* Why are you two so tense right now?"

Sloane shook her head. "It's hard to be here, being in secret, when we just spent the last few days together being so...free," she explained quietly.

I couldn't believe how honest she was with Ana.

"I understand. This must be difficult." Ana nodded, her tone sympathetic. "Well, I think Daddy wanted to take us to Martha's Vineyard. You two could have some time away there for a little bit."

Hope and excitement surged in my chest, and Sloane's demeanor brightened as she smiled.

"I think we could probably do that." Sloane glanced at me, her eyes wide with anticipation.

"Okay." Ana patted Sloane's leg as she stood up. "Go pack an overnight bag. You too, Callan. I'll go tell Daddy the plan."

* * *

I never thought I'd be in Martha's Vineyard with the love of my life, and I sure as fuck never imagined I'd be flying there on Air Force One with Jake, the President of the United States. It was still surreal to think about. We were stationed at Fort Story in Virginia, and he often got teased for being so straight-laced; he didn't drink, he didn't sleep around—he was a legit Boy Scout. I think the reason we became friends was that I was trying to stay sober, and he seemed like a good influence. He was a good guy, and now I was fucking his daughter.

I almost had a heart attack when he pulled me into a conference room on the plane. Who knew Air Force One was like a fucking mini White House? I sat on a swivel chair across from him, and he looked relaxed, one hand resting behind his chair while he crossed his legs.

"We haven't had any time to chat, have we? It's been so goddamn busy around here lately," he began, the hint of grays in his hair catching the natural light as I observed him. I knew mine probably looked the same.

"No. I think it's fair to say that when you're the fucking President, Jake," I joked.

He laughed and shrugged. "Yeah. I'm still not used to it. I don't know if anyone ever gets used to it."

"Well, you couldn't tell. You're doing great, man." I felt tense, and I hated that I felt that way around him.

"How's Sloane been? Giving you a hard time?" he asked, curiosity in his eyes.

I cleared my throat and looked away for a moment. "No, she's a sweet girl. Fucking smart, isn't she?" I tried my hardest to sound casual.

He chuckled. "Yeah. I don't know where she gets it from."

"Ana," I answered with a grin.

"Yep, that has to be it. How did she like Berkeley? I heard it wasn't her favorite." He seemed eager for my answer.

I shrugged. "She got a lot of unwanted attention. But she seemed to like the area, though," I admitted.

"I worry about her," he blurted out. "I've already seen so much shit about her online now that she's eighteen. People are sick, you know? I know she can handle herself—probably better than most—but she's still my little girl. That's why I'm glad you're around."

It felt like I'd just been punched in the stomach by a thousand bricks. I nodded and fell silent—what the fuck do I say to that?

"Yeah, man, I won't let anything happen to her," I finally said.

Just then, there was a knock on the door. Thank fucking God. But when Sloane walked in wearing tight leggings and a crop top, I felt like I was going to have another heart attack. I could barely look at her.

"Sorry, am I interrupting?" Sloane asked, glancing between the two of us.

"No, honey. Come in," Jake replied.

She took the chair next to me, and I felt my cheeks burn red hot.

"Where's your mom?" Jake asked casually, clearly unaware of how I was freaking the fuck out.

"She's working on her laptop. I wanted to see if Callan could take me on a hike while we're there. There's so many good spots, right?" She turned to Jake, resting her elbows on the conference table.

"Yeah, that's a great idea. You still climb, Callan?"

"Yeah, not so much anymore. When I can," I answered.

"Callan could win Olympic medals, Sloane. He rock climbs,

boxes...you still do Jiu-Jitsu?" Jake asked, his curiosity evident.

I nodded. "Mmhmm. All that stuff. Gotta stay in shape as an old man," I joked, sneaking a glance at Sloane for just a moment.

She giggled, and my dick twitched. *Fuck.*

"You guys aren't that old," she argued, almost flirtatiously; I wasn't sure if she realized it or not.

"We'll have to get back in the ring sometime for a friendly match. But I'm afraid you'd still kick my ass," Jake continued.

I chuckled softly. "Fuck yeah, I'd kick your ass, old man."

Just then, the pilot announced we were descending, interrupting our conversation.

"Alright. Let's get buckled up," Jake said, standing up and prompting Sloane and me to do the same.

I let out a sigh of relief. Would it always be this hard to be in the same room with Sloane and Jake together? Jake tapped me on the shoulder and gave me a brotherly side hug.

"Thanks again for being here, Callan. It's good to have you around again."

19

Sloane

Poor Callan was so tense on the flight to Martha's Vineyard. I tried my best to give him space, but I caved in the last ten minutes just to check in on him. Of course he was fine, but I think I just needed to be near him.

We had only been to the house in Martha's Vineyard a few times, and I was always amazed at its beauty. We pulled up the long driveway to the six-bedroom, two-story house that overlooked Katama Bay. It was an extravagant home nestled atop a green hill. From almost every window, you could see the bay. I just hoped Callan had the room next to mine, far from my parents' bedroom.

Callan brought my bag into the house, slowly taking in the views. I stopped beside him as he gazed out the dining room window at the endless blue sea.

"Beautiful, isn't it?" I asked quietly, our arms brushing against each other.

He quickly glanced down at our arms and shifted away just an inch. I knew he was trying to be careful, but it still stung a little bit.

"Not as beautiful as you, baby," he said quietly, glancing around to make sure we were alone.

I rolled my eyes, suppressing a giggle behind a smile.

"Stunning views, huh?" Mom appeared beside us. "Callan, your room will be next to Sloane's. Why don't you show him the way?"

She eyed us carefully before moving on into the kitchen, where Dad was speaking loudly with his two bodyguards, Leo and Julian, who were casually sitting at the kitchen island.

"Follow me," I instructed Callan.

We made our way up the stairs and down the hall, first stopping at my room.

"You can just put my bag on the bed," I said as I kicked off my Converse.

Callan smiled as he carefully set my overnight bag down. "I'm gonna hate sleeping in the room next to you. So close but so fucking far," he mumbled, watching me as he sat on the edge of the bed.

My eyes flickered to the door, then back to him. I quickly walked over, shut it, and locked it.

"Baby, we can't," he moaned, disappointment evident in his voice.

I turned to him with a smile. "The door is locked. Let's make out," I teased as I flipped my hair and slowly walked to him.

He shook his head but he didn't hesitate to take my hips and pull me onto him. I straddled him as I wrapped my arms around his shoulders and began to grind my hips onto him.

"Such a naughty fucking girl, aren't you?" He took one hand to my hair and wrapped it around his fist. He tugged my hair back and then planted his lips on my neck, his warm tongue gently swirling around my skin.

"Only for you, Daddy," I whined, my pussy wet as I felt his hard cock beneath me.

"I want to fuck you so hard that I split you into two, baby," he continued, inching his hand down into the back of my leggings and grabbing my ass.

I was so turned on by his touch and his voice that I began to work my hips faster, grinding my pussy against him.

"Make me come. I need you," I moaned into his ear.

"Fuck," he breathed out, then quickly removed his hand from my hair and stuck his middle finger into my mouth. I got it slick and felt him pull my ass cheek with his other hand. Before I knew it, he was putting his wet finger into my ass.

"Oh my God." I suppressed the loud moan that tried to escape my throat. "I'm gonna come," I whispered.

My hips continued, the pleasure from Callan's finger in my ass overwhelming as my pussy began to throb with pleasure. I let out a moan and Callan quickly covered my mouth with his hand, making me giggle as my orgasm peaked. Soon after, Callan grunted quietly in my ear, lifting his hips up and down as if he were coming too.

As my hips slowed, he let go of my mouth and removed his finger from me.

"Did you just come too?" I smiled at him as I widened my eyes.

He laughed. "Fuck yes I did. My cock was aching and I figured this was as close as we were gonna get here."

It turned me on knowing he came just from him pleasuring me as I dry humped him.

"Now I gotta go change my fucking pants," he teased, standing up and gently putting me to my feet.

"I miss you, Callan." I took his hand to stop him. "I love

you. I need to hear it from you too." I hated feeling so insecure about us in that moment.

He paused and gently placed his tattooed fingers on my chin. "I love you, Sloane Gabriela Martin. Someday you're gonna be my wife," he whispered, then pressed his lips to mine.

I melted into his kiss. If we could, I'd marry him right then and there. As we slowly parted, he walked to the door.

"Put on something easy to pull down for the hike. Just in case," he said, eyeing me with a sly smile before opening the door.

"Yes, Daddy," I replied quietly as he shut the door behind him.

* * *

I changed my bottoms before heading downstairs to wander around. I found Dad in the living room on his laptop, and he looked up and smiled at me, patting the couch beside him.

"Come sit, sweetie. I feel like I haven't seen you in weeks."

"You working already?" I asked as I settled down next to him.

He smiled and closed his laptop, setting it on the coffee table in front of us. He draped his arm over the back of the couch, resting it behind my shoulders.

"You're right. I can take a few hours off, right? That's why I wanted to come here in the first place." His voice carried a hint of sadness.

I glanced up at him. "You doing okay, Dad?"

He chuckled softly. "That's something I should be asking you. I know there's been a lot going on lately. I heard you weren't too happy about what happened in Berkeley."

I sighed and looked down at my hands. "No, it was fine. I mean, it's been happening a lot lately. I should be used to it by now," I said with a shrug.

"No, honey. That's not something you should get used to. It feels invasive, doesn't it? Your every move watched," he said gently.

I was almost teary-eyed as I looked back up at him. "Yeah. It does." I nodded.

"I'm sorry I can't be there for you more. But I'm glad you have Callan keeping an eye on you. I trust him with my life."

My heart dropped. Now I understood Callan's guilt. My dad truly loved and trusted him. And so did I. Just because we were involved romantically didn't mean Callan would be any less protective of me—if anything, he was probably more so now.

"I trust him too," I said. "I feel very safe having him around."

Dad blinked, and I wasn't sure how my words sounded, but he seemed a little surprised by my admission.

"Good. I'm glad." He finally smiled. "Hey, why don't we all go on that hike you mentioned?"

"Oh...yeah. That sounds good," I replied, my enthusiasm feigned. I wanted to be alone with Callan, but I also felt guilty for wanting to dismiss the time with Dad.

Dad stood up and held his hand out to me. I took it, and he pulled me up, then wrapped his arm around my shoulder.

"I love you, kiddo," he said, kissing the top of my head and giving me a small squeeze. "I'll go find Mom." He let go and disappeared down the hallway.

I sighed and pulled my phone out to text Callan. **Heads up. We're all going on the hike.**

Typing bubbles quickly appeared. **Okay, no worries. Maybe**

you can sneak into my room tonight, just for some company. We're being too risky lately, baby.

I rolled my eyes, but I knew he was right. **Okay. I love you. See you down here soon?**

I smiled as I watched the typing bubbles pop up again. **I love you too. Yep, just hopping out of the shower.**

My mind went wild. **Send me a shirtless selfie**

I waited as I stared down at my phone. A whole minute passed until a photo popped up. My heart leapt down to my pussy as I stared at Callan's mirror selfie with his muscular, tattooed, wet body with a towel wrapped around his hips. *Holy shit. This perfect man is mine.* And he said I was going to be his wife one day. My heart ached because I wanted to be his wife *now*.

"You ready, baby?" Mom's voice startled me, interrupting my drooling over Callan's picture.

I quickly pocketed my phone and nodded. "Uh huh," I answered, my tone higher than I expected.

Mom smiled as she put her dark brown locks into a ponytail. "What are you blushing about, huh?"

I smiled and shook my head. "You don't want to know, Mom," I answered honestly.

She rolled her eyes. "*Ay, mija.*"

And with perfect timing, Callan walked down the stairs in his casual gray joggers and a black T-shirt. Mom put her hands on her hips as she watched me watch him.

"You're behaving here, right?" she asked me quietly.

"Yes, Mom," I answered, almost with irritation.

Callan looked between the two of us, probably sensing the tension. "Are we ready to roll?" he asked casually.

I eyed him up and down, wanting to pounce on him.

"Just waiting for Jake and Leo," Mom answered with a sigh.

"We'll take the easy trail. I want to get back quickly and relax," she added.

"Yeah, we can go relax by the beach," I said to Callan.

He looked at Mom then back at me; now *he* was tense.

"I hope you brought swimming trunks, Callan. I'm sure Sloane will enjoy that view," she laughed to herself.

I felt my mouth gape wide open.

"Jesus, Ana." Callan laughed uncomfortably.

"What's so funny down here?" Dad asked lightly as he walked down the stairs.

Mom looked at me and Callan and shrugged before she turned to Dad. If she kept subtly teasing us during the trip, I was sure I would die.

"Oh nothing, papa," she dismissed him, then looked over his shoulder at Leo walking down the stairs. "Oh, good. Let's go!"

* * *

During the hike, Callan and I kept stealing glances at each other and smiling, making my heart melt every time. An hour later, we were back at the house, and everyone disappeared into their own spaces; I followed Callan up the stairs toward our rooms.

"Is it too obvious if just the two of us go down to the beach?" I whispered to him as we lingered by my door.

He shrugged, glancing over my shoulder. "If you don't remember, it's my job to keep you safe," he said with a sly smile, leaning against the wall.

God, I wanted to ride him so badly. I bit my lip and inched closer to him. "Go get your trunks on then," I ordered lightly.

Callan quickly cleared his throat, looking over my shoulder

again before staring at the ground. He subtly stepped back a little.

"What are you up to now, sweetie?" Dad's voice called from down the hall.

I turned around quickly and stepped further away from Callan.

"I was asking Callan if he could take me to the beach," I answered nervously.

"Oh, let him rest. He's been doing so much. I can take you, honey," Dad replied casually, standing in the middle of the hallway with his hands in his pockets.

I froze—did Dad sense something between us?

"I mean, I can just go by myself," I said with a smile. "Unless you want to come," I quickly added.

Dad shrugged. "I don't mind spending some time with my baby girl." He smiled back at me and nodded at Callan.

"Cool. Thanks, Jake. I'll see you guys later," Callan said, nodding at both of us before disappearing into his room.

I looked back at Dad, who raised his eyebrows expectantly. "I'll wait for you downstairs."

"Okay," I replied, practically throwing myself into my room.

Fuck. Is Dad suspicious? He definitely seemed like it. Callan was right—we were being too risky. I sighed as I pulled out my phone and texted him. **Boo** ☹

He quickly responded. **Probably better this way. Not sure if I'd be able to keep my hands off of you in a bathing suit.**

I smiled and then stripped my clothes off. I put on my tiny neon green bikini and quickly took a mirror selfie in my best angle, showing off my ass. I sent it to Callan.

Fuck, baby. When we're back in DC, I want to see you strip for me in that.

I smiled again, biting my lip. **When we're back in DC, I'm gonna do a lot more than strip for you**

I giggled and put on a sheer black cover up before slipping on sandals. He responded quickly. **Fucking tease. Let me know when you're back.**

I smiled and headed for the stairs but stopped when I noticed Mom and Dad at the bottom, their backs to me.

"I miss doing things as a family. Sloane never wants to do anything with me anymore," Dad said quietly.

Mom put her arm around him. "She's eighteen now. She's too cool for her dear old papa," she teased.

He smiled at her. "What about my *senorita*? Do you still love dear old papa?" he asked flirtatiously.

Ew. I cleared my throat and slowly walked down the stairs.

Mom turned and quickly stood up. "There she is! Sexy mama. Come on, we're all going to the beach as a family."

"And Julian," I added, glancing at Dad's bodyguard, who was heading down the stairs.

Mom laughed. "And Julian. One big happy family."

20

Callan

Being around Sloane with her family was fucking terrifying, only because I had such a hard time not being able to touch her or think about how she looked with my cock in her mouth. Stealing quick glances and secretly flirting was driving me crazy, only intensifying my desire for her. Jake started looking at me like I was a threat—he had to be sensing something between us. To avoid any more suspicion, I kept my distance for the rest of the day. I stretched out in my room, scrolling through pictures of Sloane on my phone—her in that tiny bikini and the ones of us together. I even jerked off to our little video a couple of times.

It wasn't until Ana knocked on my door and told me to come down for dinner that I felt comfortable showing my face again.

Sloane was sitting at the dining table, one leg drawn up to her chest, her head resting on her knee. She perked up when she noticed me, and my heart dropped at the sight of her big smile, showcasing her little dimple—one she seemed to reserve just for me.

"He's alive," she joked, and I was about to tease her back

until I noticed Jake and Ana in the kitchen beside us.

"Jake barbecued some chicken," Ana announced.

"He's vegetarian," Sloane quickly interjected. "Like me."

It was one of the first things we realized we had in common.

"It's alright. I can eat everything else." I shrugged.

"What? Since when?" Jake asked, looking bewildered.

I rested my hand on a dining chair, trying to remain casual in Sloane's presence. "Um." I cleared my throat. "About six years now, I think." I shrugged and turned to smile at Sloane like a total idiot before quickly looking back toward the kitchen.

"Well, Sloane made a quinoa and lentil salad thing," Jake replied, now unfazed.

Sloane stood up from her chair, wearing a tight crop top—of course, she was braless—and high-waisted shorts that accentuated her amazing ass. I stole a quick glance, but I caught Ana watching me. I nervously licked my lips and walked into the kitchen with everyone else, using every ounce of strength to avoid looking at Sloane.

"Here it is!" Sloane announced as she pulled a bowl out of the fridge, revealing the dish she had made.

She put it on the counter in front of me and I nodded with a smile.

"Looks great," I observed, quickly glancing at my girl.

"Tastes great too," she quipped back as she leaned on the counter.

I almost choked on my own spit.

Ana was quick to chime in. "Let's dig in!"

I sat across from Sloane at the table, mostly staying quiet as the family, Leo, and Julian mingled together casually. Ana attempted to make light conversation but I was too focused on not looking at Sloane. I was probably being too fucking obvious but I wanted to play it safe; if Jake was suspicious, I didn't want to give him any more reason to be.

After dinner the guys sat on the back patio with a beer. Being the sober one, I opted on staying inside with Ana and Sloane. We sat in the living room in front of the TV and I finally felt relaxed being away from Jake. It felt fucking awful that I couldn't even hang out with my good buddy because I was too busy trying not to think about fucking his daughter.

"You're being too obvious, Callan. Ease up a little, *hermano*," Ana murmured as she eased onto the couch next to Sloane, across from where I sat in the armchair.

I sighed. "It's too fucking weird. I can't act natural about this," I explained, gesturing between me and Sloane. "Wouldn't it be hard for you to pretend you and Jake weren't in love while being in the same room?"

Ana gave me a sad smile, and Sloane looked like she was on the verge of tears. I couldn't tell if they were happy or sad tears. *Fuck.*

"I'm sure it's very hard. I couldn't imagine. Perhaps we should just tell him. Let it all air out. Better to come from you two than for him to find out from someone else," Ana suggested quickly.

I shook my head immediately. "Nope. We're not doing that, Ana," I argued.

"Dad would never let me see him again if he found out, Mom," Sloane chimed in, her voice heavy with despair.

She looked absolutely heartbroken, and I wanted to reach out and hold her hand. This was killing me too.

"*Ay*, this is just...it's hard on me too, keeping this from him," Ana admitted quietly.

God, what have I done? I was hurting the two best women in the world because I couldn't keep my dick in my pants. But it was more than that, obviously. I was so in love with Sloane that I was willing to risk it all. *Maybe I should tell Ana that.*

"Ana, I want to marry Sloane. This isn't just some fling or something. I plan to love and protect your daughter for the rest of my life," I confessed quietly.

I heard Sloane's breath hitch, and I quickly took her hand, squeezing it to show my baby that I was serious.

"Even better to tell Jake that, Callan," Ana replied.

Sloane let go of my hand and stood up to face Ana. "Please don't pressure us, Mom. This is hard enough. We'll do it when we're ready, okay?" she whisper-yelled.

Ana put her hands up. "Fine. *Lo que sea.* I won't say any more." She stood up quickly and disappeared upstairs.

Sloane placed her hands on her hips and hung her head. "I just want to be back in your apartment. I hate this sneaking around; it's too nerve-wracking," she said quietly.

I sighed. "I know, baby. I hate it too. But I meant what I said—let's just fucking get hitched." I wasn't sure if my proposal was serious or just born out of desperation.

Sloane looked up at me, her eyes wide. "What's that gonna do?" she asked, curiosity in her voice. "If we still have to sneak around, why do it? When I marry you, I want the world to know. I won't hide it anymore if I'm your wife." Her frustration and passion made me love her even more. And fuck, she was right— I wouldn't want to hide the fact that she was mine if we got married.

"I know, baby. I'm just thinking out loud."

Suddenly, the back door opened, and Jake and the guys walked in. Sloane crossed her arms and slumped back down on the couch. I pulled out my phone, desperate to look at anything but Jake. Luckily, he walked straight through the dining room and up the stairs, seemingly unaware of us.

"I love you, baby," I whispered to Sloane, glancing over at her.

She gave me a small smile. "I love you too."

Shortly after, I headed upstairs to inevitably toss and turn in bed. I had just turned the light off when my phone vibrated—it was a text from Sloane. **I wish I could be in your arms right now.**

I hated that she was so fucking sad. **Me too. What I would give for a fucking kiss right now.**

She responded quickly. **Too risky to sneak in for one minute?**

The fucking sad face emoji. *Fuck it.* I pulled the blanket off of me and quietly opened my door. I glanced down the hallway and everything was quiet. I crept down the hall and gently opened Sloane's door, quickly slipping my body through. Her room was dark but I heard her sweet voice whisper out, "Callan?" She flipped her bedside lamp on. Her gorgeous face appeared near the dim lighting, with half of her body still under her covers.

"Hi baby," I whispered as I sat at the edge of her bed.

She quickly wrapped her arms around my neck and kissed me fervently, almost desperately. I pulled her closer to me but a thought immediately occurred to me.

"Wait, the door—" I stood up and made sure the door was locked. It wasn't. *So fucking reckless.* That didn't stop me from pushing her back down on the bed and hovering over her, pulling my hard cock out of my boxer briefs as she shrugged down her underwear. I immediately found her wet pussy with the tip of my cock and slammed myself into her. God, she felt so fucking good. She quietly moaned as she wrapped her legs around me and lifted her hips to meet me in the middle.

"Fuck, I love you, Sloane," I said quietly into her ear. I was so fucking desperate for her that I was already about to come.

"I love you, Callan," she whispered back.

We quickly came together, and I swore to myself that I'd get the fucking courage to make her my wife. But first, I needed to figure out how to tell Jake. Ana was right: he needed to hear it from me. I'd need to put on my bulletproof vest and man the fuck up. I needed Sloane to be entirely mine, and the only way to do it was to stop fucking sneaking around.

21

Sloane

We were finally back in DC, and all I wanted was to be alone with Callan—preferably in his apartment, or anywhere else we could just be ourselves. He had been so tense in Martha's Vineyard. It was understandable, but it made me realize how hard everything was for him. My dad's suspicious behavior didn't help either, and while we hadn't talked about it, I knew Callan sensed something too. At least now Dad would be busy with work and less likely to notice anything unusual, just like always.

Callan went home for a few hours to change and prepare for the state dinner that night. I lay in bed, fantasizing about living in his apartment—making it *our* apartment. Or maybe we'd get a little house somewhere in California, where I could attend school online and he could fix up his motorcycle for our nightly cruises around the city.

A knock on my door pulled me out of my daydream. I sat up and pulled my knees to my chest, knowing it was either Mom or Dad.

"Come in," I called out.

Of course, it was Mom. She closed the door behind her and slowly came to sit on the bed.

"How are you feeling, *mi vida*?" she asked quietly.

She crossed her legs towards me, waiting for an answer.

I wanted to tell her that I felt stuck, that I wanted to run away with Callan and live our lives freely.

I shrugged casually. "I'm fine."

She tilted her head and gave me her "I don't believe you" look.

"Now your real answer? I know you're having a hard time being so secretive, baby." She placed her hand on mine and gave it a gentle squeeze.

To be honest, I was a little pissed at her for pushing us to tell Dad; it was only making Callan more tense, and I felt like she was cornering us.

"I don't like sneaking around, but there's no other option, Mom," I replied coldly.

She raised her eyebrows at me. "I'm an ally here, Sloane," she snapped.

"It doesn't feel like it when all you've been doing is trying to guilt-trip us into telling Dad. You know what he'll do, Mom. He'll fire Callan and ruin their friendship. Unless you're just trying to wash away *your* guilt," I argued.

Her jaw dropped. "Wash away *my* guilt? Sloane Gabriela, I've done nothing but try to be supportive of you. I'm not going to sit here and let you talk to me this way." She stood up, stormed to my door, and slammed it shut.

God, what am I doing? Starting a fight with my mom, my best friend, the only person I could talk to about this—besides Callan.

I grabbed my phone and tapped on his name to call him, and he answered after one ring.

"Hey, everything okay?" he asked, concern clear in his voice.

I'd never called him before, so I knew he must have thought something was wrong.

"I'm about ready to pack a bag and come stay with you," I said quietly.

"I'd fucking love that, but what's wrong? Did something happen?" he asked gently.

I closed my eyes. "I just want to be with you, Callan. I hate this."

He sighed heavily. "Baby, I want to be with you too. Why don't you pack a bag and after the state dinner, we'll flee to my apartment and fuck like animals?"

I giggled. "Yeah. I like that idea. I get to see you look all hot in a suit tonight, huh?"

He chuckled. "Yep. What are you gonna wear? Please not something I'm gonna fucking get hard over right away," he teased.

"I don't know. Guess you gotta wait and see."

A couple of hours later, I slipped into a black, tight midi dress with spaghetti straps and a very low, lace-cupped bust. I paired it with tan, four-inch platform heels that strapped at the top. After applying my makeup and letting my hair fall in soft waves past my shoulders, I looked in the mirror and felt confident. My boobs had never looked better; I looked amazing. *Callan is going to freak out*, I thought with a smile.

I walked into the hallway to find Mom and Dad sitting in the yellow oval room with Leo and Julian. Mom looked stunning in a pink Louis Vuitton gown, and Dad even looked dapper in his suit. Everyone's heads whipped around as they noticed me enter.

"Wow," Mom announced with a smile.

"Sloane, sweetheart. You can't wear that," Dad immediately chimed in.

I felt my eyes widen in disbelief. Mom looked at Dad with a confused, bewildered expression.

"What? Why not?" she argued.

"She's..." He trailed off, gesturing toward me. "That's not appropriate for a young lady."

Mom scoffed. "She looks very classy and beautiful and grown-up. Is it not appropriate because it makes you uncomfortable?"

Dad closed his eyes in irritation. "I didn't say that. I just—"

"No," she interrupted. "You've said enough."

She waved him off like she was dismissing him. I wanted to hug her. She was always on my side, calling out sexist bullshit no matter who said it.

As if the tension in the room couldn't get any thicker, Callan casually walked in looking incredibly hot. He wore a navy blue suit with a vest jacket, a white shirt, and a black tie. His hair was slicked back, and the side of his neck tattoo peeked out from his collar. I was dying to know what he was thinking as he took me in for a few seconds, eyeing me up and down, almost in a panic. He quickly blinked and turned to look at everyone else.

"Sorry if I'm late. Everything is good to go downstairs," he said.

Mom and Dad remained silent, the tension palpable.

"Good. Let's go," Mom replied, standing up and leading the way.

I glanced back at Dad; he looked between Leo and Julian and nodded. I hurried after Mom and Callan, trying to catch up with her.

"Thanks, Mom. I'm sorry about earlier," I whispered.

She shook her head. "Don't worry about it, baby." She smiled at me and took my hand as we walked down the stairs.

I glanced back at Callan and he winked at me. I giggled to myself, looking down at the steps.

"Take your time, baby. Your dad just doesn't get it sometimes," she said quietly, shaking her head.

I sighed with relief as we walked down to the state dining room. Callan quickly moved ahead of me and Mom, pulling the door open for us. Inside, the large dining room was filled with guests in their finest gowns and suits, chatting amongst themselves until they quieted at our entrance. The chandelier sparkled with shades of purple and pink, casting a warm glow across the room.

Several round tables filled the space, and a long rectangular table stood at the front. Callan guided us to that table, where guests had already filled one side. Mom took a seat in the middle, I sat down next to her, and Callan promptly settled beside me.

Callan leaned over and whispered into my ear. "You're fucking killing me, baby."

I smiled as I looked down at my plate and silverware. "That's what I was going for," I whispered back, biting my lip to hide my smile.

He sighed and looked around, then put his hand on my thigh. He gave it a tight squeeze but released his grip once the room grew silent as Dad walked in with Leo and Julian. The Norwegian Prime Minister, the guest of honor, stood up to greet our family as Dad approached the table, and the party had begun.

Callan took every opportunity to put his hand on me. When

Dad got up to make a toast, I kept squirming under the touch of Callan's palm as he softly caressed my thigh. I didn't think anyone could sense what was going on underneath the table, but Mom nudged me with her arm as she glanced down at my lap, shaking her head.

"Too much," she warned me, then looked over at Callan.

"Fuck. Sorry," he muttered under his breath.

Everyone seemed to have a good time but all I could think about was what Callan and I would do once we left. My mind wandered to the strap-on we purchased in Berkeley. Would Callan really be into that? The idea of *me* fucking Callan almost made my brain explode. How amazing would it be to be in control of Callan's body, of his pleasure, dominating him in the way that I knew I could?

A rush of adrenaline hit me; I was gonna go for it. "When we get to your apartment, I want you on your knees for me," I whispered in Callan's ear with shaky breath. As turned on as I was, I was nervous—never in my wildest dreams did I think I would be doing this, especially with someone like Callan.

I leaned back into my chair to gauge his reaction. His face gave him away immediately—a slow, sly smile spread across his lips as he swallowed hard and licked his lower lip, then side-eyed me and nodded. I knew he was into it.

After we took pictures with the prime minister and his family, I almost raced up the steps to grab the bag I had packed for Callan's place. He waited for me at the end of the stairs and quickly walked ahead of me to open the side door toward the SUV.

We carefully drove off toward his apartment, not even bothering to say goodbye to anyone. This way, no one could ask any questions.

"Do you know what I want to do to you, Daddy?" I asked, sitting in the passenger seat and crossing my legs toward him.

"I think I have a feeling, baby," he answered, gripping the steering wheel tightly.

I giggled. "And if you're good, I'll let you fuck me however you want after."

"*Fuck*," he breathed, quickly glancing over at me. "You're gonna make me come just talking like that, baby."

I reached over to his hard cock, already begging to be released. My hand glided up and down his length, the heat between my legs growing with every stroke.

A few minutes later, we pulled into the parking garage. Callan didn't bother being discreet as he took my hand and guided me into the elevator. He put his hand to the back of my head and pulled me in for a kiss, but I quickly put my hand between our lips.

"Did I say you could kiss me?" I teased, raising my eyebrows.

Callan bit his lip and eyed me longingly. "*Please*, baby," he begged.

I smiled as the elevator door pinged open on his floor. I took his hand and led him to his door, waiting for him to unlock it as he fumbled with his keys.

"The longer you take, the longer it'll be until I fuck you," I whispered as I pressed my body against his back.

"Fuck," he muttered, then unlocked the door.

We walked in and I immediately headed for the bathroom. "Get the butt plugs and prep your ass. I'm strapping up."

I didn't look back as I closed the bathroom door behind me and squealed to myself. "Oh my *God!*" I whispered, my hands shaking.

I carefully took my dress off and hung it on the hook behind the door. I opened my bag that revealed a few nights' worth of pajamas and clothes. Underneath everything was the strap-on harness and a purple, double ended dildo that vibrated. I held the harness up in my hand and wondered how in the hell I was going to figure out how to put it on. I had never done anything like this before and I was starting to think I was in over my head. I took my phone out and found an instructional video on the manufacturer's website. I stepped into the harness, tightened the front and back straps, and inserted the dildo into the middle hole. I gasped as I stuck my side of the dildo into my already drenched pussy. I looked in the mirror and smiled at my reflection. I was still sporting my four-inch platform heels, and with the strap-on in place, I looked like a fucking queen. I turned around and my exposed ass looked amazing with the harness on. I took a few deep breaths and shook my hands out to get rid of the nerves. I took one last deep breath and flung the door open, finding Callan naked and on his knees, stroking himself as he took me all in.

"Holy fuck," he breathed out as he looked up at me.

I smiled. "Is your ass getting stretched out for me?" I asked as I put my hand on my hip.

"Yes, baby. I'm ready for you." His voice was deep and eager.

My heart raced as I inched toward him and put my hand to his hair.

"Suck my cock," I demanded, then let go of his hair and took the purple dildo in my hand.

Callan looked up at me, almost hesitantly. I wondered if I was taking things too far.

"It's not a real cock, Callan. But if you don't want to, you don't have to," I said gently.

He licked his lips as he eyed me, then leaned in and pressed his lips to the purple dildo I was holding. He slowly took it in and began to move his mouth up and down the length. Watching him suck on my dildo sent a wave of goosebumps all over my body—I had no idea how much this would turn me on.

"That's a good Daddy," I said with a smile, watching him as he found a steady rhythm and as I began to move my hips. *Holy shit, this is amazing.* Was this the type of power Callan felt while I sucked his cock, or did I feel this way because I now magically had a dick? He looked *so* sexy the way his lips wrapped around the dildo. I was starting to really get into it—I took his head in my hands and started fucking his face. I didn't even have the vibrator turned on yet but the nub atop of the dildo pressed against my clit perfectly, building up to an orgasm.

"I need to fuck you now," I said as I pulled out of his mouth and took a step back.

He nodded and stood up, jerking his hard cock quickly. I pulled him close to me and planted my lips firmly onto his, needing to feel his soft mouth against mine. I pulled away and glanced at the bed on the other side of the room.

"Get on the bed. On all fours," I instructed.

Callan immediately walked to the bed and got onto it, putting his hands and knees underneath his body and looking at me expectantly. Seeing Callan and his muscled, tattooed body waiting for me to fuck him had my pussy pulsing. I grabbed the lube that sat on his dresser and slowly walked to Callan, observing his ass that somehow looked even better propped up for me. I could see the little stainless steel butt plug in his ass as I inched closer to him.

"I'm pulling it out now. Are you ready for me?" I asked, running my hands along his ass.

"I'm ready for you, baby," he answered softly.

I gently reached for the butt plug and slowly pulled it, hearing him gasp, then dropped it on the floor where he had conveniently laid a towel. I slathered lube onto the dildo and Callan, now experienced to know that with anal, the more lube the better. Callan looked over his shoulder at me, his forehead creased in anticipation.

I took the dildo and slowly pressed the tip into him, waiting for a reaction.

"Oh, fuck," he breathed out.

"Everything good?" I asked with concern.

"Yes, baby. Keep going," he quickly responded.

I smiled and bit my lip as I inched into him slowly, his grunts of pleasure turning me on even more. I was finally fully inside of him and started to slowly move my hips.

"Oh, fuck baby. Yes," he moaned out.

"Yeah, Daddy? You like being fucked?" I grabbed his hips and began to pump quicker.

I had never heard him moan in pleasure so much—it drove me wild. As I turned the vibrator on, I knew that with just a few more thrusts, I'd come easily.

"Oh fuck, Sloane," he said in between quickened breaths.

I giggled as I began to thrust harder, the friction on my clit, combined with the vibrator and pounding into Callan, pushing me closer to coming.

"I'm gonna come. Fucking your ass feels so good," I breathed out.

"Oh fuck, baby. Me too."

We both moaned in pleasure at almost the exact same time, Callan's loud grunts only intensifying the euphoria of my orgasm.

I had to turn the vibrator off—it was too intense, and my

pussy still throbbed with need. I pulled out of Callan and he fell onto the bed on his side, catching his breath. I quickly pulled the harness and dildo off and climbed onto the bed to straddle him. He gave me a sleepy smile as he took my hips.

"How was that?" I asked curiously.

He sighed. "Sloane, that was fucking amazing. You're such a fucking goddess," he said as he squeezed my ass.

A blush spread across my cheeks; any compliment from Callan always made me giddy. "Yeah? Well, you're gonna need to fuck this goddess before we fall asleep. The dildo is fun, but I need your warm cock inside of me."

Callan's face grew serious as his lips parted. "You just got me so fucking hard again. Come on, baby," he said as he sat up and pushed me onto my back, holding my legs to his chest. "Let me please my fucking goddess."

22

Callan

It was official: I needed to get Sloane a fucking ring. I was going to propose to her. I didn't know how, but I wanted to have it ready for the right moment. With the way she made me feel, I knew I needed to keep her close so I could feel that way forever. She made me believe I was a good man, someone worthy of love. I didn't give a fuck about anything else—all I cared about was her.

I was ready to tell Jake, and if he fired me and hated me for it, then so be it. Sloane and I were stronger than whatever the outside world thought. I knew I needed to come clean about my past, but I still couldn't figure out how to do it. If she found out later without me telling her, I'd look guilty as fuck. But I cared about what she thought of me, and I worried that revealing my history could shift her feelings. Would she be scared of me? Would she feel betrayed? I didn't know, and that uncertainty was eating me alive inside.

The next morning, we lay in bed after an unexpectedly intense night. Sloane slept soundly in my arms as I recalled how incredible the night before had been. I didn't realize how fucking good it would feel to be fucked by Sloane. She was a natural at it. And she was so fucking into it that it made *me* even more into it. I would do whatever the fuck she wanted to try, as long as she was happy.

She blinked her eyes open after I watched her sleep for a few minutes. The morning sun crept through the curtains and cast a faint glow to her body.

"Good morning, baby," I said softly, running my fingers gently across her arm.

She smiled, slowly opening and closing her eyes. "Good morning."

"I love you. Do you know that?" I wanted to shout it from the rooftop. In fact, I fucking might once I told Jake.

She gave me a soft laugh. "I love you too," she said in her cute, hoarse morning voice.

"Last night was fucking amazing, baby," I continued, feeling better this morning than I had in a long, long time.

She nestled her nose into my chest and wrapped her arm around me. "It really was. I love that we can explore sexually with each other." Now she was fully awake.

I laughed quietly. "You tell me what you wanna do and I'll do it. Any fucking thing, any fucking time," I said confidently.

She laughed back. "Let's get breakfast. Maybe go outside of the city or something."

"Like where?"

"Maybe like, a little town in Maryland or something. Let's just hop on your motorcycle and find something."

I smiled to myself. "You like riding on a bike with me, huh?"

She giggled. "So what if I do?"

I suddenly sat up and hovered over Sloane, pinning her arms down on either side of her.

"Does it turn you on?" I teased, staring down into her big, brown eyes.

She bit her lip and began to breathe heavily. I loved how easily she got turned on for me. "Yes."

"Yeah? It gets your perfect pussy wet?" I went on, pressing my hard cock onto her belly.

She smiled. "So fucking wet. Just for you, Daddy."

That was all it took. I fucked her hard, making her gorgeous little mouth moan out my name, and we showered afterward and headed out to find a diner.

We rode for about thirty minutes before spotting a diner off the highway. It was nestled in a small town in Maryland, and I knew why Sloane had wanted to come here—there wouldn't be dozens of people staring at her like they did in the big cities.

The diner was tiny—the smallest I had ever seen—sandwiched between a few other businesses. We walked in, and there were only a few patrons seated. Sloane wore a baseball cap, as if that would make her less recognizable; anyone who glanced her way would still know she was the stunning fucking daughter of the President. The way her tits looked in her tight T-shirt would have anyone's attention, really.

We sat in a booth by the window and looked over the menu. I could tell Sloane was excited to be out without being noticed. I wondered if she would still be as popular when Jake wasn't president anymore. I knew that was something she thought about.

After Sloane ordered an omelet and I opted for Belgian waffles, she sighed and smiled, tilting her head at me.

"I really love being with you," she said earnestly.

Fuck, my heart melted. "I love being with you too, baby," I smiled.

She glanced around briefly before reaching for my hand on the table. I didn't care who saw; I took her hand in mine and gave it a gentle squeeze.

"I want to tell Jake soon," I blurted out.

Sloane's face fell. "Why?" She pulled her hand away.

I looked out the window, letting out a sigh as my empty hands rested on the table. "Because I want us to be together. *Really* be together. I don't want to hide anymore, baby," I explained.

Her brows knitted together as she stared at me. "He's going to fire you. You won't get to be around as much," she argued.

I shrugged. "So what? I'll find another job. You can be with me at my apartment. We'll figure it out. You're eighteen, baby. You don't need his permission, even if he *is* the fucking President," I joked.

She didn't laugh. "What about...your friendship?" she asked hesitantly.

I paused before answering. "You're more important." It was the truth; this girl, the love of my life, mattered more than my twenty-year friendship. Admitting it was hard, but I knew it was true.

She shook her head, sadness flickering in her eyes. "Really?"

I nodded. "Of course, baby. You're it—you're the one. We're gonna get married, and you're going to be stuck with me for another forty or fifty years until I croak."

That brought a smile to her face. "I hope it's longer than that." *Thank fuck, she's happy again.* "But...how are we going to tell him?"

I shot her a serious look. "*We're* not telling him; *I'm* telling him. I don't want you to see your dad punching me in the fucking face," I explained.

She rolled her eyes. "I'm not letting you do it alone," she huffed.

I blinked at her, realizing I couldn't argue with her resolve. "We'll figure it out. It doesn't need to happen today. We'll... we'll prepare for it," I assured her.

She sighed and nodded. "Okay."

We ate our food, chatting as the diners around us came and went, mostly keeping to themselves. After I paid the bill, I took her hand and led her to my bike.

"Anywhere else you want to go, baby?" I asked, leaning against the bike and pulling her close by the hips.

Traffic was light, and I wasn't worried about anyone seeing us. *Fuck 'em.*

Sloane placed her hands on my arms and shrugged. "Let's go back to your apartment. I just want to spend time with you," she replied earnestly.

Fuck, this girl was giving me a toothache. I smiled and gently pressed my lips to hers. She moaned quietly, pulling me closer. Once we parted, I gave her a playful tap on the ass. "Let's go."

* * *

Sloane and I sat on the couch together, her legs resting on my thighs as we watched some reality show on Netflix that she liked. It was complete trash, but it was entertaining. Just being with her, spending lazy time together, made me so fucking happy. I rubbed my hands over her legs, and she looked up at me with a sly smile.

We were suddenly interrupted by her phone buzzing violently on the coffee table. I leaned over to grab it for her, and my heart dropped when I saw Jake was calling. In all the time

Sloane and I had spent together, he had never once called her. I handed her the phone, feeling sick to my stomach. She eyed it with confusion.

"Hey, Dad?" she answered.

Her eyes widened slowly, and her face went pale. She looked up at me, lips parted in shock.

"I'm...I'm out shopping. Why?"

I waited, watching intently, wishing she would put the call on speaker.

"I'm not going to come home *right this instant*. What's going on?" Her brows furrowed as she glanced back at me.

"Oh, Dad...it's—" she began, but his voice cut her off.

Her chest rose and fell quickly, panic evident in her demeanor.

"I—I will explain everything when I get home, okay?" she said quietly.

Her eyes suddenly darted to mine. *Fuck, he knows. How does he know?* "Yes." She paused for a moment before speaking again. "He'll be there too." Her eyes squeezed shut tightly, and she lowered the phone.

"What's going on?" I asked impatiently.

Sloane opened her eyes and shook her head. "Someone... someone took pictures of us at the diner. And outside of it. My dad said it's all over the Internet," she explained quietly, tears welling in her eyes.

"Oh, fucking shit," I blurted out. "What the fuck? I didn't even see anyone around!"

She continued to shake her head. "We need to get back. We need to diffuse this," she thought aloud.

Her phone began vibrating again. This time, it was Ana calling. Sloane burst into tears, covering her face with her hands.

"I can't. I can't—" she started, so I took her phone and pressed it to my ear.

"Ana," I answered.

"Callan! Where's Sloane? I told you two to be fucking careful. Did you hear? I'm sure you heard because Jake is furious, and I just heard him yelling at her. Fuck. Where is she?" She spoke in one long breath.

"She's here. We'll be there soon," I said, keeping it brief before I hung up.

I hadn't expected shit to escalate so quickly. And this wasn't how I wanted Jake to find out. I didn't want the world to know about us this way, either.

I pulled Sloane into my arms as she cried. "We'll get through this, baby. Remember? We need to be strong together," I said, needing to remind myself just as much.

"I know," she said between hiccuped breaths. "I know. I love you. I love you, Callan," she repeated.

I took a deep breath and rubbed her back in soothing circles. "I love you, baby."

This was going to be the hardest fucking moment of my life.

23

Sloane

What the fuck has he done to you? Dad's words echoed in my head as Callan and I got into his SUV. Why would he say that, as if I were some helpless victim with no say in this? Why blame him when I was the one who initiated everything? Dad didn't know that yet, but he would soon find out. I'd tell him everything, even that we wanted to get married. He'd have to understand how serious we were, and maybe Mom would back me up.

"What are we gonna do?" I asked Callan after we pulled onto the main street outside his building.

"We'll remain calm. I'll tell him I'm crazy about you," he explained quietly. "If he doesn't get it, then he doesn't get it, Sloane. He may need time to adjust to us being together. We just need to stand our ground."

He sounded so sure of himself.

"Okay." I nodded. "If he fires you, I'm coming with you."

Callan glanced over at me, confusion flickering across his face. "Like, you're leaving with me?"

"Yes. Is that okay? If I stay with you?" I didn't want to

impose, but I also couldn't bear the thought of being apart from him.

He smiled quickly. "Of course it's okay, baby. Fucking bring your stuff and never leave if you don't want to."

That was all the reassurance I needed. We pulled up to the house, and I took a deep breath before opening my door. Callan reached over and took my hand. "It's gonna be okay, baby. You and me. We got this."

I nodded with a smile, but my heart raced and my stomach curled into knots. My hands felt weak and shaky as we walked up the stairs to the living quarters where I knew Dad was waiting for us. As expected, we approached the yellow oval room, and he was sitting there, suit jacket off, staring down at the ground before looking up at us through his lashes.

"You've got a lot of fucking nerve showing your face here again, Callan," Dad hissed, disdain dripping from his tone as he stood up and put his hands in his pockets.

I glanced at Callan. His jaw was clenched, but he held his head high.

"I don't think you fully understand the situation, Jake," he muttered.

Dad scoffed. "No? What don't I understand about you taking advantage of my eighteen-year-old daughter?"

"Dad, that's not what's happening here," I quickly chimed in.

I saw Dad's eyes flicker over my shoulder. I turned back to see Mom standing at the beam that separated the room from the hallway, arms crossed, looking at us with an icy glare.

"Then tell me what's happening here, Sloane. I'd love to hear it from you." Dad wasn't holding back any indignation.

My shaky hands clasped in front of me, held up to my chest

almost like a prayer. "I started all of this between us," I began, gesturing with my clasped hands between me and Callan. "He fought his feelings. He didn't give in easily. But I knew from the beginning, Dad. I knew that I loved him and that he was the one." I was surprised at how clear and concise my words were, how freely they flowed from me.

Dad suddenly burst into laughter. Confused, I looked over at Mom, who had her eyes closed in irritation, shaking her head. A quick glance at Callan showed the annoyance clearly written on his face.

"Sloane, you think you're in love with Callan? *Him*? This fucking almost forty-year-old ex-junkie?" Dad asked, exasperated.

"Jake!" Mom quickly scolded him.

"Nah, I can take it, Ana. Just fucking clear the air, Jake. Take it all out on me," Callan said calmly, his hands firmly in his pockets.

"You mean the man you asked to come look after your family because he was the only person alive that you trusted for the job?" I butt in.

Dad's eyes widened. "Yeah, the man I thought I trusted with my life. The one whose life I've saved more than once, pulling him out of more shit than I can count—that I'm sure he hasn't told you about," he spit out, pointing his finger at me.

Callan sighed. "Alright, Jake. We're all heated here. Why don't we just take a bit to cool off before—"

"Fuck you, Callan!" Dad shouted suddenly. "Telling *me* to fucking cool off when you've been fucking my daughter?!"

Callan blinked, his chest rising and falling rapidly. "You already heard it from her, Jake. I'm in love with her. I'm sorry, but I'm fucking in love."

His words hit me hard, but before I could process anything, Dad lunged at Callan, backing him against the wall. He raised his fist and struck Callan across the face. Instinctively, I rushed toward them, hearing Mom shriek for Leo and Julian. Dad shoved me aside as he lifted his fist again, but Leo and Julian quickly flanked him, grabbing his arms.

I turned to Callan, who stood against the wall, stone-faced and breathing heavily, his eye already beginning to swell.

"Get the fuck out of here! If I see your face around here again, you'll be in fucking prison for life!" Dad shouted, pointing to the hallway.

Tears streamed down my face. This was bad—worst-case scenario bad. Callan looked at me, uncertainty in his eyes, before turning to leave. I started to follow him, but Mom tugged on my arm. "Wait, baby. Let's all talk."

I shook my head. "No. I have to go with him," I pleaded, watching him walk down the stairs.

"Sloane." Dad was already beside me, tugging my arm along with Mom. Fear surged through my body—were they really not going to let me go?

"Let me go," I warned him, my voice deeper than I expected.

"Sloane, you need to know something about Callan," Dad insisted, easing his grip. "Something I defended him for—that I helped him get off scot-free. But now, after this...I'm not so sure anymore."

I glanced at Mom; she looked as confused as I felt. "What are you talking about, Jake?" she asked quietly.

He let go of me and placed his hands on his hips, walking toward the middle of the room.

"Leo, Julian. Make sure he's off the premises. I need to speak to my family alone," he instructed, waving them away.

My hands trembled as I held my breath, waiting for Dad to explain.

"Dad," I muttered angrily. "Tell me now, or I'm leaving."

Dad turned, looking between me and Mom, who stood beside me with her arms crossed. "Ana, do you remember the case I was asked to testify on? The one I couldn't discuss?"

"Yes," she replied quickly.

Dad sighed, lowering his head. "It was a sexual assault case. It was against Callan."

24

Callan

I knew Jake was going to fucking hit me. I expected it. I should have spoken to him alone, but I knew Sloane wouldn't have it. I also anticipated insults—Jake always thought he was so much fucking better than me. Born wealthy, straight-laced, and a straight-up fucking nerd, yet I loved him. We were so different when we first met in the Navy—the only thing we had in common was our sobriety. Yet somehow, we became the best of friends, going through hell and back together in the SEALs.

I was required to go through therapy for my PTSD, but I didn't want to dwell on that. Maybe that's why I made such bad decisions before I left the Navy. I didn't technically get kicked out, but I sure as hell didn't re-enlist—not after nearly facing a dishonorable discharge.

Jake had just been promoted to E7 as an officer. Meanwhile, I was struggling. My relationship of three years was tanking—not just because of me, but because of her too. Sarah. She was a fucking verbally abusive smoke show who tested every one of my limits. At twenty-six, I didn't know any better. I was only thinking with my dick and living for the drama she created. We were both fucked up, but I convinced myself it was love. She was sweet as pie when we were around other people. That's why everyone believed her when she accused me of sexually assaulting her.

It was right after I relapsed. I was drinking all the time, even while working. I don't know how I didn't get caught—maybe it was just luck. Sarah sure as fuck gave me hell about it, calling me a fuck-up and a pathetic loser who couldn't control myself, and then we'd hate-fuck until the sun came up.

One particular evening, after we'd been drinking, I told her I was leaving. I was determined to get clean and fix my life. From what I remembered, she screamed at me while I packed my things, then started pounding on me with her little fists. At 5'2" and 110 pounds soaking wet, it didn't do much, but I pushed her off, and she stumbled back against the dresser, sending everything crashing down beside her. I checked to make sure she was okay—she was, just fucking drunk and too unsteady to stay upright. She kept screaming until I locked myself in the bathroom to get the hell away from her.

I woke up with a text from Jake. **There's a warrant for your arrest. Sarah claims you sexually assaulted her.**

I found myself on trial in the military court. Sarah put up a convincing front—she had friends testify that I was a fucking monster. They presented texts where I called her a stupid fucking cunt, a worthless bitch, an evil slut. I was angry, but she had hurled far worse insults at me. Even in my drunken state, I never laid a hand on her. We had rough sex, but she asked for everything we did.

But then pictures of bruises surfaced as evidence. I had no fucking idea how she got them. I'll admit, I blacked out more than once when we were drinking, but I knew I'd never hit her—I wasn't that much of a scumbag. The bruises spanned several days, covering the last few months of our relationship. She claimed I'd blacked out and tossed her around like a punching bag. People were shocked—they sided with her, convinced that the fucking junkie with tattoos and muscles was the monster she made me out to be.

Yet somehow, I was acquitted. The officers judging my case listened to character witnesses on my behalf, including Jake's. They saw the evidence of Sarah's verbal abuse through texts and voicemails. I lost rank, but I only had a few months left until my enlistment was up. And then I ran.

That's when I went back to Philly and lost everything. I never got clean. I traveled around with my tent and a single bag of belongings, using any spare change I had to buy booze. I lost all track of time, and by the time I was suicidal, two years had passed. That's when I called Jake. He had been searching for me since I disappeared off the radar. Thank fuck I remembered his number; otherwise, I probably would have ended my life. He got me into rehab, helped me with money when I got out, and then set me up with a decent job.

And now, here I was, sitting alone in my DC apartment after he just clocked me in the face. I deserved it. After everything he did for me, I repaid him by fucking his daughter. What the fuck was I thinking? But Sloane was the most perfect person I had ever laid eyes on. It wasn't just her beauty—I was in love with her intelligence, her quick wit, and her sweetness. And she loved me. I didn't deserve her. I knew I had to cut out the misogynistic bullshit, but it was true: everyone could see it—she was too good, too pure, too fucking perfect for me.

I was spiraling. *Where the fuck is Sloane?* I texted her with shaky hands: **Everything okay? Where are you?**

I stared at my phone for a full five minutes before tossing it onto the couch and gazing out the window. Across the street was a mini market, and I craved whiskey so fucking badly. I needed to know where Sloane was and what Jake was telling her. With how quick he was to badmouth me, I had no doubt he was dragging up Sarah's name. Now I looked guilty as fuck for not telling Sloane sooner.

I picked up my phone again—still nothing. Sighing, I grabbed my wallet, took the elevator down, and walked to the mini market across the street.

25

Sloane

"*What?*" Tears streamed down my face. "Callan wouldn't do that."

"Jake...you can't be serious," Mom said, her voice filled with disbelief.

Dad shrugged, shaking his head. "He was acquitted, partly thanks to me. His ex-girlfriend who accused him wasn't a good person, so it was clear she was lying. But now...now that he's done this, I don't know if I ever really knew Callan at all. I can't be sure if he was guilty or not."

My heart dropped. "So...he *didn't* do it, though. He was accused, but he didn't do it," I said, mostly to reassure myself.

"Jake, how could you keep this from me?" Mom asked harshly. "*Sarah* did all of that?"

I shook my head at both of them. "Sarah?"

Mom frowned at me, then turned back to Dad. "Answer me, Jacob."

Dad nodded.

"Well then he definitely didn't do it. Sarah was crazy!" Mom threw her hands in the air. "That woman was no good."

Dad shook his head at her and shrugged. "And *Callan* isn't crazy? The fucking ex-junkie drunk who I had to save off the streets all those years ago? The one who is now fucking our daughter?" He was yelling and talking about me like I wasn't right in front of him.

"Dad!" I butt in. "He's not just *fucking* me, as you so eloquently put it. It's not even about that," I argued.

His face turned red. I wasn't sure if he ever heard me say *fuck* before.

"What's it about then, huh? How do you have *anything* in common with a man twenty years older than you?" I could tell he was trying to remain calm.

I crossed my arms. "What exactly do you have in common with Mom?" I challenged him.

"Your mother isn't twenty years younger than me, Sloane," he disputed.

"What does that even matter, Dad? Shouldn't all that matter is that I'm happy?"

Dad scoffed and put his hands to his head, exasperated.

Mom sighed. "Let's all just take a few minutes to ourselves, okay? Let's all calm down and collect our thoughts," she suggested.

I immediately perked up, wanting to go find Callan, needing his side of the story. Dad shook his head and pointed at me, as if sensing the shift in my energy.

"Sloane, you're not going anywhere. I'm not letting you see a fucking perverted child molestor who's been taking advantage of you."

"Jake!" Mom scolded.

My jaw dropped. "*Excuse me?* Do I *look* like a child, Dad? None of this started until I was eighteen, and I've consented to everything we've done together," I argued, my voice raised.

Dad raised his eyebrows. "He's still a fucking pervert, Sloane. You have no idea how *wrong* this is. A man his age should want nothing to do with a girl your age."

Anger surged through me. "I am not a fucking little girl anymore, Dad. And you cannot tell me that you won't 'let' me see him. Because legally, I can walk right out of here and never come back."

"*Ay dios mio.* Jake, Sloane...we need to all take a breather, okay? Otherwise we're going to say things we regret in here," Mom cut it in, taking my hand and squeezing it.

Dad's widened eyes never left me. His voice was low and deep as he said, "You and Callan have ruined my reelection. My whole legacy as a president is shattered. The only thing anyone will ever remember is how my fucking thirty-eight year old bodyguard and my eighteen-year-old daughter were fucking."

A deep ache spread through my chest. Dad had never talked to me that way before, and hearing those words out loud made me start bawling. I already felt guilty, but now it weighed down on me like sandbags were tied to my ankles.

"Jacob Harold Martin," Mom's low voice reprimanded Dad as I ran out of the room and into my own.

My heart was shattered. Had we really ruined Dad's entire career? Would people be *that* offended by my relationship with someone older than me? Why did it even matter? It had nothing to do with him.

I locked my door and pulled my phone out, my breath hiccuping from the sobs that still escaped my chest. There was a text from Callan: **Everything okay? Where are you?**

I quickly texted back with shaky fingers: **No. I am not okay.**

I need you.

I stared at my phone, waiting for Callan to respond. A loud knock on the door jolted me, pulling my attention away from the screen.

"Sloane, honey. Are you okay?" Mom's worried voice called out.

I shook my head. "No, Mom. I'm not okay. I need to get out of here," I cried. I looked back down at my phone, waiting for Callan. There was nothing. Impatient, I dialed his number.

"Baby, please let me in. We can talk," Mom continued.

I listened as the ringtone droned on; Callan's voicemail picked up, and I hung up. I dialed again, desperate to hear his voice.

"Sloane." Mom wasn't giving up, but I didn't respond.

I began to lose it when Callan didn't answer the second time. I grabbed a small suitcase and began to pile in clothes, books, my laptop, extra chargers. I grabbed my purse, phone, and closed the suitcase as I unlocked the door and swung it open. Mom was standing there with her arms crossed and a sad, concerned frown on her face.

"Baby." She looked down at my bag and shook her head. "Please don't leave. I know Daddy said some harsh words but you have to understand how this is all making him feel," she said quietly.

I shook my head. "How do you think *I* feel? Dad doesn't care about me! He only cares about how he looks to the public." I took a step aside and began to walk away.

"Where are you going?" she called out.

"Where do you think?" I responded as I looked over my shoulder and headed for the stairs.

"At least have someone take you there, baby. I don't want

you out there by yourself," her voice followed closely behind me.

I hurried down the stairs and found Leo and Julian waiting at the bottom.

"Ma'am, the President asked that no one leave or enter the premises," Julian said to Mom as she stepped down beside me.

She scoffed. "Well, we're not just anyone, are we? Move," she snapped.

They exchanged glances, their feet still firmly planted.

"I said fucking move or I'm firing you both right now!" she yelled.

Leo huffed and took a step back, making room for us to pass. Julian shook his head as he followed suit.

Mom held my hand as we walked toward the row of SUVs. She waved over one of her guards, pointing to one of the vehicles. "I need you to drive Sloane somewhere safely." She turned to me with wide, nervous eyes. "Baby, tell him where to go, okay?"

I wanted to cry even more; I was so thankful for my mom at that moment.

"Thank you, Mom." My lip quivered as I reached for a hug. She wrapped her arms around me snugly and gently rubbed my back.

"I'm here for you, okay, baby? Please let me know when you get there." She let go, kissed my cheek, and stormed back into the house. I was afraid for Leo and Julian and the wrath they would endure from her.

The guard, whom I hadn't spoken to much, opened the door for me and took my bag. He set it in the back, and then we were on our way. I gave him directions to Callan's apartment, and ten minutes later, we pulled up in front of his building.

Worry consumed me as I stared down at my phone, waiting for a response from Callan.

"Ma'am, can I carry your bag for you?" the guard asked as he opened my door.

"No, thanks." I smiled and took my bag, heading for the lobby.

I pushed the button for Callan's floor and waited, my heart racing. *Why hasn't he responded? Will he even be home?*

I raised my shaky hand and knocked on the door. After a moment of silence, I knocked again, straining to hear any movement inside the apartment.

"Sloane."

Relief flooded through me at the sound of his voice, but it quickly shifted to worry as I turned around. Callan stood there, his eyes unfocused, wobbling slightly with a brown paper bag in his hand. I could smell the alcohol on him from a few feet away.

"Cal," I whispered, tears welling in my eyes. "Come here." I dropped my bag and opened my arms.

His face twisted into a frown as he slowly approached me. He began to sob, and I wrapped my arms around him, crying with him. Had being with me driven him to this? Had his guilt overtaken his strength to stay sober? Even more guilt hit me as I rubbed gentle circles on his back.

"Come on, baby. Let's go inside," I finally said, not wanting to let him go.

"I'm no good for you, baby girl. You shouldn't be here," he slurred.

"Well, I'm not going anywhere. Remember? You're stuck with me," I teased, trying to lighten the mood as he released me.

He shook his head, tears still streaming down his face. "Look at you. Then look at me. How does this make sense?"

I tried not to let it sting; I knew it was the alcohol talking.

"Come on, baby. Let's go inside," I repeated, pulling him toward the door.

He wobbled beside me. "It's open, I think."

I twisted the knob and the door swung open. Relieved, I grabbed my bag and pulled Callan inside with me.

"Let's make you some coffee," I said, setting my bag down in the kitchen and beginning to open his cabinets.

The stool near the kitchen island dragged on the floor as Callan tried to sit on it. "My sweet fucking baby. Why do you love me?" he asked, taking another swig from the paper bag.

"Can I have that, please?" I asked, pointing at the bag.

He looked down at it, as if surprised it was in his hand, then held it up, offering it to me. I immediately took it from him and poured the contents down the sink.

"Baby, you just wasted it," he slurred softly, watching the alcohol swirl away.

"Why don't we go lay down?" I suggested, hoping to change the subject.

He groaned. "Sloane, you're so fucking perfect. Am I taking advantage of you? Am I just a disgusting pervert corrupting your beautiful innocence?"

I sighed, resisting the urge to roll my eyes—I knew he was carrying the weight of my dad's words.

"Do you think you could take advantage of someone that fucked your ass last night?" I asked lightly.

Callan chuckled, smiling. "Doesn't seem like it. God, baby. I love you. Let's go get married. Right now." He stood up, steadying himself by holding onto the counter.

I smiled and took his hand, pulling him out of his self-loathing, even if just for a minute. "Why don't we take a nap? When we wake up, we can decide what to do next."

He nodded. "Yeah. I'm tired. Come on, baby." He waited until I tugged on his hand and led him to the bedroom. I closed the curtains, pulled down the comforter, then brought him onto the bed with me.

As we lay down, he began to kiss my shoulder, rubbing his hands gently around my breasts and thighs. He was turning me on, but I didn't want to take advantage of him while he was in such a vulnerable state, especially since I was sure he wouldn't remember it later.

"Come on, Cal." I took his hands and pressed them to my lips, gently kissing them. Then I scooted lower on the bed, resting my head on his chest and wrapping his arm around my shoulder.

"I love you, Sloane," he whispered, and just a few seconds later, he began to snore.

I sighed, letting a tear fall down my cheek. Now that I was safe in Callan's arms, my mind drifted back to Dad. His words echoed in my head: *You and Callan have ruined my re-election. My whole legacy as a president is shattered.* Was that really true? How would he ever forgive me for that? And how would Callan and I ever live it down?

My thoughts raced as I held Callan closer. *He is not capable of hurting someone the way Dad claimed. Who is this Sarah that accused him of something like this?* I was determined to find out what really happened. But first, I needed to take care of Callan.

26

Callan

My eyes weren't even open yet when I felt the throbbing pulse of a headache. I knew the feeling all too well—I was hungover. The memories of what happened with Jake flooded back, and I shot up, gasping for air. *Sloane.*

"Baby, it's okay." Her sweet voice was beside me in bed, and I instantly burst into tears. Tears of relief, pain, guilt, shame, and love.

I felt her warm body nestle close as I cried into my hands. "I'm sorry, baby. I fucked up. I fucked up," I repeated through sobs.

I never cried, and I hated how shameful I felt doing it in front of Sloane.

"It's okay, baby. I'm here. Everything is gonna be okay," she whispered softly, rubbing circles on my back.

I gasped for air as my sobs began to subside. I lifted my head; the only light came from the faint glow seeping in from the hallway. I glanced over at Sloane—she stared at me, wide-eyed and worried. I fucking hated that I made her feel like that.

"Sloane, I have to tell you something," I blurted out, afraid that she already knew. I waited for her to stop me, but she only kept her eyes on me, listening intently as she continued to rub circles on my back. "I was accused of something terrible by an ex-girlfriend of mine."

She didn't say anything; she only nodded knowingly. "I know," she whispered.

My heart dropped to the fucking floor. "You know?"

She nodded again. "My dad told me. But I don't believe it," she said quietly.

I swallowed hard and shook my head. "It's not true, baby. I swear it's not. I'd never lay a hand on a woman."

She bit her quivering lip, like she was trying not to cry. "I know you wouldn't, Callan. I know," she whispered.

Relief washed over me like a warm blanket. I exhaled and lay back on the bed, gently tugging her down with me as I wrapped my arm around her.

She held onto me tightly. "Why didn't you tell me before?" she asked quietly after a moment of silence.

I sighed heavily. "Because I was afraid of what you'd think of me. I was afraid that you'd be scared of me," I admitted.

She sat up suddenly, gazing down at me with sad eyes. "Callan, I would never be afraid of you. I know you, and despite what you may think, you're a big fucking softie." A small smile tugged at her lips.

I laughed. She was right. I only put on the facade of being a big fucking tough guy, but she really knew me—she brought out the best in me.

"Can I ask you something else?" she hesitantly asked, looking down at my bare chest.

I was nervous again. "Anything, baby. I'll tell you everything."

She tilted her head as her gaze lifted to mine. "Did you drink because you felt guilty about...about us being together?" The pain was unmistakable in her voice, and it broke my fucking heart.

"No, baby," I assured her as I sat up, taking her hand. "I jumped to conclusions when you didn't answer your phone right away. I thought Jake told you and then I thought you were just gonna...I don't know, fucking hate me or something," I admitted. "It's my own fault, baby."

Tears filled her eyes as she knelt beside me on the bed, then swung a leg over to straddle me, her body aligning with mine. I doubt she intended to turn me on at that moment, but my cock instantly hardened.

"I'll never stop loving you, Callan, no matter what. Don't ever assume anything like that ever again," she said sternly as she gazed into my eyes, my goddess taking charge.

I couldn't help but grab her ass and begin to grind her on top of my hard cock. "I won't, baby," I said, squeezing her plump ass as her hips began to move, her lips slightly parting.

She began to moan quietly. "My pussy is the only thing you'll ever need," she said with a sly smile.

Fucking hell. "Goddamn, baby. I love when your pretty little voice talks dirty to me," I said as I grazed my lips to hers, trying to tease her, but she knew she was in charge.

She giggled and my cock twitched. "I wasn't trying to seduce you, but now that I have your hard cock underneath me, I need you inside of me."

I let out an involuntary moan. I swear to fucking God, her dirty talk could easily make me come.

"Yeah? You want me to fill up your perfect pussy?" I was already lifting her shirt over her head, exposing her bare tits in my face, and I eagerly planted my lips on her nipple.

"Fuck yes," she moaned, moving her hips against my cock, and I was ready to burst already.

I lifted her up and tossed her onto her back on the bed, and she began to pull her underwear down as I took out my cock.

"I want you to be rough with me, Daddy," she said, right as I put the tip of my cock to her slit, but her words stopped me.

"Yeah?" I asked nervously. For some reason, now that she knew about the accusation against me, I hesitated to be rough with her.

"Yes. *Please.* I want you to do everything you want with me. Use me, Daddy," she begged, lifting her hips in search of my cock.

I didn't want her to know how much that turned me on. I didn't want her to know that was the only sex I knew before she and I got together. I loved degradation, hair pulling, spitting, and choking. I was afraid to show her that side of me because she was my perfect girl. I was her first, her only, and I didn't want her to think less of me. I just wanted to make her happy—I wanted to make *her* feel good.

I was too inside my head. I pulled away slightly, just enough to resist the urge to pound into her tight pussy. "You sure, Sloane? What if you don't like that?" I asked quietly, searching her face as I spoke.

Her eyebrows pulled together. "You know I'll tell you how I feel, Callan. If I don't like it, I'll tell you to stop. I trust you." She grabbed my hips and pulled me close to her again.

Fuck. That's all it took—I guided my cock to her pussy, and I thrust hard and deep into her, then took her wrists with my hands and pinned her to the bed.

"Tell me, baby. You want to be Daddy's good little slut? You want me to pound your pussy and ass so hard, you won't be able to walk straight for a fucking week?" I growled quietly, just loud enough for her to hear over her own moans.

"Yes, Daddy. Let me be your good little slut. Fuck me hard, slap me, choke me," she whined, her gaze not once leaving mine.

Holy fucking shit. She really is my dream girl.

"You sure, baby?" I asked, still hesitant, unsure of myself.

"Yes!" she responded with an attitude, and I smiled, knowing exactly what I wanted to do with my little fucking brat.

I released one of her wrists, bringing my hand up to her lips, parting them with my thumb and forefinger. Letting saliva build up behind my lips, I spat down at her, and it landed perfectly in her mouth. She smiled as she swallowed, and I moved my hand away, then gently slapped her cheek. She gasped, but her wide, eager eyes met mine, full of anticipation.

"Like that?" I asked for reassurance, fucking her harder.

"Yes!" she whimpered as her eyes rolled back with pleasure.

Fuck. I wasn't going to last long being rough with my sweet girl.

"More!" she demanded loudly, wrapping her legs around me and pulling herself even closer to me.

"God, such a naughty fucking slut. You like when Daddy degrades you, calls you his little whore?" I asked, pulling her legs up and against my chest, and she felt even fucking tighter.

"Fuck yes. I wanna be your good fucking whore. I want you to use me in every way you want," she moaned, prompting me to thrust harder and faster, making her scream.

"Come on, baby," I said as I reached down to thumb her clit, rubbing furiously. "Come on my cock like a good girl."

She began to scream as she clenched her thighs around my

body, her perfect fucking face writhing in pleasure.

I let go of her as she loosened her grip on me, and I picked her up and tossed her around, positioning her on her stomach. She got on her knees and looked back at me with a smile, biting her bottom lip in anticipation. Her plump ass jiggled as I grabbed her hips and thrust hard into her, and she whimpered as she fisted the blanket underneath her, letting her head hang low. I watched her ass bounce against my body as I fisted her hair, tugging it back as she arched her back and let me pull hard.

"Fuck, baby. I need to fuck your sweet little ass next. It's begging me to fuck it," I growled as I tugged her hair back harder, lifting her body to rest her back against my chest as I continued to pound her.

"Yes, Daddy, fuck my ass," she cried excitedly.

I let out a primal moan as I pulled out and quickly grabbed the lube from my bedside table. I generously lathered my cock with the cold liquid and brought her back into the same position, this time gently wrapping my hand around her throat.

"You wanna prep, baby? Or do you want Daddy to fuck your ass just like this?" My lips grazed against her ear as I teased her ass with the head of my cock.

"Fuck my ass *now*," she demanded, and it brought a smile to my face—my baby knew what she wanted, and she was gonna get it.

I slowly pushed my cock into her ass, wanting to pound into her but not wanting to hurt her, so I took my time. I began to thrust my hips gently as she moaned, and I tightened my grip on her throat, ready to burst already.

"Oh my God," she growled as I continued to inch in, and I finally lost control as she reached her hand down to her pussy and began to rub herself.

I pounded my hips against her ass, igniting more screams from her mouth. I let go of my grip on her throat to hold onto her hips, and she caught herself on her hands on the bed. I hadn't heard my baby moan so loudly before, so wildly, and it brought out a fucking beast in me. I continued to pound her ass as she fell down onto her belly on the bed, and my balls tightened as I neared my orgasm. I reached around to her clit and began to rub quickly as I growled out with pleasure, spilling myself into her ass, and she screamed out, "I'm coming! Fuck, I'm coming!"

Holy fucking shit. I couldn't believe how satisfying it was to be so rough with Sloane, and she fucking loved it. *Right? She loved it?* My mind began to race before I even pulled out of her.

"Baby," I said as I caught my breath, trailing kisses on her shoulder.

"Hmmm?" Her eyes were closed and a small smile tugged on her lips.

I didn't want to pull out yet, so I fell onto the bed, pulling her down with me as I positioned us on our sides, leaving my cock in her ass as I spooned her.

"Baby, did you like that?" I asked worriedly, getting into my head again.

"*Oh my God*, Callan," she moaned, still lost in pleasure. "I fucking *loved* it."

I smiled and exhaled a chuckle, relieved. I also loved that my fucking foul mouth was rubbing off on her so much.

"Sloane, I love you. I'd be so fucking lost without you," I blurted out, my emotions running high.

"Aw, baby." She turned her head and raised her arm to pull me into a kiss. "I love you too, Callan. So, so much."

I wanted to see her beautiful face so I begrudgingly pulled

out of her and turned her around to face me. Her big, brown eyes found mine and she smiled that big, dimpled smile. All of the guilt that had consumed me before suddenly vanished. I was knocked the fuck out by Jake, but I deserved it. But it was done with—now he knew. Now we just needed to face the scrutiny of whatever the fuck the press was saying about it. *And the Sarah shit, fuck. How the fuck—*

"What are you thinking about?" Sloane pulled me out of my head as she gently placed her palm on my cheek.

I thought about where to start first.

"I don't remember going to sleep. What happened when...did I do anything stupid when you got here?" I hesitantly asked.

Her smile faded slightly, but she shook her head. "No. You were trying to feel me up, but I distracted you. You were the same Callan as always, just slightly slurred and wobbly," she said with a small laugh.

Thank fuck.

"I'm sorry, baby. I should have been sober. I should have been clear-headed so we could've talked about everything that happened," I said quietly, still ashamed of myself.

She shook her head. "It's okay, Cal. That was rough—I can understand why you did it." She began to rub circles on my arm, and I wondered how I ended up so lucky. What the fuck did I do in a past life to deserve the most amazing, special woman in the world? I must have been the fucking Pope or some shit.

"How are *you* doing, baby? Are you okay?" I asked, sitting up on my elbow, desperately wanting to take care of her for once.

She shook her head and blinked, then rolled onto her back. I could see tears welling in her eyes and my heart fucking broke into a million pieces.

"I'm okay. My dad said some harsh stuff, but…I know he didn't mean it. It's just…" she trailed off, staring at the ceiling.

"What, baby?" I asked, taking her hand in mine.

She looked back at me and frowned. "The internet is saying a bunch of shitty things. About me, about you, about my dad. I know I shouldn't look at that stuff but…I just don't understand why any of this matters." Her voice was small and weak, a tone I hadn't heard from her much.

I sighed. My baby was smart, but she hadn't yet realized how cruel the world could be.

"Don't go on the internet, baby. Fuck 'em," I said, offering the weakest fucking advice, but she still smiled and nodded.

"Let's hide out here for a while. Now that it's out there, and I basically moved out, you're gonna be stuck with me for a while." She laughed, and she was back to my usual sweet girl.

I rolled over and onto my knees, then flung a leg over her so I could straddle her. I pinned her wrists against the bed and she bit her lip with a smile, eagerly waiting for whatever I was gonna do to her.

"Good. Now tell me all the things you liked about Daddy being rough with you, and I'll do them all over again."

27

Sloane

Over the next few days, my mom texted me constantly. She mentioned that Dad felt bad about what he'd said, but I needed to hear it from him directly—and there was nothing but radio silence on his end. Mom, though...she was supportive and caring, checking in on how I was doing and if I needed anything. She was the strongest person I knew, and knowing she was holding up gave me a sense of comfort amidst the chaos of the outside world.

And Callan—God, being around him 24/7 just reaffirmed that everything that had happened was worth it. He was trying to take care of me; he was cooking, running me baths, waiting on me hand and foot. We would laugh until the sun came up, we'd have sex all night, and we'd lounge around all day while I read or while we watched trashy reality shows. We were in the little bubble I had longed for and I never wanted to leave it.

I had no idea what the media was saying about us because I stayed off social media and the internet. The first night that it came out, I spent hours looking at articles about how Callan was a creep, how my dad was an idiot for hiring him, how I was this pure little innocent eighteen-year-old that didn't know any better. It was infuriating, and I hated that it got to me so much. But now...now I didn't know anything. I didn't know if my dad had made any statements about the "scandal." Dozens of texts poured in from old friends and family members, but I didn't know how to respond. Some asked if I was okay; others wanted to know what on earth I was thinking. Eventually, I just silenced all notifications except for my mom's.

And then there was Sarah—who was she, really, and why did she say those things about Callan? I was sure he hadn't done what she accused him of, but there was still that tiny sliver of doubt, a whisper of uncertainty I couldn't shake. I'd always been taught to believe women who spoke out about abuse, and it tore me apart to even consider the possibility that she might be telling the truth. Callan had admitted to blacking out when he drank—what if he'd done something in a fit of anger and just didn't remember? Deep down, I knew that wasn't who he was, but I also knew that alcohol or drugs could make people do unimaginable things. With a confusing mix of guilt and uncertainty weighing on me, I decided to ask my mom for help in contacting Sarah. I wasn't even sure she'd speak to me, but I needed to try and hear her side. The idea of going behind Callan's back made me feel sick, but I couldn't figure out how to explain to him why I had to reach out to her.

I lay awake one night, next to a peacefully sleeping Callan, staring at the text my mom had sent with Sarah's details: **Sarah Jordan, Baltimore, 33**. My mom understood why I needed to talk to her, though even she was cautious. Sarah was less than an hour away, and I could easily find her. *Fuck, I can't do this to Callan.* I sighed and texted my mom back: **Do you think she'll talk to you?**

As I waited for her response, I decided to google Sarah. I found her instantly. I wasn't sure how I knew it was her, but something just clicked. She was beautiful—her mixed-race heritage gave her striking high cheekbones and large brown eyes. And the kicker: she was a nursing director at a rehab facility. That gave me hope—she was probably sober now. Maybe it would be easier to reach her.

Mom's text finally came through: **No. We don't have a great history. But she might talk to you.**

I closed my eyes and shut off my phone, the guilt pressing hard on my conscience.

* * *

I woke up to Callan massaging my ass, feeling his hard cock teasing between my ass cheeks. It was how I was usually woken up and I loved it. Ever since I realized how much I loved being roughed up during sex, I started seeing more of Callan's kinky side. But outside the bedroom, he was still the big, tattooed teddy bear I knew and loved. It was an interesting dynamic—despite his tough exterior and dominance in the bedroom, I ended up being the dominant one in every other part of our relationship. And Callan seemed to love it.

"Baby, let's go for a ride today. Let's get out of town. Let's just fucking wander and stay in a shitty hotel off the highway," Callan excitedly suggested as I lay in his arms after he spanked me and came in my mouth.

I laughed softly. "I'd love that. We probably need a little sunshine after being cooped up here for a few days, huh?" I lifted myself up to look at him; I wondered if I'd always get butterflies whenever I caught a glimpse of his face.

And then an idea hit me—Sarah. *Baltimore.* "Do you wanna ride to Baltimore? The Peabody Library is there and I've always wanted to go." I was instantly mortified with myself; I was being selfish, but I *needed* to talk to Sarah.

Callan hesitated for a moment. "Yeah, why not?" He didn't seem thrilled, and I wondered if he knew that Sarah lived there.

"I mean...we don't have to," I said, immediately backing out, feeling extremely guilty.

"No, no." He smiled. "My little bookworm. So fucking smart. Maybe you can teach me how to read there," he joked.

I laughed, resting my head on his chest. "I don't know," I teased, smirking. "Can you handle books without pictures?"

"Oh, I see how it is." He chuckled, pulling me closer. "Guess I'll just stick to the coloring books then."

An hour later, we were on the road to Baltimore. I held onto Callan's solid body, wishing I could ride with him forever; being with him, anywhere, was my happy place. I was safe with him.

But I wasn't sure I was ready to be out in public. Even though I'd suggested the Peabody Library, it suddenly felt too crowded, too much attention on us. And the guilt gnawed at me for lying to Callan about my real reasons for coming to Baltimore. As we entered the city, I spotted a small motel and pointed it out, suggesting we stop there. Callan pulled into the parking lot and cut the engine in front of the lobby. I tightened my grip around him, deciding at that moment to come clean.

"Sarah lives here. I wanted to talk to her. That's why I suggested Baltimore. I'm sorry, Callan," I said, my voice muffled through my helmet and my eyes squeezed shut as I clung to his torso.

I felt his body tense. "Sloane..."

"I'm sorry," I repeated, tears spilling instantly. "I just wanted to hear her side of it. I needed to know. I'm so sorry, baby." My words came out in a desperate rush.

He let out a deep sigh, his hands resting over mine, allowing me to cry. After a moment, he reached up, removed his helmet, and slowly stood, pulling me away from him. I looked up as he ran a hand through his hair, his forehead creased and an unmistakable frown darkening his face.

"I'm sorry," I repeated, my shoulders slumping in defeat.

He sighed again, quieter this time. "Come on, Sloane. Let's get a room and talk." He held out his hand, and I reluctantly stood, pulling my helmet off and placing my hand in his. Once I was on my feet, he led the way into the lobby, rented a room for the night, and we headed up the stairs together.

We walked into our small room with a king-sized bed in the middle, with a TV and dresser directly across from it. Nestled in the corner was a small armchair and lamp. Callan tossed the keycard on the dresser and sat at the foot of the bed with his head hung low.

"Why do you want to talk to Sarah?" he asked quietly, looking down at his hands.

I slowly walked toward the bed and sat down next to him. "I just...I want to hear her side of the story. Maybe she'll admit that she lied," I thought aloud.

He looked up at me with pain in his eyes. "And if she doesn't? What if she tells you that I beat her senseless? Are you gonna believe her?" Tears filled his eyes, and I began to hate myself.

I shook my head. "She's not going to. She's gonna tell the truth. She's sober now—she works at a rehab center," I blurted out. If I was being honest with him, I wanted him to know what I'd been up to.

His eyes widened and he shook his head. "How do you know all of this? How did you find her?"

I looked down at the floor. "My mom told me." Guilt continued to sting in my chest.

Callan was silent and I couldn't stand it. I began to cry as I put my face in my hands, hating the doubt that had planted itself inside my mind. I felt Callan's arm wrap around my shoulders, which made me cry harder; I didn't deserve to be comforted, not after lying to him like this.

"Alright," he said after my sobs slowed. "Go talk to her. Go do what you need to do."

I looked up at him in surprise. He stared down at me, his eyes filled with pain and sadness.

"Callan—"

"Just go, Sloane. If you need to talk to her to fucking believe me, then do it," he said harshly, letting go of me and standing up.

Fuck, what have I done? "Callan," I repeated, but he walked away and slammed the bathroom door shut behind him.

I sat there, stunned. *I got myself into this mess—now I need to get out of it.* I had to talk to Sarah now, whether I wanted to or not. The mere fact that Callan was intent on me talking to her for the truth only strengthened my opinion that he wasn't guilty of hurting her.

I looked over at the bathroom door, then I took my phone out and ordered an Uber. My destination: Sarah's place of work.

28

Callan

I couldn't tell what hurt more—the fact that the love of my life doubted my character, or that even I was starting to doubt myself. I had been so certain I hadn't done it, but the mere fact that I blacked out that night made me question everything. What if I *did* hurt her? What kind of man would that make me? And what would Sloane think? What would she do? Would she leave me? Would she forgive me? Could I even forgive myself? The guilt from that time in my life consumed me—what if I really did hurt Sarah? What the fuck would I do then?

After a few minutes of sulking in the bathroom, I heard the front door open and close. I knew that Sloane had left. *Fucking Ana.* I knew it wasn't fair to be angry at her, but I was. As I spiraled with my fucking guilt, I dialed her. She answered after a few rings.

"Callan," she said, surprise clear in her voice.

"Guess where Sloane and I are right now? Baltimore. Wanna know why?" I paused for a moment, but continued. "Sloane thinks I fucking did it. She thinks I'd hurt someone like that." I began to cry, the phone shaking in my hand as I brought my elbows to my knees, trying to pull myself together.

"Oh, Callan," Ana replied softly. "She doesn't think that. You know what I think? I think she wants to talk to Sarah to clear your name. She wants to make this right."

I scoffed. "Nah. She thinks I'm a piece of shit. And Sarah does too. I know what she's gonna say, and everything's gonna end because she's a fucking liar," I spat out. "Or maybe she's not. Maybe I did fucking hurt her because I can't remember." Tears welled up again. The amount of crying I'd done in the past week made my head fucking spin—it was more than I'd ever cried in my life.

"Do you really think that, Callan? You think you did that?" Ana asked with frustration.

"No," I immediately replied. "I don't fucking know anymore."

Ana sighed on the other end. "Sloane loves you, Cal." The softness of her voice returned. "You know that much is true."

"Yeah, but for how long? She's on her way to Sarah right now. I'm at a fucking Red Roof Inn, sobbing in a tiny fucking hotel room. What the fuck am I supposed to do while she's gone?" I stood up and began to pace, and the urge to drink was stronger than ever.

"Stay on the line with me. Tell me about what you and Sloane have been doing."

Did she know how close I was to relapse again?

"I don't know if you want that information, Ana," I said with a small, embarrassed laugh.

"*Ay, dios mio.*" She laughed in return. "I mean, what else? Tell me what you love about Sloane." She was trying to distract me, and it was working.

I sighed and sat down on the armchair in the corner of the

room. "I love her laugh. I love how when her smile gets real big, that little dimple comes out on the side of her cheek. I love how smart she is. She fucking corrects me all the time, and I love it. I love how she makes me feel. She makes me feel like I'm not a piece of shit. She makes all of this fucking worth it," I said in one long breath. "And I don't know what I'm gonna do without her," I choked out.

"Callan, don't jump to conclusions," she responded. "Don't write this all off just yet."

She was right; I had jumped to conclusions before, and I fucking relapsed. Running a hand through my hair, I sat back and took deep breaths. Then, I did what I should have done before—I called my sponsor.

29

Sloane

I had no idea if Sarah would be at work or not. It was a weekday, in the middle of the day, so I could only hope. As the Uber got closer to the rehab center, the ache in my chest grew. Callan was devastated when he told me to go. I felt incredibly guilty for luring him to Baltimore under false pretenses—pretenses that could possibly harm our relationship. I wasn't sure what I would do if Sarah gave me a detailed account of what Callan had done to her. I prayed to every God I could think of, hoping she would admit she had made it all up. People on drugs or alcohol made mistakes, and they lied. But if Callan had hurt her...I wasn't sure how I would feel. Would it make me love him any less? I believed in redemption, in people growing and taking accountability for their past. I knew the Callan I loved wasn't the same person he was eight years ago—lost and addicted.

I walked into the lobby of the brick building. It was clean and homey, and the front desk receptionist immediately recognized me. She was young, and she jumped up with a smile as I walked closer. "Oh my God. Sloane Martin?"

"Hi," I said with a smile. "I'm um...I'm hoping to see an old friend. Is Sarah in today?"

She looked surprised. "You know *Sarah*?"

I nodded. "Yeah." I shrugged.

"She never told me that! Oh my God, yeah...she's here. One sec, I'll go get her!" She quickly scurried off down the hallway.

Nerves swirled through my belly, and I crossed my arms as I glanced out the window, wondering what the hell I was gonna say to her.

"Sloane?"

I turned, and there was Sarah. She looked exactly like her picture, though she was much more petite than I'd realized—and even more beautiful. Her hair was styled in long braids, and an oversized knit cardigan hung low, nearly reaching the ground. She wore tortoiseshell glasses, her gaze intense. Her eyebrows were drawn together as she gave me a wary smile.

"Hi, Sarah?" I asked hesitantly.

The receptionist had returned to her desk and watched us intently. Sarah crossed her arms and took a step closer to me.

"Are you here because of Callan?" Sarah asked quietly.

Of course she knew I was connected to Callan—we were all over the internet. I'm sure anyone with a TV or phone knew that Callan and I were together.

"Yeah, um..." I glanced at the receptionist and then back at Sarah. "Can we talk?"

Sarah regarded me for a moment, staring me up and down. I suddenly felt uneasy under her gaze. "Okay." She turned and began down the hallway, and I quickly followed her.

We ended up in a room down the hall, and she closed the door behind me. I guessed it was her office; she had a desk with a nameplate on it, with touches of plants, bohemian decor, and some certificates and diplomas on the wall.

"Why are you here?" she asked coldly as she sat behind her desk, cutting straight to the chase.

I swallowed hard as I sat down, trying to wrack my brain for words.

"I, um...I heard about your past with Callan. About when... you two were together," I began.

Her expression hardened and she crossed her arms as she sat back. "Okay. And?" She was already defensive.

I shook my head slightly. "I just want to know what happened that night," I answered honestly.

She stared at me for a moment before her expression softened, and she looked down at her desk in front of her.

"I was a drunk too, you know," she began as her gaze lifted to meet mine. "I was young. Not as young as you but..." She raised her eyebrows, as if she was judging me—there wasn't a doubt in my mind that she thought the age difference between me and Callan was weird too. "But I was young and fucking stupid. And Callan was all I had, you know? I didn't have any family, no friends—no one. And even though our relationship was toxic, I was in love. And when he told me he was going to leave me, that he was gonna get clean and get far away from me, I panicked."

My stomach dropped.

"I was drunk, and I started screaming at him, hitting him, pushing him and egging him on. I *wanted* him to do something, you know? But he didn't budge. He pulled me off of him and I kept going. I was so fucking mad when he locked himself in the bathroom, that I fucking drove to my friend's house and called the military police." She lowered her eyes again. "We were on base, and I thought they'd kick him out of the military, and he'd be stuck with me. I fucking lied because I was scared. I was terrified of being alone." She glanced back up at me, tears welling in her eyes. "And since then, I've been scared to tell the truth, because I fucking ruined his life. It kinda ruined mine too."

I didn't even realize tears were streaming down my face.

"I got clean a few years later, and I wanted to reach out to him, but it seemed like it was too late. And I didn't know how to get in touch with him anyway." She sighed and uncrossed her arms, clasping her hands together on the desk. "Is he doing okay?"

I nodded, still shunned by her confession. "Yeah. I mean, we're dealing with...all of this," I said, waving my hand in the air, searching for words. "But he's good. He's gonna be okay." I nodded.

She sighed heavily, letting her shoulders fall a little. "Good." She nodded back. "Um...I can't face him. Not right now. But... would you give him a note from me?" She pulled out a notepad and pen and let the pen hover over the notepad as she waited for me to answer.

"Of course," I answered gently.

She began to write and I pulled out my phone, hoping I didn't miss anything from Callan. But there was nothing. I put my phone back in my pocket as Sarah finished up, folding the paper and then handing it to me.

"It's an apology. Long overdue," she said with a small smile.

I nodded as I took the note. "Thank you for your honesty, Sarah. I'm sure that wasn't easy."

Her eyebrows twitched as her lips curled into a smile. "You're eighteen?"

I laughed and nodded. "Yeah. Why?"

She shook her head. "I don't know. You just seem older. Too

smart for an eighteen year-old." She shrugged, opening up her office door.

"I hear that a lot," I admitted.

She gave me a small smile. "I'll see you later, Sloane."

I was still shaking as I walked down the hall, relief flooding through me. I had to call Callan right away. After I stopped for a selfie that the receptionist requested, I exited the building and pulled out my phone. My phone vibrated with a text, and as I stared at the message from an unknown number, a wave of anxiety surged through my chest. *What the fuck?!*

You're just as bad as your dad, keeping dirty little secrets. Better tell him to confess everything, or I'll ruin your whole family.

30

Callan

I just ended the call with Nick, my sponsor. He always managed to talk me down whenever I called him to vent or when I was just feeling like shit—which was often. He was like a therapist, but also a friend. And I didn't have to pay him. I hadn't wanted to admit to relapsing, but I needed to take accountability. I needed him to know how close I was to slipping again. As always, he helped me calm down.

Then Sloane called. I stared at my phone, my heart sinking—was she calling with good news or bad? I answered and put her on speaker, sinking to my knees and clasping my hands together on the bed like I was praying. I hadn't prayed in a long time, but I sure as fuck was doing it now.

"Sloane, baby," I managed to choke out.

"Callan." Her voice was just as shaky as mine was. "Callan, I'm sorry. I'm so sorry I doubted you," she cried.

Relief washed over me, and the tears I'd been holding back came pouring out. I didn't do it. I didn't fucking do it. I couldn't understand why I had doubted myself so much in the first place—I knew I'd never do something like that. Sarah was fucking crazy, but for once, she'd told the truth. Of course, it was only after she'd already ruined my life.

"Baby, it's okay. Just get back here. I need to fucking hold you. You need me to get you?" I was already up on my feet before I waited for her answer.

"Yeah, I'm outside a coffee shop down the road from Sarah's work. I'll send you the address. But Callan, something weird happened—not with Sarah, but right after I left," she explained, and I could hear the sounds of traffic passing by on her end.

I was already hopping on my bike, but I paused as I waited for her to continue. "What, baby? What happened?"

"Someone texted me. They said I'm keeping dirty little secrets just like my dad. And that... that he needs to confess, or they'll ruin our family."

Instantly, my vision clouded with rage. *Who the fuck is threatening my girl? And what the hell did Jake do?*

"You know something I don't, baby?" I asked, trying to keep my voice calm.

"No! I have no idea what this means! Who is this person, and how did they get my number?!" Her voice was full of frustration.

I slipped my helmet on and swung my leg over the seat. "I don't know. But I'm gonna find out, baby. Anyone threatening my girl has some fucking hell to pay."

* * *

Sloane was obviously shaken up; we sat on the bed in our hotel room, and her hands trembled as she stared down at them. I stared at the text for what felt like an eternity, wracking my

206

brain for answers. I knew the only way we were going to find out anything was by getting help from someone with a lot of resources and power. And we both knew someone in that position.

"We gotta tell Jake," I muttered, knowing exactly how Sloane would react.

She looked up at me with a frown, her brows drawn together in frustration. "You really think he's gonna take it seriously? I'm sure we get threats all the time, and they obviously lead nowhere."

"Well they've never been sent to you directly, Sloane. This feels serious. You know it's serious too, baby," I said softly.

She sighed and shook her head, tears forming in her eyes. She looked back down at her hands and shrugged. "He's the last person I wanna talk to right now," she whispered.

I know the feeling. "I know. But maybe, I don't know...your mom could help. Once she hears about this, I know all hell will break loose," I teased.

She laughed as she took her phone from my hand, then looked down at it for a few moments, seemingly deep in thought. "Oh, I almost forgot..." She grabbed her purse from the floor, dug into a pocket, and handed me a piece of paper. "It's from Sarah."

Fuck. My heart pounded against my ribcage as I took the paper and studied Sloane's face, waiting for her to continue.

"She said it's an apology," she said with a shrug. "Read it."

I loved when she was so fucking bossy.

I hesitantly glanced down at the note and slowly opened it.

Callan,

I've thought a lot about the past—what I did, what I said. I wish things had been different. Life has a strange way of making us face what we've done, doesn't it?

I'm sorry, if that means anything now. I hope you've found what you deserve.

Sarah

I re-read it over and over, and I couldn't shake the feeling that she was full of shit. But it was done with, Sloane knew the truth, and we could move on—*I* could move on. I had spent so many years hating myself, convincing myself that maybe I was the monster she claimed I was. But now, I could finally see it for what it was—a twisted game of manipulation. The weight I'd been carrying, all the fucking guilt and shame, began to lift. I was innocent all along.

"Good fucking riddance," I said, tossing the note aside on the bed.

Sloane grabbed it and read it, then looked up at me with her eyebrows pulled together. "I expected a better apology letter than this," she muttered, tossing it aside like I had.

I didn't want to think about Sarah anymore. I wanted to take care of my girl, and we needed to figure shit out right away.

"You gonna call Ana, or should I?"

She lifted her phone and tapped it a few times before putting it on speaker as it rang. Ana answered almost immediately.

"*Hola, cariño, ¿estás bien?*" Her voice was warm, but there was a slight undertone of worry.

"Hey, Mom. Yeah, I'm okay. Well, actually…" Sloane glanced up at me, as if she needed guidance on how to start explaining.

"Sloane got a weird text, Ana. They were threatening your family," I chimed in.

"I'm screenshotting and sending it to you, Mom. I think you should show Dad," Sloane continued.

"What?!" Ana's voice was deep and laced with anger. "*¡Qué*

coño?! What do they mean Daddy has secrets?"

I stood up and began to pace. "We were hoping you could find out," I offered. "And maybe call what's his face, the security advisor. And homeland security. Get their fucking tech people on it." I realized there was panic in my voice and I stopped pacing, looking over at Sloane. She was watching me intently, and I think it started to sink in how serious this was.

"Jacob!" Ana yelled after a moment, a door slamming in the background. "Someone is threatening Sloane. They're saying you have dirty little secrets. Do you know what the fuck they would be talking about?"

Sloane and I glanced at each other worriedly. There was muffled chatter before the call ended.

"We should go back to the house. You'll be the safest there. We can figure out what to do from there," I said as I picked up Sloane's purse, reaching for her hand.

She sat still on the bed, her worried eyes staring into mine. "I'm not going unless you're there too," she said quietly, and tears started to fill her eyes.

Fuck, my heart. I had no idea if Jake would let me be there or not, but I wasn't going to just drop Sloane off and say, "Alright, see ya!" But if me not being there meant Sloane was safe, I'd have to leave. Although, there was no doubt in my mind that Sloane wouldn't let that happen—she always got what she wanted, after all.

31

Sloane

An hour after we called my mom, we were pulling up to the house. My mom stood at the gate, making sure we got in without a problem. *Already a bad sign.* Callan parked in his usual spot and my mom greeted each of us with a tight hug.

"Did you get anything yet?" Callan asked before my mom could get a word in.

"No." She shook her head with a frown. "Jake has been on it, though. We need your phone, baby," she said as she turned to me.

Shit. My worst nightmare was my dad going through my phone. *All the texts, pictures...*

"Uh, alright," I started, pulling my phone out. "Let me just... " I began deleting my text threads and "hiding" any risqué pictures.

"Don't worry, baby," my mom said as she put her hand on my arm. "I'm not gonna let anyone snoop."

I sighed as I handed it over. "Where's Dad?"

She returned a sigh. I could tell by the look on her face that she was upset. "Somewhere around here. I'll go find him. You two go upstairs; there's extra detail at every entrance, and I'm re-hiring you, Callan. Don't leave Sloane's side." The firmness and confidence in her voice made me feel even safer in her presence.

"You couldn't fuckin' pay me to leave Sloane's side," Callan responded, taking my hand, and then guided us toward the door.

We headed up the stairs to the living quarters and down the hall to my room. It felt so strange to hold Callan's hand out in the open like this—strange, but freeing.

My room was still in the condition I left it in when I packed in a hurry. Callan shut the door behind us and locked it, then pulled me in for a deep, passionate kiss. Tension melted from my body as I wrapped my arms around his shoulders, and I could feel him relax as his hands slid down my back to my ass. His erection pressed against my stomach as he lifted me up and I wrapped my legs around him, desperate for more. He carried me to the desk and set me down, his lips lingering on mine before he began to lift my shirt, his eyes filled with desperate need. Just then, a knock at the door made us both freeze.

"Sloane," my dad called out.

"*Fuck*," Callan muttered as he pulled me off the desk and straightened out my shirt.

"Sloane," Dad repeated with more frantic knocking on the door.

"One second, Dad!" I called out, irritated and anxious.

Callan took my hand and kissed the top of my knuckles. "We got this, baby," he assured me.

I took a deep breath and smiled at him. He released my hand and leaned against the desk, crossing his arms as I made my way to the door. I cleared my throat as I unlocked it and slowly pulled it open, finding my Dad standing there with his hands on his hips and a scowl on his face.

"Where's Callan?" he asked angrily.

"Hi, Dad. It's nice to see you too. Me? Oh, I'm fine," I muttered out sarcastically.

"Sloane, stop. Where is he?" He didn't wait for my answer as he pushed the door wide open to find Callan walking up to him, his expression mirroring my dad's.

My chest tightened as I watched them approach each other.

"He's not going anywhere, Dad. If you make him leave, I'm leaving too," I said before either of them got a word in.

Callan stood firmly and silently beside me as my dad glared at him, his jaw tight, as if I wasn't even there.

"You're not staying under my roof," Dad said through clenched teeth.

I rolled my eyes. "The White House is federal property of the United States govern—"

"Sloane, you know what I mean. Don't get smart with me," Dad quipped back.

"Okay, I'm leaving then." I turned around and headed for my purse, but then I heard Mom's voice.

"*Nadie va a ningún lado,*" she yelled as I turned and saw her appear in the doorway. "Sloane and Callan stay, Jacob. She's your daughter—and he's family, whether you'll admit it or not."

Dad sighed heavily and turned around, taking Mom's shoulder and moving into the hallway.

I could hear them arguing but I didn't bother to listen in. I glanced at Callan and his expression was somber, but he gave me a small, reassuring smile as he took my hand.

"Maybe it *is* better that I leave, baby. Jake has every right to kick me outta here," he said quietly, squeezing my hand lightly.

Tears welled in my eyes instantly. "No. You're not leaving. You're staying, or I'm going with you," I demanded.

He sighed as his jaw clenched. I could tell he wanted to argue, but all he said was, "Okay, baby. We're staying together."

The arguing outside the door stopped and Dad walked in quickly, as if he'd catch us doing something.

"Once we figure this out, you're out of here, Callan. I'm doing this to protect my stubborn daughter, otherwise I'd fucking kick you out myself," he spit out as he pointed his finger at him.

"Don't worry, Dad," I snapped. "Once we figure this out, you won't have to see either of us again."

My heart sank when my dad's expression shifted from anger to utter devastation. To my surprise, he didn't say a word—he just shot a quick glance between me and Callan before angrily storming off. I watched as my mom followed him down the hallway.

"I fucking hate that this is straining your relationship with Jake," Callan said, placing his hand on my cheek. His eyes were wide with worry.

Tears streamed down my cheeks as I leaned into his touch. "It's not your fault, Callan. It's his," I said after a moment. "He should be happy that you love me so much and want to protect me. All he cares about is keeping me away from you, no matter how much it hurts me," I finished, my voice cracking. "But he doesn't understand, Callan. He doesn't understand how much I need you."

He didn't say a word; instead, he pulled me close and wrapped his arms tightly around me.

"I need you too, baby. I need you so fuckin' much," he whispered into my ear as he stroked my hair.

As I melted into his embrace, the warmth of his arms around me felt like the only thing keeping me grounded. It wasn't just love—it was something deeper, a connection so intense it was almost unbearable. He was my safe haven...and my anchor in the storm that had become my life.

* * *

Callan and I locked ourselves in the room for the rest of the night. It was late as we cuddled in bed, watching Netflix, and I nuzzled my face into his chest. He hummed deeply, as if my touch ignited something in him, and he grabbed my hips, guiding me to straddle him. I felt his erection growing beneath me, and as I stared into his eyes, I began to grind my hips against him. A lustful smile appeared on his lips.

"You think this is a good idea? I think Jake is one step away from fucking murdering me in plain sight," he joked, but his hands gripped my hips firmly.

I shook my head. "Don't think. Just fuck me," I exhaled softly.

He smiled wider before he lifted me up and pushed me down onto the bed, face first. I giggled excitedly as he eagerly pulled my jeans down and threw them on the floor, and I glanced back as he began to pull his zipper down.

"Better be quiet, baby. Let's see how hard I can pound you before you scream into that pillow," he muttered quietly before he thrust his hard cock into me.

I bit my lip hard to stay quiet as I gripped the sheets beneath me, his hips slapping hard and quickly against my ass. His hand was suddenly at my neck, and he slowly began to squeeze as his breath quickened. As the friction of my clit rubbed against the bed, along with Callan's cock pushing in and out of me, my pussy began to seize with pleasure, and my moans were low as my airflow depleted. I heard a faint chuckle in my ear as he took his other palm and pushed it against my mouth, trying to quiet me, but then a deep and low grunt escaped his throat as he released his hands from me. I gasped as I caught my breath as Callan's hips slowed to a stop, draining himself in me.

Even a quickie like that satisfied me beyond belief. The sheer fact that we were in the White House, with my parents just down the hall and security detail practically outside my door, turned me on immensely. Was it the thrill of possibly being heard or caught? Or was it because I was free to fuck Callan in my bed without anyone being able to stop us?

Callan finally pulled out of me and lay on his side, wrapping his arms around my hips and pulling me into a close cuddle, making himself the big spoon.

"Fuck, I don't ever want to leave this spot," he whispered in my ear. "My girl, naked against me, with my cum dripping out of her," he went on, his voice deep and velvety.

As I giggled and backed my ass against him, there was a quick and sudden knock at the door. Callan and I jumped up like springs before a voice came through.

"Sloane, baby. We need you and Callan in the sitting room to discuss some things," my mom called out calmly.

Callan let out a deep sigh, one that sounded like pure relief.

"Okay. We'll be out in a minute," I responded loudly.

I looked over at my nervous, beautiful man and laughed. "Let's get back to that soon," I said, pointing my eyes to the bed.

He laughed as he stood up and began to pull his boxer briefs and jeans on, shaking his head at me. "So fucking naughty," he teased.

Five minutes later, Callan and I walked hand in hand down the hall to the yellow oval room. We found my parents sitting on the couch that faced the hall, and my dad's already hardened expression turned into a glare as he glanced at me and Callan, his eyes trailing down to our clasped hands. I glanced at a few familiar faces, vaguely recognizing them as part of the administration. They were scattered around in the armchairs, leaving the couch parallel to my parents open for us. Leo and Julian stood by the windows, watching us intently. Callan let go of my hand as we made our way to the couch, gesturing for me to go first. I sat stiffly across from my dad, while Callan sat next to me, across from my mom.

"Is it necessary for him to be here?" Dad asked through clenched teeth, clearly trying his hardest to keep it together.

"Yes," I replied straightforwardly, holding my gaze with his.

"Sloane, we need to know if there's anyone that's been acting strangely with you," Mom started, ignoring our staring contest. "Someone you know. We are trying to rule out people that you know first. The security team couldn't trace the number because it's a burner phone and it's not giving off a location. They believe it's been disposed of," she explained.

My heart began to race. *Someone I know?*

"Where was Callan when you received the text?" Dad asked bitterly, his gaze now fixed on Callan.

"I wouldn't do anything to hurt Sloane, Jake," Callan responded quickly, a hint of anger in his voice.

"And where exactly were *you* when you received the text,

Sloane?" Dad went on, turning toward me.

Does he think we planned this? Does he think we're both in on this?

"I was…" I began, wondering how truthful I should be. Did it really matter where *I* was?

"We were in Baltimore. She wanted to talk to Sarah, since you decided to delve into the past," Callan answered, putting his elbows to the tops of his thighs. "And Sarah admitted to lying. That make you feel better now, Jake?"

Dad's eyes widened and his face turned white. I wasn't able to think about it before Mom cut in.

"See? I knew he wouldn't do such a thing, Jacob," Mom said, slapping my dad's thigh with the back of her hand.

"How did you find Sarah?" Dad asked suspiciously, looking between me and Callan.

"What about that one boy, the governor's son? James?" Mom asked quickly, diverting the topic.

Was it possible that it was James? Did he find out about me and Callan, get jealous, and decide to try to scare us? But why involve Dad in it?

"I don't think so," I said as I shook my head. "Why would he?"

"Because he fucking liked you, and you rejected him so now he's trying to hurt you," Callan concluded angrily.

"Get his name," Dad said to the man sitting in the armchair beside him. "Check every device he has. Find out where he was when that text came through," he demanded sternly as he stood up.

I shook my head, muttering to myself as I stared down at the floor, trying to focus. "No, it can't be."

Callan put his hand on my thigh. "It has to be, unless there's someone else you think would be capable of this," he said quietly as the commotion and chatter around us became loud.

But I couldn't think of anyone else—logically, James was the best and easiest explanation. But was it too easy? He was a sweet guy; I didn't think he'd do anything like this. Then again, did I really know him?

"Let me go with them," Callan said as he stood up, and I realized he was talking to my dad. "If it's that kid, I'm gonna beat the fucking shit out of him," he spit out.

Dad paused as he regarded Callan with bemusement. "No." He shook his head and then looked down at me as his expression softened. "Stay with Sloane. They'll get this figured out. Keep her safe here," he said quietly as he turned back to Callan.

My heart melted—did Dad finally *get it* now? I glanced over at Mom and she was smiling at me warmly. Maybe Mom knocked some sense into him.

I stood up and took Callan's hand, entwining my fingers with his. I knew he was wound up and angry, ready to do something about James possibly sending the threat.

"Come on, Daddy," I whispered in his ear. "Now you need to fill up my ass."

He turned to me with wide eyes, his anger shifting to desire. "Yes, ma'am."

32

Callan

I didn't want to think about any threatening texts or Sloane being around that fucking kid. I had never felt so angry in my life. Someone threatening my girl—my future fucking wife— had me reeling. However, she successfully calmed me down after I drained every last drop of myself into her ass.

I guess we fell asleep, because the next thing I knew, faint morning light crept through the curtains, and Sloane had her hand on my hard cock as she stroked me gently.

"Good morning, Daddy," she said as she looked up at me with a smile, already on her fucking knees and ready to blow me.

"Fuck," I moaned as I put my hands behind my head, watching her. "Good morning, baby."

"Sloane!" Jake's voice called out from the other side of the door.

God fucking damnit. Sloane rolled her eyes and let go of my throbbing cock.

"Yes?" she called out sweetly.

"Can I come in?" he asked, and I heard the doorknob rattle as he tried to turn it.

My eyes shot wide open, panic rising in my chest, and I checked her door—thank fuck it was locked.

"Well, um...give me a sec, Dad," she huffed as she got up from bed and I hurriedly put my cock away.

Sloane shrugged on sweats and left her perky, hard nipples under a tank top on display. If she answered the door like that for anyone else, I'd be fuming. I pulled up my jeans and straightened my shirt out, then began to put my shoes on when she opened the door.

I glanced up and noticed Jake's tired eyes on his daughter before they shifted to me. "Can I speak to you alone, sweetie?" His tone was gentle, but it only raised my suspicions.

Sloane turned to me with sad eyes. I nodded, but her brows furrowed, her expression hardening. She was still upset with her dad, and it seemed a soft tone and a "sweetie" weren't enough to change that. She turned back to Jake, crossing her arms.

"No. You can speak to me right here," she said, her voice firm.

A smile flickered across my face as I looked down, tying my shoes. I wasn't about to object—not with that attitude of hers—because any attempt would be shut down right away.

Jake sighed, crossing his arms. "It wasn't James. His dad gave us a hell of a time, but we got the information we needed, and he's in the clear," he explained.

"Nah," I cut in immediately. "It's gotta be him, Jake. Who the fuck else could it be?" I asked as I stood up and walked towards them.

Jake's jaw tightened as he watched me. "That's what we're

trying to figure out, Callan," he responded, irritation seeping into his voice. "That's why I'm here. Sloane," he said, glancing back at her. "Can you think of anyone else?"

Sloane was about to respond when Leo approached Jake, tapping him on the shoulder. "Mr. President, there's an urgent call for you," he said, and Jake immediately turned and followed him in the other direction.

Sloane looked up at me, worry etched across her face. "What could that be?" she asked, her voice quiet and timid—nothing like my usual confident, fiery girl. She was scared.

"Don't worry, baby. You don't ever have to be worried or scared with me. I'll fuckin' protect you with my life," I said with a smile, wrapping her in my arms.

She only nodded, offering me a small smile. Just as I leaned in for a kiss, my phone started vibrating in my pocket.

"Go ahead and check it. It could be important," Sloane urged.

I groaned and fished my phone out of my pocket. I was pissed the moment I realized an unknown number was calling. "Spam," I said as I held up my phone for Sloane to see.

"No," she said, shaking her head. "Answer it—what if it's them?"

I eyed her with concern, though I did my best to keep it hidden. I answered and slowly put the phone up to my ear. "Callan Holt."

"She's really pretty, Cal. But so *young*. And Jake's daughter? Guess you're not afraid to stoop low. *Real* low."

Fuck. "Sarah, how the fuck did you get my number?"

I glanced down at Sloane and her eyes were filled with confusion. Sarah just laughed, and I had never been so fucking annoyed in my life.

"You act like you're fucking royalty or something. I used

Google, moron. It was a lot harder to get Sloane's number, though. But I managed. I have my ways," she said with a chuckle.

Sloane was whispering to me, but I couldn't make out a word—my vision blurred with anger, and my face burned with fiery fucking heat. "*You* sent that text? *You* fucking threatened Sloane?"

Sloane gasped and took a step back. My free hand clenched into a fist, and I had to fight the urge to punch the wall beside me.

"It's not all about her, Callan. Have you asked your best friend what he's been up to? Hasn't he told you yet?"

I started pacing. "What the fuck do you mean?" I demanded through gritted teeth.

Sarah's laughter echoed, sending a chill through me and making every hair on my body stand on edge.

Her tone turned ominous. "Just ask him. And tell him he's got forty-eight hours to tell Ana, or I'll tell the whole world." The line went dead.

I was down the hall before I even had the chance to think. *If Jake has something to do with this shit, I don't fucking care—I'll punch the fucking president.*

"Callan, what's going on? What did she say?" Sloane asked as she trailed behind me as I paced down the stairs to head to Jake's office.

"She sent the text to you," I spit out, my vision still blurred with anger. "I think Jake has something to do with this."

"Callan!" Sloane's voice cracked as she cried out, stopping me in my tracks. I turned around to find her standing there, wide-eyed, tears streaming down her face.

"Baby." I closed the distance between us, pulling her

into my arms. She buried her face in my chest, her sobs echoing through the hall. The bodyguards watched, their gazes lingering longer than I liked. "What the fuck are you lookin' at?" I growled at one, and he quickly shifted his eyes to the far side of the room.

"I don't know what's going on, baby," I whispered in her ear. "Sarah made it sound like, I don't know, she has some shit on your dad. I just want to go talk to him and figure out if he knows anything," I explained softly.

She looked up at me with tear-soaked eyes. "Tell me exactly what she said," she demanded sharply, the firmness in her tone a striking contrast to her fragile expression.

I hadn't even finished explaining when Sloane spun around and stormed down the hall toward the west wing. My anger still simmered, but I couldn't help the way my eyes followed her, the sway of her hips and the jiggle of her ass impossible to ignore as she stomped toward the Oval Office. I needed to be inside her pussy soon or I'd fucking implode.

"Is he in there?" Sloane asked Leo who stood next to the oval office door.

"Yes," he responded, not even looking her in the eye.

"What the fuck is your problem, Leo?" I snarled, itching for a fight, my anger looking for any outlet. Leo barely had time to react before Sloane swung the door open with force. She quickly walked in and I spotted Jake sitting on the couch, surrounded by stacks of documents, oblivious to the storm brewing in the hallway.

"Sloane," he said with surprise, then glanced at me as I closed the door.

"Why is Sarah telling Callan that you have forty-eight hours to confess something to Mom, or else she'll tell the whole world?" Sloane's voice cracked, the anger obvious in her words as she stood with her hands on her hips.

I inched closer, my jaw clenching tight as we waited for his answer. His eyes darted between the two of us but he shook his head, hesitation clear on his face. "I don't know, Sloane. Sarah has a tendency to lie about things—you know that," he said calmly, then turned to me. "What exactly did she say?" he asked.

He was eerily calm, as if he'd rehearsed this or had been expecting it. When I relayed the message, he laughed quietly and shook his head. "I'll handle it," he said with a nod.

Sloane glanced at me, hesitation flickering in her eyes, before turning her focus back to Jake. "Why aren't you jumping up and taking care of it then? Why are you so calm about this?" she demanded, her voice rising.

"Because she's not a threat, Sloane!" Jake snapped.

"She's threatening your family, Jake. How the fuck is she not a threat?" I shot back, my anger flaring as I stepped forward, refusing to let him dismiss it so easily.

He let out a heavy sigh. "I need you two to leave, alright? Let me sort this out," he said, his calm demeanor slipping back into place.

Sloane scoffed, shaking her head in disbelief before spinning on her heels and heading for the door. I lingered for a moment, shooting Jake an angry glare, but I didn't say a word. Instead, I turned and followed her out, the tension still simmering in my chest.

I followed her out of the west wing and back into the main house. She remained silent as she marched up the stairs, and I trailed behind, unable to shake the feeling that Jake was fucking lying—he seemed too calm.

"My dad is lying, I can tell," Sloane said, as if reading my mind. "I'm gonna talk to my mom," she added.

We made it to the hallway on the main floor, and I took her hand, squeezing it gently to stop her. She turned to me, her eyes wide and filled with fear. "Something bad is gonna happen, Callan. I have a really, really bad feeling," she whispered, her voice cracking as tears welled up in her eyes.

"I'm not gonna let anything happen to you, baby," I murmured, placing my hand gently on her cheek. I wanted nothing more than to kiss her, to take away the fear in her eyes, but I held back, knowing it wasn't the right moment.

She nodded. "I know you won't, Cal. But it's not me I'm worried about—it's my mom."

33

Sloane

I didn't know what my dad was hiding, but I knew he was hiding something. He was acting so strange—too calm, almost like he was trying to keep us from seeing the cracks. I needed to confide in Mom because she would know what to do—she always knew what to do. And if Dad was lying, she'd be the one to uncover the truth.

Callan and I found her in her private office on the second floor of the living quarters. The moment I barged in, she ended the call she was on and stood up quickly, the worry clear in her eyes.

"Sloane," she said, her voice full of concern. "What's wrong?"

Callan stepped forward, explaining the call with Sarah, but he paused and glanced at me, giving me the space to continue with how Dad had reacted. Mom's expression said it all—she was furious.

"*¿Qué coño?* What could he possibly be hiding from me, especially something that Sarah knows and I don't?" she asked, her frustration clear.

I shook my head and shrugged, unsure of what to say.

"*¡A tomar por culo!*" she muttered under her breath, storming toward the door. "You two stay here. I'm going to speak to your father, Sloane, *y lo juro por Dios...*" The door slammed behind her and I jumped, my nerves stretched to the breaking point.

Callan turned to me, placing his hands gently on my waist. I could see how much he wanted to comfort me, but we were both too frustrated, too on edge to find any relief in the moment.

"My dad wouldn't..." I started, my voice trailing off as my thoughts spiraled toward the worst possibilities. "He wouldn't have cheated on my mom with Sarah, right? That can't be it."

Callan's eyes widened, and he shook his head slowly. "I don't know, baby. But whatever it is, we're all gonna get through it, okay?"

I couldn't hold it back any longer—the lump in my throat gave way, and tears streamed down my face. Desperation took over as I grabbed Callan's face, pressing my lips hard against his, seeking comfort in the only place that felt safe. He pressed his body against mine, pulling me close as his hands slid around my waist, but just as quickly, he pulled away. His eyes darkened, and his voice dropped to a deep, commanding tone.

"Down the hall. In the bathroom. I need to fuck you right now, Sloane," he said, his words dripping with authority and raw desire as he took my hand and led me out the door.

He slammed the bathroom door behind us and quickly peeled down my sweats as he pressed his lips against mine. My shaky hands began to unzip his jeans before he took over and let his hard cock spring free. I couldn't even let my underwear fall to the ground before Callan ripped them off and lifted me up from my ass, walking me over to the counter as I wrapped my legs around him. He plunged his cock into me before he even set me down, and I gasped with relief as he filled me up, my mind going completely blank aside from the overwhelming pleasure.

"Fuck, baby," Callan whispered in my ear before gently trailing kisses on my neck.

"Fuck me hard, Daddy. I need it," I whispered back, clawing my nails on his back.

"Yeah, you need it? You need Daddy's cock to make it all better?" he moaned out quietly, probably highly aware of how easily we could be heard.

I whimpered as he began to thrust harder, my body trembling under his intensity. I bit down on his shoulder, stifling my moans, trying to keep quiet. He let out a low grunt, his hips pounding against me, before he released me, pulling out and swiftly turning me around. He quickly plunged back into me, and I watched us in the mirror as he gripped my hips, his gaze fixed on the curve of my body before his eyes finally met mine in the reflection. A slow, wicked smile spread across his face as he reached for my hair, wrapping it tightly around his hand in a firm fist, pulling me even closer.

"Rub your needy clit, baby. Eyes on me while you come on my cock," he demanded in my ear as he inched his other hand up to my neck, lightly squeezing.

My hand trailed down to my clit and I began to furiously rub myself, close to climax as I watched us in the mirror. Seeing Callan's hand around my throat as his body pounded against mine, my boobs bouncing up and down, and his cock hitting just right suddenly had my pussy seizing around him. My eyes involuntarily closed as a wave of pleasure coursed through my core, and Callan's grip on my throat tightened as he grunted deeply.

"Come on, baby. Get on your knees. I need you to finish what you started this morning," he growled, his voice thick with need. My eyes fluttered open, locking with his intense gaze, as I slowly pulled off of him and lowered myself in front of him.

He held his cock in his hand as he eyed my body, then put his other hand softly to my cheek. "Open wide, baby girl," he ordered gently.

My mouth shot open, the sight of Callan's thick cock in his hand sending a tingle to my pussy. All of a sudden, he rammed his cock into my mouth, taking both hands to the side of my head and fucking my face. I steadied myself on my knees with one hand on my thigh, and I couldn't help myself from rubbing my clit again, needing more release. The force from his thrusts made it hard to look up at him, but I caught a glimpse of his wild, widened eyes as he stared down at me, his full lips parted and his brows pulled together in concentration. My pussy began to seize again, just as Callan let out a deep, guttural moan and his warm cum shot to the back of my throat. I let out a quiet moan of satisfaction, my eyes locked on his face as it contorted into a look of sheer pleasure.

I swallowed every last drop as my mouth parted from his cock, licking my lips with the mixture of his taste and mine.

"Fuck, baby. You're my fucking dream girl," Callan breathed, putting his thumb to my lips and stroking gently.

I smiled as I looked up at him. "Next time, I want *you* on your knees."

* * *

We sat restlessly in Mom's office, the tension thick in the air as we waited for any kind of update. I kept glancing toward the door, itching to join her during the interrogation with Dad, but Callan reassured me that they probably needed to handle this alone. Still, my mind wouldn't stop racing—Dad and Sarah together? It didn't make sense. Sure, she was beautiful, but why would he cheat on Mom, who he was desperately in love with? And with someone they both knew, someone they had never really gotten along with. The thought twisted in my chest, making it harder to breathe. I couldn't imagine what life was going to be like if my mom and dad weren't together.

Callan held my hand as I stared out the window at the long stretch of grass, my thoughts tangled. Even with him beside me, the minutes we waited felt endless, every second stretching on in torturous silence. Then, when my mom finally walked in, her face sullen, eyes swollen and red from tears, I knew instantly what had happened. The truth I had dreaded was written all over her face.

"Mom," I said softly, standing up and taking her hand. "What happened? What did he say?"

I glanced at Callan, and without a word, he nodded, instantly understanding that this was something I needed to face with her alone. He quietly slipped out the door, closing it gently behind him, leaving us alone.

"Your father didn't even have to say anything. Sarah sent me a video of them while I was walking over there," she said, holding her phone up briefly before tossing it onto the couch in disgust. "And he *still* denied it. *La madre que te pario*," she spat, her voice sharp as she cursed him in Spanish. The words hit me like a punch to the chest, tightening with a mix of grief and anger.

"Mom, I'm..." I began, but the words caught in my throat. What could I say? Not only had my dad shattered his marriage, but he had broken our family, too. *How could he? Why would he do this to us?*

"Come on, baby. Pack a bag. We're getting out of here," she said suddenly, her voice still thick with emotion as she sniffled and turned on her heel, heading for the door.

I didn't hesitate or question her. I just followed, feeling the weight of the situation settle in. As we stepped into the hall, I saw Callan waiting, his eyes searching mine as we moved toward him.

"Don't ask me any questions, Callan. Not yet," Mom said firmly as she marched past him.

He locked eyes with me, concern written all over his face, but I shook my head, trying to keep my tears at bay. All I could do was take his hand and follow my mom.

A few minutes later, Callan and I sat at the piano in the hallway, waiting for her. After I explained everything that had happened, he shook his head, his gaze drifting down the hall.

"And I thought us being together was bad," he joked lightly, trying to ease the tension, but I couldn't even manage a smile. I just frowned, the weight of everything still too heavy to let any humor in.

"I'm sorry, baby," he added, placing his hand gently on my thigh. "I don't know what the fuck to say, so I'll just keep my mouth shut. I'm just...fuck," he muttered, frustration clear in his voice.

His choice of words caught me off guard, and despite every-thing, I let out a small giggle. In that brief moment, the weight felt just a little lighter. I was grateful he was there—he was my rock through all of this, steady when everything else felt like it was falling apart. I couldn't imagine going through this without him by my side.

Just then, a door at the end of the hall slammed shut, and out came my mom with a suitcase in tow. Her steps were purposeful, her expression set with determination as she stopped at the top of the stairs.

"Where are your things?" she asked, already sounding exasperated.

I glanced at Callan, then back at her. "Most of my stuff is at Callan's," I replied with a shrug.

Mom nodded, a flicker of relief crossing her face. "Okay, good. Let's go. Callan, we'll take your SUV." She didn't wait for a response as she headed for the stairs, her focus sharp.

We didn't even make it out the door before Dad's voice echoed down the hall, frantic and panicked.

"Ana! Where are you going? You can't just leave—where are you going?" he demanded, Leo and Julian trailing closely behind him.

"Wherever the fuck you're not, *tramposo hijo de puta*," Mom shot back, her voice sharp and resolute as she kept walking, not even sparing him a glance.

"At least take Leo or Julian with you," Dad called out, defeat heavy in his voice as we stopped by Callan's SUV.

"No," she replied with disgust, finally turning to face him. The sound of his footsteps echoed on the concrete, and her glare cut through the distance between them. "I have Callan if I need anything. You'll be getting divorce papers soon."

Callan looked down at the ground, stone-faced, as he opened the backseat door for my mom. The tension between my parents was unbearable, and I couldn't stand being caught in the middle of it. Without a word, I walked around the SUV and slid into the passenger seat, slamming the door shut behind me, desperate to shut out the chaos.

Mom climbed in right after me, followed by Callan, and we drove off in heavy silence. Through the rearview mirror, I caught a glimpse of my dad standing there, watching us sullenly as we left him behind.

"*Mamá, ¿estás bien?*" I asked as I turned to look back at her.

Callan quickly glanced over at me, then shifted his focus back to the road ahead. Mom sighed heavily as she stared out the window, slipping on her sunglasses. "Sloane, *déjame calmarme primero*," she muttered, her voice strained.

"Okay," I replied with a nod. She wanted to be left alone, and I could understand that. I turned back to the road, my mind swirling with questions I wasn't ready to ask.

"Where are we going?" Callan asked quietly, his eyes darting to me for a moment, as if I had any idea.

"Head east on I-50. We've got a lake house in St. Michaels. We'll figure things out from there," Mom instructed hurriedly, her voice steady as I stared out my window.

The car fell into silence for a while before Callan rested his hand gently on my thigh, his eyes still focused on the road. I glanced over at him with a small smile, then turned to look at Mom, who kept her gaze fixed on the scenery outside her window, seemingly lost in thought.

"Why don't you ever speak Spanish to me?" Callan asked quietly, his tone light and teasing.

I snickered as I glanced back at him. "*¿Hablas español?*"

He shrugged, flashing me a wide grin. "Nope." He shook his head, letting out a soft laugh.

I rolled my eyes with a smile, turning my gaze forward. "*Por eso.*"

The road stretched out before us, the quiet hum of the tires the only sound filling the car. Callan's hand stayed steady on the wheel, his other resting on my thigh. I tried to focus on anything but the storm brewing inside me, gazing at the passing trees on the open road.

Without warning, a loud crash shattered the calm. The SUV jerked violently to the side, metal screeching against metal. My body slammed against the door, and my breath hitched in my chest as the world outside blurred into a chaotic swirl of color and sound.

"Callan!" I screamed, but the car kept spinning, completely out of control. Callan's knuckles were white on the steering wheel, struggling to regain control as the SUV fishtailed, tires screeching against the pavement.

The impact hit again—harder this time. Glass shattered, raining down around me like tiny daggers, and the world seemed to move in slow motion. My heart pounded in my ears, drowning out everything else. I could hear Mom yelling, but her voice was distant, like it was coming from another world. I didn't know which way was up or down anymore. The SUV skidded off the road, and everything stopped in an instant with a sickening jolt.

Then there was silence.

My head throbbed, my vision blurry. I blinked, trying to make sense of what had just happened. Everything felt distant, disjointed, like I was floating outside my own body.

Suddenly, hands grabbed me, strong and unyielding. I tried to push away, tried to fight, but my limbs felt heavy and useless. A wave of panic rushed over me, but before I could react, I was being pulled out of the wrecked SUV.

"Callan!" I choked out, my voice barely more than a whisper, but there was no response.

The last thing I saw was a flash of movement, a dark figure looming over me, and then everything went black.

34

Callan

My ears rang from the crash, the chaos still spinning in my head as I tried to piece together what had just happened. The scent of burning rubber filled my lungs, but I forced myself to focus. *Sloane.*

My head spun, but my body moved on instinct. I glanced at the passenger seat—empty. Sloane was gone.

"Ana!" I whipped around, barely catching a glimpse of her struggling to push open the backseat door. She stumbled out, her hand pressed to her forehead, looking around, dazed and disoriented.

"What happened?" she mumbled, her voice shaky as she stared at the wreckage, still trying to piece it together.

I couldn't focus on her right now—Sloane was missing. Panic consumed me as I staggered out of the SUV, my muscles screaming in pain, but the fear swallowed everything else.

"Sloane!" I yelled, my voice hoarse, searching the deserted road and the tree line. Ana wobbled beside me, her expression lost and confused. She kept muttering, "What happened? Where's Sloane?"

The emptiness around us was suffocating, and the cold realization hit me hard—someone took her.

"Someone—someone fucking took Sloane, Ana. She was just here. She's gone," I stammered, my voice shaking, feeling like my heart was splitting in two.

Ana blinked, still trying to catch up, her face pale. "What? What do you mean? How...?"

What the fuck just happened? My mind raced, trying to piece it together. Then it hit me—*those two cars we'd passed just a few miles back. Dark SUVs, just like mine.* I hadn't thought much of them at the time, but now it made sense. There was only one person who'd go to these lengths, someone who wanted to hurt not just Jake, but me, too.

"Sarah. It was fucking Sarah," I growled, the realization burning through me as I rushed back to the SUV to search for my phone.

"What? No," Ana muttered, disbelief creeping into her voice, as if she couldn't accept that my psychotic ex would actually do this. But I knew her. I knew what she was capable of.

I tore through the car, my mind spinning with one thought: find Sloane. My hands shook as I shoved aside everything in my path, looking for my phone. This wasn't just about getting help—this meant calling the fucking piece of shit who did this.

She wanted me to reach out, to panic. She fucking got what she wanted. But she wasn't going to win. Not this time.

I found my phone, my heart pounding as I dialed the number. My fingers trembled, rage building in my chest.

"That didn't take long," Sarah answered with a devious laugh.

"What did you do?" I spit out. "What the fuck did you do? Where is she?"

Ana was already screaming into the phone next to me. "*¿Qué coño has hecho? ¡Maldita zorra!*"

Sarah's laugh echoed through the line, cold and taunting, as if she was savoring every second of our desperation.

"God, that woman drives me nuts!" Sarah spit out. "Tell her to shut the fuck up if she ever wants to see her daughter again."

I was trembling with rage. "Shut the fuck up, Sarah. Where is she? What do you want?"

Ana was talking on her phone now, presumably to Jake or hopefully the fucking secret service.

Sarah's laugh cut through the line again, sharper this time. "Oh, Callan, always trying to be the hero," she sneered, her voice dripping with mockery. "It's cute, really. Like you've got any control over this."

She paused, letting her words sink in before continuing, her tone turning vicious. "What do I want? I want you to feel as powerless as I did. I want you to watch everything you care about crumble. And that sweet little thing you're so desperate to save?" She chuckled. "She's just the start. You think this is about Sloane? No, baby, this is about you. I want *you* to hurt as much as I did."

I gripped the phone tighter, the urge to break something almost overwhelming. Ana was still speaking urgently into her phone, but my focus was locked on Sarah, every word of hers stoking the fire burning inside me.

I gripped the phone tighter. "You think you've won, Sarah?" My voice was low, steady, barely holding back the rage. "You're nothing but desperate, clinging to whatever you can to feel powerful. But you've already fucking lost—long before you pulled this shit."

There was silence on the other end for a moment before Sarah's cold laugh returned, though I could tell my words had hit a nerve.

"Okay, Callan. Let's see who's really won after I tear your precious girl apart." She hung up.

"Goddammit!" I shouted, nearly hurling my phone to the ground, but stopped short—this was my only connection to Sloane.

"Secret Service is en route," Ana said, her voice steady with the phone still to her ear. "Did you catch anything we can use to track her?"

"Two black SUVs like mine. I—I don't know which direction," I stammered, my voice breaking as hopelessness swelled in my chest.

I stared down at my phone, my mind scrambling for answers. There had to be a way to get to Sarah. If all she wanted was me, I could use that. I began pacing, thoughts racing, a whirlwind of desperate ideas spinning through my head...

35

Sloane

A dull throb pulsed in the back of my head as I slowly came to. Everything was blurry at first, like I was waking from a nightmare, but the cold, hard surface beneath me quickly grounded me in reality. I shifted, wincing as the stiffness in my limbs reminded me I was somewhere far from safe.

I blinked, my eyes adjusting to the faint light filtering through cracks in the walls. Concrete floors. Metal beams. The faint sound of dripping water echoed in the distance. It had to be a warehouse. The air was thick, stale, and carried the faint scent of rust and something else I couldn't place.

I swallowed against the dryness in my throat as the memories came rushing back. The car. The hands grabbing me. Then—nothing. Panic twisted in my chest, but I forced it down, trying to focus. My hands were bound behind my back, but my legs were free. The silence was deafening, until suddenly... there were footsteps.

They were coming closer, slow and heavy, echoing off the walls.

My heart jumped into my throat. I was overwhelmed with

a sense of relief—*someone's here.* I tried to sit up, forcing my body to move, every muscle aching from whatever they'd done to me. Then I saw him.

I almost laughed from sheer relief. "Leo," I croaked, my voice trembling with a mix of hope and exhaustion. "Thank God."

But he didn't rush to help me. He didn't move at all.

Something cold washed over me as I looked at his face. He was too calm, too detached. His eyes didn't meet mine, and didn't carry any of the urgency I expected.

"Leo?" I tried again, the excitement in my voice fading. "What...what's going on?"

He finally looked at me, but his expression was unreadable, his lips pressed into a thin line. "I didn't want it to be like this," he muttered, a hint of regret in his voice. "But I owed her."

I blinked, confused. "*Her?* Do you mean...Sarah?" I already knew, deep down, that she was behind this. But why Leo?

Leo exhaled, running a hand through his hair. "She needed me, Sloane. I couldn't turn my back on her...not after everything she's done for me."

"You're *helping* her?" My voice cracked, disbelief and betrayal flooding my body. "Why? Leo, you're like an uncle to me."

His jaw clenched, and for the first time, he looked at me with something other than indifference. "And I've always been there for you, haven't I? But...this is different."

"Different how?" I snapped, the words spilling out before I could stop them. "She's trying to hurt me, and you're on her side?"

"It's not about sides, Sloane." His voice lowered, almost like he was trying to make me understand. "Sarah saved me when no one else would. When I hit rock bottom, she pulled me out. She's like family to me…and I couldn't just walk away from that."

"But you're choosing her over me," I whispered, the words catching in my throat.

"I'm not choosing," he said softly, his eyes finally meeting mine. "I'm trying to repay a debt."

I didn't understand, and I wasn't sure if I ever would. "Please, Leo," I begged, my voice breaking as tears welled in my eyes. "Please let me go." My words came out in fragile, desperate whispers as tears streamed down my cheeks.

He hesitated, his expression conflicted, like he wanted to say something but couldn't bring himself to. After a moment, he shook his head. "I'll get you some water. She'll be here soon." His tone was almost apologetic as he turned to leave.

"Leo, *please*," I cried out, my voice raw, grasping for him, for anything that could pull me out of this nightmare. But he didn't look back. He disappeared into the shadows, leaving me alone.

A scream tore from my throat, frustration and fear crashing together as I wrestled with the zip ties biting into my wrists, my hands numb and useless against the restraints. Then, I saw it—light creeping in, the outside world flickering for just a moment before the figure blocked it out. *Sarah.* The doors closed behind her with a heavy clang, and for a fleeting second, I wondered just how many people were helping her.

The sharp click of her heels echoed through the warehouse, each step deliberate. A smug smirk stretched across her face as she approached, her eyes narrowing with contempt. One hand rested on her hip as if she had all the power in the world.

"Well, well…there's the little princess," she sneered, her

tone dripping with mockery. "Did you enjoy your beauty rest?"

"Why am I here, Sarah? What the fuck do you want from me?" I spat, the anger surging through me, momentarily masking my fear.

She laughed. "Oh, sweetie, it's not about *you*." She leaned closer, her eyes gleaming with malice. "I want to hurt Callan, just like he hurt me. I want to rip away the thing he cherishes most—just like he did to me. And you, Sloane, you're that thing." Her smirk deepened as she straightened up. "But why stop there? Jake and Ana...they're guilty too. They helped him. So really, it's a two-for-one special."

Her words sliced through me, the cruel reality sinking in. This wasn't just about revenge—this was about destroying lives. And she was using me to do it.

"So what's the plan, Sarah? You're gonna kill me?" I challenged, forcing my voice to stay steady even as panic clawed at me from the inside. "You're really going to murder the President's daughter? You won't get away with it. You'll spend the rest of your life rotting in maximum security."

My voice sounded strong, defiant, but beneath it, my heart raced and fear gnawed at my chest. I needed to make her doubt herself, to buy some time—anything to get out of this.

Sarah's smirk widened as she crossed her arms, her eyes gleaming with amusement. "Oh, sweetie, do you really think I haven't thought this through? I'm not stupid enough to kill you outright. That would be too easy, too quick. No, I want Callan to *suffer*."

She stepped closer, her voice dropping to a cold whisper. "I want him to watch as I tear you apart piece by piece. Mentally. Physically. I want him to know it's all his fault, that *he* couldn't protect you. And by the time I'm done, no one will care that you're the President's daughter. Not even you."

She straightened up, her eyes burning with hatred. "As for prison? Let's just say I have a few friends in high places who owe me a favor or two. Maximum security won't be much of a problem."

My heart sank as the weight of her words pressed down on me, heavy and suffocating. But I couldn't let her see my fear. I forced my voice to stay strong, even though I felt the panic swirling just beneath the surface.

"My dad will find me. *Callan* will find me," I said, meeting her gaze with all the conviction I could muster. "You won't get away with this, Sarah. I'm sure they're probably tracking this exact location as we speak."

I prayed I was right. Every second that passed felt like a race against time, and I needed to believe that help was on its way.

But all Sarah did was laugh, a cold, humorless sound that echoed off the walls. "Oh, honey, do you really think anyone's going to find you?" She shook her head, amusement flickering in her eyes. "Leo's been helping me this whole time, right under your father's nose. Jake didn't have a clue."

She stepped closer, her voice laced with mockery. "What makes you think he's smart enough to find you now? You're alone, Sloane. No one's coming."

Her words cut deep, gnawing at the flicker of hope I was holding onto.

The door creaked open again, and Leo stepped in, holding a bottle of water. His expression was carefully neutral as he walked toward me, his movements slower than before. My hands were still bound behind my back, and the reminder of how helpless I was sent a fresh wave of panic through me.

Sarah eyed him impatiently. "Took you long enough," she

snapped. "Just give her the water."

Leo didn't say a word as he crouched beside me, twisting the cap off the bottle. He lifted it toward my lips, his hand steady but...there was something off. There was something in the way he moved, something almost hesitant. I parted my lips and let him pour the water into my mouth, careful not to gulp it down too quickly.

For a moment, his eyes met mine, and I caught something— maybe guilt, maybe regret. But it was gone as quickly as it appeared.

"Not too much," Sarah snapped, her voice sharp. "She doesn't need to get comfortable. We just need to keep her alive. For now, anyway."

Leo pulled the bottle away, his expression hardening again as he stood. His jaw was tight, and I noticed the way his fists clenched briefly before he let them go. Sarah didn't seem to notice, her focus entirely on me.

"You're not going soft, are you, Leo?" she teased, her tone mocking. "Don't tell me you're growing a conscience. You owe me, remember?"

His face remained impassive as he turned toward her. "You don't need to overdo it. She's not going anywhere."

Sarah rolled her eyes, stepping closer to me. "Oh, Leo. Always the protector, even when it's not your job anymore."

He didn't respond. He just glanced down at me one last time before he turned and walked toward the door. His face gave nothing away, but something in the air had shifted. I wasn't sure what it meant yet, but I could feel it.

Sarah didn't miss a beat. "I'll be back soon, princess. Don't get too comfortable," she sneered before walking out after him.

The door slammed shut, leaving me alone in the cold, empty warehouse. Silence pressed on, broken only by the pounding of my heart. My wrists throbbed from the zip ties, and my mind raced, replaying the past few minutes.

Leo hadn't said much and he barely looked at me. But something was there—a hesitation, a flicker of doubt in his eyes. It wasn't much, but it was enough to stir something inside me.

Maybe he's not fully on her side. Maybe there's still a chance.

The thought settled in, fragile but real. I clung to it, letting that small spark of hope push back the darkness closing in around me.

36

Callan

I sat in a private room at the small-town police station, the closest one to the crash site. Ana had already flown back to D.C. with Julian to meet with the tech team, leaving me here. Jake sat across from me, his expression unreadable, while Secret Service agents swarmed around us, busy with my phone. They were running every possible trace on the call I made, hoping to track down Sarah and Sloane.

As I sat there with the steady hum of activity around me, something felt off.

Leo.

He wasn't here, and that didn't sit right with me. He'd been involved in every major situation, and even every minor situation like Jake knocking me the fuck out. But now, in the middle of all this, he was missing.

I glanced at Jake, his face as stoic as ever. "Where's Leo?" I asked, trying to keep my voice even, though a sense of unease coursed through me.

"He's following a lead," Jake replied simply, not breaking his usual calm demeanor.

I nodded, but something still didn't sit right. Maybe it was nothing, just nerves from everything happening...or maybe Leo's absence was something more.

"What lead?" I dug deeper.

Jake leaned back slightly in his chair, keeping his tone steady. "One of our sources reported seeing a black SUV matching the one from the scene a couple of towns over. Leo was the closest, so we sent him out."

It sounded plausible—logical even—but it still didn't ease the tightness in my chest. A black SUV was a solid lead, something worth investigating, but something still gnawed at me.

"Why was he so close?" I pressed.

Jake shrugged slightly, keeping his tone even. "Just coincidence, I guess. He was already out working some smaller leads when everything happened. He's always been good about staying close when things heat up."

It made sense, but there was still something that didn't add up. Leo's absence now felt too coincidental, too perfectly timed. My gut told me there was more to this than just chance.

"Isn't he always by your side?" I asked, digging deeper. "I've never seen him leave you for anything this important."

Jake paused for a moment, the question hanging between us. His eyes flicked to mine, and for the first time, I saw a hint of uncertainty flash across his face. "Yeah, he usually is."

He seemed to mull it over for a second before shaking his head, as if dismissing the thought. "Look, Leo's good at what he does. He wouldn't go off like this unless it was important."

But now, I could tell—something didn't sit right with Jake either.

"Might be a good time to call him, get an update," I suggested, sitting back in my chair, arms crossed. I tried to keep my tone casual, but my eyes stayed fixed on Jake.

Jake hesitated, just for a second, before nodding. "Yeah, good idea."

He pulled out his phone and dialed, holding it to his ear. I watched his face closely, noticing the slight tension in his jaw as the line rang. After a few long moments, he lowered the phone and glanced at me. "No answer."

A pit formed in my stomach. "That's fucking weird, isn't it?"

Jake didn't respond right away, his brows pulled together as he stared at his phone. "Yeah...it is."

His frown deepened, and he stood up, turning toward the Secret Service agents working around us. "I want a team out looking for Leo, now," he ordered, his voice firm. "Track his last known location and send someone to check it out. Something's not right."

The agents exchanged quick glances before nodding and moving into action, tapping at their earpieces and communicating the new orders.

I watched it all unfold, the knot in my stomach tightening. If Leo had just gone dark, that could only mean one of two things: he was in trouble, or he was hiding something. Either way, it wasn't good.

Jake sat back down, his expression more tense than before. "We'll find him," he said, though I wasn't sure who he was trying to convince—me, or himself.

The room buzzed with movement as the agents followed Jake's orders, but before I could process what that meant, one of them walked over and handed me my phone.

"We've done what we can for now. You'll get updates as we

track everything," he said.

I barely nodded, feeling the weight of the phone in my hand. But before I could put it away, the screen lit up. A number I didn't recognize flashed across it. My heart lurched.

I swiped to answer, bringing the phone to my ear. "Sarah?"

Her laugh on the other end was cold, chilling. "Miss me, Callan?"

"Where is she?" My voice was tight, controlled, though panic bubbled just beneath the surface. "What the fuck are you doing with Sloane?"

"Oh, you'll find out soon enough," she sneered. "But I'll give you a little hint: she's not looking too good right now. I've got your precious girl, and I'm about to show you what it feels like to lose everything."

My grip on the phone tightened, blood pounding in my ears. "If you fucking hurt her—"

"Oh, I *will*," Sarah interrupted, her voice dripping with malice. "And you'll watch it all unfold."

The line went dead.

I stared at the phone, my pulse racing. Sloane was running out of time.

I shot out of my chair, adrenaline flooding my system. I rushed over to the nearest agent with my phone clutched in my hand.

"Can you trace this?" I asked urgently. "Sarah just called me. She's got Sloane."

The agent looked at me, then down at my phone. Without missing a beat, he nodded. "Give me a second." He motioned to another agent and quickly hooked my phone up to their equipment.

Jake stood nearby, watching with sharp eyes, his usual

calm demeanor giving way to a sense of tension that was unmistakable. His arms were crossed, and I could see the slight strain in his jaw as he kept his focus on the agents.

"We'll need a minute to pull the data," the agent said as they worked, fingers flying over keyboards. I stood there restlessly, every second feeling like an eternity. Jake paced just behind me, running a hand through his hair, his frustration evident.

"Come on," I muttered under my breath, my fists clenching and unclenching as I watched the screens.

Finally, the agent turned to us, his face set in concentration. "We've got something. It's a burner phone, but we're triangulating the location from the nearest cell towers."

I glanced at Jake. He'd stopped pacing, his eyes locked on the agent as the information sank in. "How close?" he asked, his voice low and controlled, but I could sense the urgency.

"Close enough for us to move. We'll get a team ready," the agent said, but before he could finish, I stepped forward.

"I'm going," I said firmly.

Jake chimed in quickly. "So am I."

The agent didn't even flinch. "Mr. President, I'm sorry, but you can't come. You know the protocol."

Jake clenched his jaw, not arguing because we both knew what that meant, but I could see the pain in his eyes as he wrestled with staying behind.

He turned to me, his voice low. "You're going, then."

I nodded. "I'll bring her back."

The agent motioned to me. "We'll gear you up and move fast. Let's go."

Jake locked eyes with me, his expression tight with fear and frustration. "You find her, Callan. No matter what." He still trusted me, despite everything that had happened.

"I will," I said, and I meant it.

Without another word, I followed the agents out. The weight of everything fell hard on my shoulders, but there wasn't time to think about anything else now. Sloane was out there, and I was going to bring her back—no matter what it took.

37

Sloane

The metallic clang of the door echoed through the dark warehouse as it creaked open. I'd been sitting in the same spot for what felt like hours, my wrists raw from struggling against the zip ties. My throat was dry, my body aching, but I wasn't going to give Sarah the satisfaction of hearing me beg for anything.

Her heels clicked against the concrete floor, that sound alone enough to set my nerves on edge. I couldn't see her at first, but I could hear her moving closer, the smirk practically audible in every step.

"Hello, princess," she taunted, stepping into the faint light that leaked through the cracks in the walls. She carried a small, shiny metal case with her, and just the sight of it made my stomach twist.

I swallowed hard, forcing myself to stay silent.

She knelt down in front of me, her eyes gleaming with sadistic amusement. "You know, I thought about what to do with you for a while," she said, slowly opening the case. Inside were various small instruments—small, but enough to cause pain. She lifted one, a small blade, holding it up to catch the light. "Hurting Callan has always been on my mind. Fucking your dad was supposed to be my revenge, just a little way to ruin his life from a distance."

She smirked. "But then I found out who Callan was with. And you...oh, that made it even better. Callan with Jake's daughter? It was like a fucking gift. You're someone he actually cares about. Something I can take away from him."

Her voice grew sharper, bitter. "It's been eight years, and the world moves on. But I didn't. I couldn't. And then, those pictures leaked. Seeing the two of you so happy? It made me *sick.*"

Her eyes narrowed as the blade skimmed my arm, just enough to send a sharp sting through my skin. "Breaking you mentally? That's going to be so fucking satisfying," she murmured. "I'm not going to kill you—not yet. You're far too valuable for that. But I will show you what it feels like to lose everything. Piece by piece."

She leaned in closer, her breath hot against my ear. "How long do you think Callan can handle watching you fall apart?"

I flinched instinctively, but there was nowhere to go. Fear coursed through me, but I forced it down. *Don't give her the satisfaction.*

Before she could say anything else, the door burst open. Leo rushed in, his face pale, urgency in his voice. "Sarah, we've got a problem. They're on the way. Callan and a team. We need to move—*now.*"

Sarah froze, glaring at him. "What do you mean, they're on the way?"

"They were onto me. They traced your call. They'll be here any minute," Leo said quickly, his gaze flicking toward me for a split second before turning back to her.

Then, faint but unmistakable, the sound of a helicopter whirled in the distance, growing louder by the second.

Sarah's body tensed. "Shit," she hissed. She spun around, yanking me up by the arm. I winced as she pressed the cold blade to my throat, her breath coming faster now.

"Leo, go!" she snapped, her voice shaking, her angry tone now laced with fear. "Get out there and distract them! Buy me some fucking time!"

Leo hesitated, his eyes darting between me and Sarah. For a brief moment, it seemed like he was going to refuse, but then he nodded and turned toward the door, his steps quick.

Sarah's grip tightened around me as she dragged me toward the back of the warehouse, the knife still dangerously close to my throat. "We're leaving, princess. Don't even think about trying to run."

She dragged me toward the back of the warehouse, her grip painfully tight, the knife still hovering near my throat. My pulse raced, my mind scrambling for a way out. The helicopter was getting closer. *This is my chance.*

With a surge of adrenaline, I jerked my head back, slamming it into Sarah's face. I heard a satisfying yelp as she fumbled backward, momentarily losing her grip on me.

Without thinking, I bolted, my legs shaky but desperate to put as much distance between us as possible. But I only made it a few steps before I felt a sharp tug at my ankle. Sarah had regained her footing and tripped me, sending me crashing to the cold, hard floor.

I gasped as the wind was knocked out of me, my wrists still bound, leaving me defenseless as I struggled to get up. Before I could move, Sarah was on me again, her face twisted in fury.

"Nice try," she spat, grabbing me by the arm and yanking

me back to my feet, the blade now pressed even closer to my throat. "You're not getting away that easily."

Before she could drag me any farther, the door burst open again. Leo stormed in, his face white and eyes wild. His chest heaved as he glanced between me and Sarah, the tension unbearable.

"I give up," Leo blurted out, his voice shaky but resolute. "I'm done with this. I'm going out, hands up." His eyes darted toward the sound of the helicopter, now deafening as it prepared to land just outside the warehouse.

I couldn't see Sarah's face, but I felt her body tense behind me, the blade pressing harder against my throat. "What the fuck are you talking about, Leo?" she spat, her voice sharp with panic. "We had a plan!"

He shook his head, his expression grim. "It's over, Sarah. They're here. I'm not going down for this." His hands raised slowly in surrender. "I'm walking out, and you should, too."

Sarah's grip on me tightened, her panic barely concealed. The blade pressed harder against my skin, but her confidence wavered. "You fucking coward. You owe me!" she spat.

He took a slow step back toward the door, his hands still raised. "I'm not dying for this. I'm going out there. You do what you want, but I'm done."

I could feel Sarah's indecision, her body rigid behind me, her breathing uneven. She didn't move, but I could tell she was torn, her plan unraveling as the helicopter outside drew closer.

Leo stepped out of the warehouse door, leaving it wide open. The sound of the helicopter hit me, the wind whipping through the large space. Through the open doorway, I saw the helicopters that had just landed outside, their lights cutting through the dust and darkness.

Leo dropped to his knees on the gravel, hands raised in surrender, his figure small against the chaos unfolding around him.

And then I saw him.

Callan was the first to retreat from the helicopter, his eyes scanning the scene, his body tense with determination. For a split second, my heart leapt at the sight of him—he was here. He'd come for me. But the sharp edge of the knife pressed harder against my neck, pulling me back into the terrifying reality.

"Don't think he's going to save you," Sarah hissed behind me, her voice shaking with desperation. "One wrong move, and I'll make sure he watches you bleed."

Callan's eyes locked on mine as he moved closer, his face tight with desperation. But the pressure of the blade at my neck grew more intense as Sarah's grip tightened. Her breath was ragged behind me, her body vibrating with anger.

"Stop right there, Callan," she spat, dragging me backward, the knife pressing harder against my skin. "You take one more step, and I'll make sure you regret it for the rest of your life."

Callan froze, his hands raised in surrender. "Sarah, you don't have to do this. It's over—just let her go."

She laughed bitterly, the sound hollow. "Over? Not yet." The blade dug into my skin, just enough to draw blood. I felt the warm blood trickle down my neck and gasped, but I fought to keep still. The terror in Callan's eyes only seemed to fuel her.

"You think you can just walk away from me after everything?" she shouted, her voice shaking with rage. "I'm going to make sure you feel the same helplessness I did."

And then, with a sudden, violent motion, she plunged the

blade deep into my side.

The pain was instant and overwhelming. I screamed, my legs buckling as my vision blurred. I could hear Callan's agonized shout, but it felt distant, muffled by the searing heat spreading through my body.

Callan surged forward, but Sarah yanked the knife out before I collapsed to the ground, blood soaking through my clothes. "Now you can watch her bleed," she hissed.

Before she could do more, the agents rushed in, tackling her to the ground as the knife clattered from her hand. She struggled beneath them, but the fight was gone from her. The damage had already been done.

Callan was at my side in an instant, his hands trembling as he pressed them over the wound, trying desperately to stop the bleeding. His face was a mask of terror, his eyes wide with fear, and seeing him like that—so broken—made my heart ache more than the pain itself. "Sloane, stay with me, baby," he begged, his voice cracking under the weight of his panic. "Please, you're gonna be alright, baby. You're gonna be okay."

I wanted to reach out to him, to tell him how much I loved him, how I'd loved him since the moment I realized what he meant to me. But the words wouldn't come. His voice grew more frantic, his grip on me tightening. "Sloane? Sloane, baby, open your eyes! Please...please don't fucking leave me."

I tried to hold on to the sound of his voice, to focus on the warmth of his hands against my skin. But the edges of my vision blurred, the world around me dimming. *I love you*, I thought. *I love you more than anything.*

Everything was slipping away now, slowly and quietly. And then there was nothing.

38

Callan

The helicopter ride was a blur of noise and chaos, but all I could focus on was Sloane. I held her hand the entire time, watching the medics work frantically to stabilize her, the blood soaking through their gloves as they shouted orders over the roar of the helicopter. I kept telling myself to stay calm, that she'd pull through, but the sight of her—so pale, so still—made it feel like the world was collapsing around me.

I didn't let go of her hand, not even when we touched down at the hospital and they wheeled her into the ICU. Now, sitting here in the small, sterile room, the machines beeping softly around us, I couldn't stop watching her chest rise and fall. It was the only thing keeping me grounded—those small, shallow breaths telling me she was still here.

The doctors said she was going to make it, that the knife had missed anything vital, that she was lucky. *Lucky.* The word rattled in my brain, but I didn't fucking feel lucky. All I could think about was how close I'd come to losing her.

I squeezed her hand gently, my thumb brushing over her knuckles. "You're safe now, baby," I whispered, my voice barely holding together. "You're gonna be okay."

I leaned in closer, resting my forehead gently against her arm, letting the sound of the machines fill the silence.

"I'm here, baby," I whispered. "I'm not leaving."

* * *

The steady beeping of the machines was a constant reminder that Sloane was still alive, still here. I held her hand, guilt gnawing at me. I had tried to stop Sarah, tried to talk her down, but it hadn't been enough.

Jake stood by the window, his arms crossed, his face hard and unreadable, but I could feel the weight of his anger bearing down on me. We hadn't spoken about what had happened yet, at least not in detail. Ana sat on the other side of Sloane, her eyes flicking between the two of us, her frustration barely contained. The air between us felt like it was ready to explode, and I was tense as fuck.

Finally, Jake broke the silence, his voice low but sharp. "You should've stopped it."

I looked up, already feeling the knot in my stomach tighten. "What?"

"You were there," Jake continued, turning to face me, his eyes narrowing. "You should've stopped it. The car crash, the kidnapping, Sarah stabbing her—you were there for all of it. How the hell did you let it get this far?"

I could feel my frustration boiling over. "You think I wanted this to fucking happen?" I shot back. "I tried to stop her."

"Tried?" Jake's voice rose, his anger surfacing. "My daughter's in that bed because you didn't stop Sarah. You didn't fight her. You let it happen."

"I didn't *let* anything happen," I said, standing up, my voice rising. "I tried to talk her down. I didn't get a chance to fight."

"But you didn't stop her, did you?" Jake snapped. "You were too distracted by Sloane. You were too caught up in your feelings to pay attention to the danger. And now look where we are."

Before I could respond, Ana cut in, her voice trembling with anger. "Don't you *dare* put this all on Callan. It is *not* his fault, not at all."

Jake's eyes flicked toward her. "What the hell are you talking about?"

"I'm talking about *you*," Ana snapped, standing up from her chair. Her eyes were blazing, her voice shaking with fury. "You ruined this family, Jake. You fucked Sarah. You *knew* she was crazy. You knew she was capable of lying and manipulating, and you didn't care. You didn't care about what it would do to us—what it would do to Sloane."

Jake's face tightened, his fists clenching at his sides. "Ana—"

"No," she cut him off, her voice rising. "*Esto es culpa tuya.* You let Sarah get close enough to manipulate her way back into our lives because you wanted a quick fuck *con la maldita diabla.* You didn't care about anything—about the costs, about your family. You knew what she was capable of, and you didn't care."

Jake flinched, his jaw tightening, but he didn't respond. He turned away, unable to look at either of us.

"She wasn't after you," I added, my voice lower and tinged with guilt. "She was using you to get to me. And you let her."

Ana wasn't done—she was fucking relentless as she practically cut me off and continued. "You destroyed everything.

You failed us, Jake. You ruined this family just to have sex with her. And now our daughter is lying in that bed because of *you*."

The silence that followed was suffocating. Jake didn't say a word. His back was still turned, but I knew that what Ana said had gotten to him. How couldn't it? She was fucking ruthless, but she was right.

Ana's voice softened slightly, but the fury was still there. "Don't you dare blame Callan for this. You knew exactly what Sarah was, and you brought her back into our lives anyway. This is all on you."

It was silent again, the air tense and still. I looked down at Sloane, my heart heavy with guilt, but for the first time, it wasn't just mine to carry.

39

Sloane

It had been a few weeks since the hospital, and while the dull ache in my side was still there, things felt calmer now. The worst of it was over, and the quiet comfort of Callan's apartment had become exactly what I needed. Healing wasn't just physical—it was the peace I felt here, wrapped in his blanket, knowing I was safe.

I curled up on the couch, the soft light filtering through the curtains, and let myself relax. I never knew love like this was possible—so steady and comforting. I had never felt so completely cared for, so at home. Callan had been by my side through all of it, taking care of me, and I loved him for it. I loved him in a way I didn't know I could.

He was in the kitchen, making coffee like he did every morning. I could hear the soft clinks of mugs, the smell of the brew filling the air. Being with him like this, in these quiet moments, felt like something I'd never imagined I could have.

"You want some coffee?" he called from the kitchen, his voice gentle.

I smiled, sinking deeper into the cushions. "Yes, please,

Daddy."

A few minutes later, he came over, handing me a cup before sitting down beside me. He didn't need to say anything, didn't need to ask how I was feeling. We had been through enough, and now it was about just being here, together. Letting the rest of the world fade away while we stayed in this quiet little space we had carved out for ourselves.

I leaned my head against his shoulder, feeling his warmth. In this moment, I felt whole, like the outside world didn't matter. With him, everything else faded.

But then, as I rested my head against Callan's shoulder, my mind drifted back to the chaos that had led us here. It was crazy—terrifying, really—how everything had spiraled so quickly with Sarah. She wasn't just some random threat; she had planned it all so carefully, down to the smallest detail.

My stomach twisted as I thought about how she had leaked the sex video of her and my dad to the media. She had help—someone working in the shadows, making sure that the story exploded everywhere. The scandal was too big, too ugly for anyone to contain, and it forced my dad to resign. The weight of it all still hung over me, suffocating at times.

I closed my eyes, trying to push the memories away, but they kept coming. Sarah's twisted smile, the way she manipulated every situation, how she seemed to delight in tearing my family apart. My dad wasn't innocent, though—he had made his choices. He had slept with her, knowing what kind of person she was.

But it wasn't just the resignation that haunted me. It was my mom. She left him. My mom, always the one who held everything together, had finally walked away. I couldn't blame her, but the weight of it all had been too much for me to carry.

My family was broken, and every piece of it was a reminder of how things would never be the same.

I was angry at my dad. Angry that he had been so careless, that he hadn't thought about what it would mean for us. I wasn't sure if I'd ever be able to forgive him for that.

Callan's hand gently rested on my leg, pulling me out of the spiral. I hadn't realized how tightly I'd been gripping the edge of the blanket, lost in the whirlwind of my thoughts.

"You okay?" he asked softly, his eyes filled with concern.

Callan's hand stayed on my leg, grounding me, his presence pulling me back from the weight of everything. I took a deep breath, letting the warmth of his touch seep into me. It helped—*he* helped.

"I'll be alright," I whispered, my voice softer than I intended, but I meant it. I turned to him, meeting his eyes. "Especially with you here."

He didn't say anything right away, but the look on his face was all I needed. His thumb gently traced circles on my leg, a silent reassurance that he wasn't going anywhere.

"Being with you...it makes everything feel a little less heavy," I said, my voice steadier.

His expression softened, his eyes filled with something deep, something that made me feel safe. "I got you, baby."

And he did. Through all of it—the chaos, the pain, the anger—I knew I could lean on him. I didn't have to carry the weight of everything on my own. I had him.

"I know," I whispered, feeling the tightness in my chest start to ease. "I don't think I could do this without you."

Callan didn't say anything more; he just pulled me closer, wrapping his arm around me as I rested my head against his chest. The outside world still felt overwhelming, but with him by my side, I knew I'd be alright.

"Hey," he whispered, his hand trailing slowly along the inside of my thigh. "Why don't you sit back, relax, and open those beautiful legs of yours. Let me feast on your pretty pussy." His voice was a playful mix of seduction and warmth, sending a flutter through my chest.

Throughout my recovery, he had been so gentle—always patient, but never holding back his desire. There were times when I begged for him, needing him so badly, and he'd happily oblige. A few moments even had me worried my stitches might tear, but it didn't matter. I needed him in a way that made everything else fade away.

Before I could even respond, Callan slunk down on his knees in front of the couch, gently parting my legs as he thumbed my panties and lowered them to the floor. My heart began to race as his hands trailed back up to my thighs, his hazel-green eyes fixed on mine. I lifted my hips slightly in anticipation as he licked his lips, giving me a small smirk. He started to trail gentle kisses up my thigh, trying to tease me, and succeeding.

"Come on, Daddy. Make me come, and then maybe I'll let you come inside of me," I whispered, though my tone was firm. Callan loved when I was dominant, and seeing him on his knees for me always made me feel like the powerful goddess that I was, a title he never let me forget.

He grunted, biting on his lower lip, and I took my hands to his hair, pulling him closer. He exhaled before pressing his lips firmly to my pussy, his tongue instantly finding my clit. I watched as he lapped his tongue around, a look of desire and hunger from him as we locked eyes. The heat in my core began to swell and my hips bucked up and down in anticipation of my orgasm. Callan moaned loudly, sending a vibration through his mouth, causing my pussy to seize with release as he gripped my thighs hard. I clenched my eyes shut, my cries of pleasure echoing throughout the living room, and I immediately chased another orgasm, using Callan's tongue and mouth as my personal fuck toy, and I came again and again.

"Fuck, I can't handle it. I'm gonna fucking burst, baby," Callan mumbled before removing his mouth from my pussy, staring up at me eagerly as I blinked open my eyes.

He was waiting for permission, and I loved the way we switched roles based on our moods. I loved how much he had opened himself up for new possibilities, how open-minded he had become.

"Fine." I sighed, faking exasperation, unable to contain my smile.

"Fuck yes. Thank you, baby. Thanking you for letting me fuck your sweet pussy," he said eagerly as he lifted himself from the floor and lowered his boxer briefs, letting his cock spring free.

I giggled as I lifted my legs and set my feet on the couch, opening wide for him. I felt a tinge of pain on my side, but I ignored it, needing Callan more than anything.

"Come on then, Daddy. Show me how much you appreciate it," I said with a sly smile.

He eyed me intently as he positioned me flat on my back and hovered over me, carefully aligning himself as I lifted my legs and wrapped them around his hips. Lately he had been careful not to press his weight against my body for fear of hurting me, and that just meant I got to see his muscled, tattooed body work hard to fuck me.

He slid into me deeply and exhaled as he remained still, looking down at me with widened eyes and pure awe. I rested my hands on his biceps and smiled, slightly lifting my hips with impatience.

"What, baby? You told me to appreciate your pussy, and I'm admiring how fucking good you feel," he said with a grin, knowing he was teasing me.

"I know what you're doing. You better start fucking me fast or I won't let you at all," I quipped back.

Callan's grin widened as he began to pump his hips, slowly at first, gradually going faster. He watched as my boobs bounced underneath my thin cotton shirt, my nipples hard from his touch. His eyes trailed back up to mine, and as he perfectly fucked me, rubbing against my g-spot, I cried out with pleasure.

"Come inside me. Now," I breathed out, then my pussy began to pulse around his cock, a wave of heat enveloping my body. Only a second later, Callan grunted out with pleasure, his loud moans filling the room.

"Jesus fucking Christ," he said as he caught his breath, sitting back and letting my thighs rest around his legs, his cum spilling out of me.

Without hesitation, he got back onto his knees and lifted my legs, wrapping them around his shoulders. He began to lick me clean, and as I watched him and felt his tongue lapping around inside of me, the fire in my core began to burn again. I lifted my hips, seeking more, craving everything he had to give. I knew I would always want more when it came to Callan, and luckily, we had all the time in the world.

* * *

In the following weeks, I watched as the media tore my dad

apart. His resignation dominated the headlines, with some calling it the biggest scandal since the Clinton-Lewinsky affair. I did my best to avoid it, but it was everywhere—social media, texts from friends, people on the street hounding me for my opinion.

My mom handled it with nothing but grace. She made a public statement about their divorce, never once speaking ill of my dad—at least, not publicly—before whisking herself off to Spain to spend time with my abuela. She said she'd move back to New York when the time was right.

Sarah was being held in a federal detention center, awaiting her trial in federal court. We didn't know when the trial would be, but I planned to be there, no matter what. I wasn't going to let her slip through the cracks of the system, and neither was Callan. She had torn my life apart—torn my family apart—and I'd do everything in my power to make sure she spent as much time in prison as possible.

But as much as Sarah haunted my thoughts, I wasn't going to let her control my future. I had things to look forward to, things she could never take away from me.

Callan and I were packing for our two-week vacation to Fiji. It was the perfect escape before the next big chapter of our lives. After several acceptances from colleges, I'd finally decided on UCLA, majoring in psychology with a minor in Gender Studies. I'd be starting that fall, and I couldn't wait.

Before we packed up and moved across the country, I wanted this time with Callan, a break from everything that had happened. Just the two of us, somewhere far away, where we could leave the past behind, even if only for a little while.

And then my phone rang, pulling me from my thoughts. A gnawing ache of dread filled my chest as I saw the name on the screen—Dad. As much as I wanted to avoid him, as much as I was still angry at him for everything he had done, he was still my dad.

I hesitated, my thumb hovering over the screen before I finally answered.

"Hey, Sloane," his voice came through, softer than usual, almost cautious. "I'm glad you answered. I just...I wanted to say I'm sorry."

There was a pause, the weight of his words hanging between us. After everything that had happened, after everything he had done, he was apologizing. Part of me wanted to tell him it was too late, that it didn't change anything. But another part of me—the part that still wanted to hold on to the idea of him—couldn't let go that easily.

"I'm not asking you to forgive me," he continued, sensing my silence. "I just wanted you to know that I'm sorry. For everything."

I swallowed hard, unsure of what to say. I wasn't ready to accept his apology, not yet. Maybe not ever. But I couldn't dismiss it, either. At least not completely.

"Okay," I said finally, my voice quiet and guarded. "I hear you."

I didn't offer more, and he didn't push. The call ended, leaving things unresolved, like so much between us.

I stared at my phone for a few moments after the call ended, the weight of it still pressing down on me. The apology lingered, but it wasn't enough to wash away everything that had happened. I wasn't sure it ever would be.

Callan sensed the shift in my mood because as he walked in our room, his eyes were soft with concern. Without a word, he sat beside me, wrapping his arm around my shoulders and pulling me close. I leaned into him, grateful for the quiet comfort that only he could give.

"You okay, baby?" he asked softly, his voice low and soothing.

I nodded, though the knot in my chest told a different story. "It was my dad," I murmured, my voice cracking slightly. "He apologized...for everything."

Callan stayed silent at first, pulling me a little closer. "How do you feel about that?"

I sighed and smiled. He was so used to talking about his feelings now, and I was proud of him. I rested my head against his chest and said, "I don't know. I'm not ready to accept it yet."

"That's okay," he said gently. "You don't have to be."

We sat there for a few moments, the silence between us comfortable, and I felt the tension slowly start to ease. Callan always had a way of making me feel like everything would be alright, even when my mind was a mess.

"Come on, baby," he whispered after a while, pressing a soft kiss to the top of my head. "Let's go to bed."

I let him lead me to the bedroom, his hand warm and steady in mine. The weight of the day, of the call, started to slip away as I curled up next to him. In his arms, the weight on my chest began to lift, and I felt like I could finally breathe again. Whatever came next, I knew I had the strength to face it. With Callan by my side, the burden would always feel a little lighter.

40

Callan

The warm sun heated my skin as I lounged on a beach chair beside Sloane, the soft crash of waves filling the air. Fiji was fucking perfect, but being next to Sloane made it even better. I glanced over at her, lying on her stomach on a matching chair, her eyes closed, a faint smile curving her lips. She looked at peace, and knowing I had a part in that made my heart swell.

Sloane had changed me in ways I didn't even realize at first. It wasn't just about love—it was about everything. She taught me how to open up, to be vulnerable, to let someone in completely. She'd shown me that even though she was twenty years younger, she had a wisdom that sometimes made me forget the age gap altogether. In her own way, she'd become my greatest teacher, even if she didn't know it.

I often forgot how much younger she was, because when we were together, it didn't matter. She challenged me and made me a better version of myself. For the first time in a long time, I felt worthy. Worthy of love, of happiness—things I'd pushed away for so long, thinking I didn't deserve them. But with Sloane, I knew I was lucky. And loved. *So* fucking loved.

She stirred beside me, stretching slightly before her eyes fluttered open. She caught me looking, and that familiar smile spread across her face. "What?" she asked, her voice soft and teasing.

"Nothing," I said, grinning. "Just thinking about how fucking lucky I am."

Her smile widened, and she reached for my hand, her touch grounding me in this moment—this perfect moment where everything felt right.

"Come on," I said, standing up and pulling her with me. "Let's sit by the water."

We walked to the edge of the shore, settling in the warm sand, the gentle waves lapping at our feet. We dug our toes into the sand, feeling the soft grains beneath us. The ocean stretched endlessly before us, and for the first time in a long time, I wasn't thinking about the past or what could go wrong.

I was just here, with her. My perfect fucking girl. And that was all I needed.

41

Epilogue

I knew I shouldn't have come to this gala. It had only been six months since the complete disaster Sarah caused. I spent most of that time in Spain, trying to gather the courage to face the world again. As much as I tried to come off as strong, the whole thing nearly broke me.

Now, here I was, sitting at a table full of celebrities, a glass of champagne in hand. Oscar winners, pop stars, rock stars—they were all around me, offering kind words and encouragement, but I could see the pity in their eyes. It was overwhelming, and I was more than ready to leave.

My bodyguard of six months stood by the wall, his gaze scanning the room before landing on me. He was a kind man, not much for words, but funny when he wanted to be, with a dry sense of humor. We locked eyes, and I gave him a small nod, signaling that I was almost ready to go.

Then someone sat down next to me. I recognized him instantly—Charlie Ashford. He started out in a British boy band and later branched out on his own. He must've been in his late twenties now, strikingly handsome, with brown wavy hair styled deliberately messy and eyes the color of emeralds. He was cool—too cool—and I had no idea what to say when he smiled at me, his sharp jawline momentarily distracting me.

"Ana Martin, wow," he said with a shy chuckle.

"Del Rosario now," I corrected. "But please, just call me Ana."

I wanted nothing to do with Jake's last name anymore. I should have never taken it in the first place. Sloane was even thinking about taking my surname when she married Callan next spring, though I encouraged her to do whatever felt right. I didn't want her to feel like she was giving up her identity by changing her name to Holt.

Charlie lifted his eyebrows with a surprised grin. "Sorry, Ana." His British accent was charming, and I felt embarrassingly typical for swooning at it.

I laughed nervously, shaking my head. Why was I so flustered around this attractive, younger man? My cheeks burned with embarrassment as we made eye contact, perhaps for a little too long. It was so unlike me to feel this way, and it left me wildly confused.

"I'm Charlie. Charlie Ashford," he said, putting his hand to his chest.

"I know," I replied with a polite laugh. "I think the whole world knows who you are."

He chuckled softly and bit his lower lip. My heart fluttered. *He's too young for you, Ana.*

"I think you're much more famous," he quipped, then his eyes widened a little. "Because, you know...you're a former First Lady."

No one ever mentioned the affair, and for that, I was grateful.

"I suppose so." I shrugged, unsure of what to talk about

with him. What could we possibly have in common? He was a British rock star, and I was a former First Lady. I figured that's what I'd always be known as now, even though I had once considered running for office myself. But after everything with Jake, I didn't want to be in the spotlight anymore. I'd change the world in different ways.

"So, um..." He leaned closer to talk over the music. "Do you live in New York, or are you just in town for the gala?"

He's trying to make small talk. *That's sweet.*

"I live here now," I said. "Only a few blocks away."

Did he need to know that?

His eyebrows shot up again in surprise, making him look even more charming. "Me too."

My heart raced. *Cut this out, Ana. You need to get out of here.*

"Hmm." I nodded, trying to get out of my head. My eyes scanned the table; I felt uneasy under his gaze. It wasn't unwanted, but the way he made me feel was throwing me off balance.

"Can I get you another drink?" he asked, his eyes still fixed on me.

I glanced down at my half-empty champagne flute. "No, thank you. I was just about to leave," I said, sitting up straighter.

"Oh, well, hey neighbor," he teased lightly. "Do you want to...I don't know, meet up for coffee? Or a drink?" He placed his arm on the table as if he was thinking of reaching out.

I glanced at the tattoo peeking out from under his shirt cuff. "Are you trying to ask me out?" I asked bluntly. If he was, I needed to shut it down quickly.

He chuckled nervously, looking down before locking eyes with me again. "Yeah. What do you say?"

I let out a surprised laugh. "Charlie, I'm at least ten years older than you."

His smile didn't fade as he shrugged. "I don't care. Do you?"

Why *did* I care? I had been so accepting of Sloane and Callan's relationship, and they were twenty years apart. What was ten?

I shouldn't do this. I should say no. But what was the harm in one drink? Maybe I could use a little fun. *But perhaps I should make him work for it, if he really wanted it.*

"Alright," I said, giving him a challenging look. "How about this: figure out how to contact me, and I'll go for a drink with you."

His smile widened, his eyes lighting up with mischief.

"Challenge accepted. I'll see you soon for that drink, then."

Acknowledgments

To my alpha and beta readers—thank you for the invaluable encouragement and feedback that helped bring this book to life.

To my ARC readers—thank you so much for giving this book a chance!

To my family—thank you for your unwavering support. I feel so loved, and even if you don't read this (which, honestly, I hope you don't!), please continue supporting me blindly!

And finally, to *you*—thank you for being part of this journey. I'm grateful for each and every one of my readers.

About the Author

Cassandra lives in Southern California. In her free time she enjoys tending to her house plants, reading, playing video games with her daughter, and laughing at cat videos with her husband.

You can connect with me on:

- https://www.instagram.com/author.cassandravega
- https://authorcassandravega.com